## THE HIGH LONESOME

Smoke rode deeper into the mountains, memories of the old mountain man called Preacher all around him. Ol' Preacher had talked about this country and took Smoke through it when Smoke was a young boy. It seemed to Smoke that his friend and mentor was still guiding him on.

Smoke had crossed the Salt River Range and was not far from where the mountain man, William Sublette, had reached a particularly beautiful and lonesome place and named it Jackson Hole, after another mountain man, David Jackson. Preacher had told Smoke that was back in '29, long before the damn settlers started coming in and civilizing everything they touched.

Smoke frowned and turned in his saddle. He was going to test those men following him. He was going to give them a taste of what was in store for them if they persisted in hunting him clear up into northwest Wyoming, where peaks pushed two-and-a-half miles into the sky—and one misstep meant death.

Here in the hole is where he'd find out if those on his backtrail really meant to kill him. For if that was true, he would surely leave them to be buried among the aspen, Englemann spruce, Douglas fir and lodgepole pine—in a land where the mountain men of old had joined the wolves in their howling, lending their voices to the ever-sighing winds of the High Lonesome.

# BOOK YOUR PLACE ON OUR WEBSITE AND MAKE THE READING CONNECTION!

We've created a customized website just for our very special readers, where you can get the inside scoop on everything that's going on with Zebra, Pinnacle and Kensington books.

When you come online, you'll have the exciting opportunity to:

- View covers of upcoming books
- Read sample chapters
- Learn about our future publishing schedule (listed by publication month *and author*)
- Find out when your favorite authors will be visiting a city near you
- Search for and order backlist books from our online catalog
- Check out author bios and background information
- Send e-mail to your favorite authors
- Meet the Kensington staff online
- Join us in weekly chats with authors, readers and other guests
- Get writing guidelines
- AND MUCH MORE!

Visit our website at
http://www.pinnaclebooks.com

# WILLIAM W. JOHNSTONE

# PURSUIT OF THE MOUNTAIN MAN

## PINNACLE BOOKS
### Kensington Publishing Corp.

http://www.pinnaclebooks.com

Dedicated to L.J. and Kat Martin

PINNACLE BOOKS are published by

Kensington Publishing Corp.
850 Third Avenue
New York, NY 10022

All Kensington Titles, Imprints, and Distributed Lines are available at special quantity discounts for bulk purchases for sales promotions, premiums, fund-raising, and educational or institutional use. Special book excerpts or customized printings can also be created to fit specific needs. For details, write or phone the office of the Kensington special sales manager: Kensington Publishing Corp., 850 Third Avenue, New York, NY 10022, attn: Special Sales Department, Phone: 1-800-221-2647.

Pinnacle and the P logo Reg. U.S. Pat. & TM Off.

15 14 13 12 11 10 9 8

Printed in the United States of America

I never forget a face, but in your case I'll make an exception.

G. Marx

# 1

The young man had been eyeballing the quiet stranger for several minutes. The young man stood at the bar, sipping whiskey. The quiet stranger sat at a table, his back to a wall, slowly eating his supper and sipping coffee. The young man couldn't understand why the stranger didn't take offense to his staring; couldn't understand why the tough-looking stranger wearing two guns didn't reply to his silent insults.

He just sat there, eating his supper and drinking coffee.

The young man concluded the stranger was yellow.

"Kid," the barkeep finally said, "I'd leave that man alone. He's got bad stamped all over him."

"You know him?"

"Nope. But I know the type. Leave him be."

"He don't look like nothin' special to me."

"Your funeral," the barkeep said, and moved to the other end of the bar.

Jack Lynch looked at the barkeep and snorted in disgust. Jack had four notches cut into his gun and was considered by some—in this part of the country—to be very quick on the shoot. He was considered by others to be a loud-mouthed punk who was going to drag iron on the wrong man one day.

That day had come.

Late winter in Utah. The stoves in the saloon glowed red and the winds were cold as they buffeted the building. Four men sat playing a quiet game of penny-ante poker, a few others stood at the long bar, talking and sipping beer or whiskey or, in a couple of cases, both. A gambler sat alone at another table, playing a game of solitaire, waiting for a sucker to come in. One man was passed out, his head on the table, snoring softly.

And the stranger sat alone, finishing his supper.

Jack Lynch turned and put his back to the bar. Now he openly stared at the stranger, a sneer on his face. "You don't have much to say, do you, mister?" he called.

The stranger did not look up. He poured another cup of coffee from the pot and sugared it, slowly stirring the strong brew. Then he started in on his fresh-baked dried apple pie. It had been a long day and he wanted no more than to eat his meal in peace and get a good night's sleep at the small hotel in this Northern Utah town, not many miles from the Wyoming border.

But if this loud-mouth kept pushing him . . .

"Hey! I asked you a question, man," Jack raised his voice.

The stranger chewed his pie, swallowed, and took a sip of coffee. He lifted his eyes to the loud-mouth. The stranger's eyes were brown and cold-looking, no emotion in them. His shoulders were wide and his arms heavily muscled, his wrists thick. His hands were big and flat-knuckled, scarred from many fights. He was a ruggedly handsome man, well over six feet tall. He wore two guns, one tied low on his right side, the other worn high and butt forward on his left side. A long-bladed knife was in a sheath behind his right-hand gun.

"Since the question was probably very forgettable, I've

6

already forgotten it," the stranger said in a soft voice. "Is it worth repeating?"

"Huh?" Jack said.

"See? You've already forgotten it. So how important can it be?" The stranger returned to his pie and coffee.

The gambler smiled. He thought he knew the stranger's name. And if he was correct, this loud-mouth was standing very close to death.

"I don't think I like you very much," Jack said.

"You're at the end of a very long list," the stranger replied. He tapped the coffee pot and looked at the barkeep. "It's empty. Would you bring another pot, please?"

"My, don't he talk po-lite, though?" Jack sneered the words. "Like a sissy."

"Jack," one of the card players said. "Why don't you shut your damn mouth and leave the man alone? He ain't bothered no one."

"You want to make me?" Jack challenged the man. "Come on. Make me shut up."

"Oh, go to hell, Jack," another card player said.

Another pot of coffee was placed on the stranger's table and the barkeep backed quickly away. The stranger poured and sugared and stirred and then carefully rolled a cigarette, lighting up.

"My name's Jack Lynch," the young man called to the stranger.

"Everybody should know their name."

The card players laughed at that. The gambler smiled and riffled the cards.

"What do you mean by that?" Jack asked.

"Boy," the stranger said, "do you push all strangers like the way you're proddin' me?"

"Just the ones who think they're tough. I usually prove they ain't."

"And how do you do that, Jack?"

"By stretchin' 'em out on the floor!"

"Did you ever stop to think that one of these days

7

it might well be you that's stretched out on the floor?"

"That don't ever enter my mind," Jack said.

"It should."

"You think you're the man who can do that?"

"Yes," the stranger said softly.

Jack flushed deeply, the color rising to his cheeks. The only reason he hadn't called them old coots at the card table out after they laughed at him was that none of them was wearing a gun. "Stand up!" Jack shouted.

The stranger pushed back his chair and stood up.

"Big," a card player said.

Jack Lynch stood with his legs spread, his hand by his gun.

The front door opened and a blast of cold air swept the saloon. The town marshal stepped in and sized up the situation in about two seconds. "Back off, Jack," he barked the words. "And I mean right now, boy."

"Marshal, I . . ."

"Shut up, Jack!" the marshal hollered. "Put that hammer thong back in place and do it slow. Ahh. That's better. Now settle down." He looked at the stranger. "Been a long time."

"Five years ago. Your horse threw a shoe and you stopped in town. You're looking well."

"Feel fine."

"I recommend the apple pie," the stranger said. "It was delicious." He picked up his hat and settled it on his head.

"I'll sure have me a wedge. And some coffee, Ralph," he said to the barkeep.

"Comin' right up, Marshal."

"See you around," the stranger said.

"See you."

The front door opened and closed and the stranger was gone, walking across the still frozen street to the hotel.

"Sorry, Marshal," Jack said. "I didn't know he was a friend of yours."

8

The marshal sipped his coffee. "Jack, do you have any idea at all who that was?"

"Some yeller-bellied tinhorn," Jack replied.

The gambler smiled.

The marshal's eyes were bleak as he turned his head to look at the young man. "Jack, you've done some dumb things in the years that I've known you. But today took the cake. That was Smoke Jensen."

Jack swayed for a moment, grabbing at the bar for support. The gambler kicked a chair across the floor and the marshal placed it upright for Jack to sit in. Jack Lynch's eyes were dull and his face was pale. A bit of spittle oozed out of one corner of his mouth.

"I knew it was him as soon as he stood up and I seen that left-hand gun in a cross-draw," the gambler said.

"And . . . you didn't say nothin' to me?" Jack mumbled the words.

"Why should I? It was your mouth that got you into it. You're a loud-mouth, pushy kid. It would have served you right if Jensen had drilled you clean through."

Jack recovered his bluster and now he was embarrassed. He stood up from the chair. His legs were still a little shaky and he backed up to the bar and leaned against it. "You can't talk to me like that, gambler."

The marshal was more than a little miffed at Jack's attitude. He'd pulled him out of one situation; be damned if he'd interfere in this one. He walked over to a table and sat down.

Across the street, in his room, Smoke had taken pen and paper and was writing to his wife, Sally.

"Don't push me, kid," the gambler said. "I've lived too long for me to take much crap from the likes of you. Jensen just didn't want to kill you. He's tired of it. I haven't reached that point yet."

"You son of a . . ." Jack grabbed for iron.

The gambler shook his right arm and a derringer slipped into his hand. He fired both barrels of the

.41. Jack coughed and sat down on the floor.

Smoke thought he heard gunshots and paused in his writing. When no more shots were heard, he dipped the nib into an ink well and began writing.

*Dear Sally,*

*How are you? I miss you very much but hope you are having a good time visiting family and friends back east . . .*

The gambler broke open the .41 derringer and reloaded. Jack's eyes were on him. The front of Jack's white shirt was spreading crimson.

"I don't want to die!" Jack cried.

"You should have thought about that before you strapped on that iron, boy," the marshal told him.

"It hurts!"

"I 'spect it does."

*. . . Nothing seems to change here, Sally. The only place where I am reasonably assured of being left alone is on the Sugarloaf. But you know the urge to see the land is strong within me, and I shall not be tied down like a vicious yard dog. This evening, while I was having supper, another young punk tried to goad me into drawing . . .*

"I want you out of town on the next stage, gambler," the marshal told the man.

"Would you have told Jensen that?" the gambler asked.

The marshal met his eyes. "Yes."

The gambler nodded his head. "Yes, I think you would have. All right, marshal. I'll leave in the morning."

"Fair enough."

*. . . I must go still further, up into Wyoming, then maybe across into Idaho, to find the bulls I'm looking for, Sally. If it were just a little bit warmer, I would sleep under the stars and not even enter towns except for provisions. But I fear this married man has grown too accustomed to comforters, feather ticks, and rugs on the floor on cold mornings. And, I must add, the nearness of you . . .*

"Put on my headstone that I was a gunfighter,

10

will you, Marshal?" Jack said, his voice growing weak.

"If that's what you want, Jack."

"It don't hurt no more."

"That's good, Jack."

"I can't hear you, Marshal. Speak up. They's a roarin' in my ears. I'm a-feared, Marshal Brackton! Is there really a hell, you reckon?"

*. . . I'm in a little town just south of the Uinta Mountains, Sally. I knew the marshal here, and he intervened this evening and saved a young man from death, at least at my hands. I'm going into the high country tomorrow, Sally. Where there are no towns and hopefully, no young hellions looking to make a reputation. I shall build a lean-to for my shelter and think good thoughts of you and the children . . .*

"Marshal!" Jack cried. "I can't see! I'm blind. Oh, God, where's that holy-roller. I thought he'd done come in to comfort me."

"I'm right here, son. Are you a Saint?"

"I ain't nothing," Jack whispered.

*. . . I send all my love over the miles, Sally, and pray that I shall see you soon.*

*Your loving and faithful husband, Smoke.*

The barkeep leaned over and looked at Jack Lynch. "Yeah. He's something, all right. He's dead!"

# 2

Smoke posted his letter to Sally at the hotel and left before dawn the next morning, amid a light falling of snow. The big Appaloosa he rode was rough and shaggy-looking, with his winter coat still on. His pack horse was tough and had been patiently trained by Smoke.

Smoke rode for five miles before dismounting and building a small fire to prepare the coffee and bacon he'd resupplied back in the town. After he ate the bacon he sopped chunks of bread into the grease and finished off his meal with another cup of hot, strong coffee.

He camped for the night close to a little river, with snow-capped Marsh Peak to his east. The morning dawned pristine white, with several inches of new snow on the ground.

The country he was riding through was wild and high and beautiful, but already being touched by the hand of man. Smoke remembered when he rode through this country as a boy, years back, with the legendary mountain man, Preacher. The two of them could ride for days, sometimes weeks, without ever seeing a white man. No more.

For the most part, the Indians no long posed any threat. Only occasionally would a few young bucks bust loose from some reservation and cause trouble. The west was slowly being tamed. The outlaw Jesse James had been killed, shot in the back by a man he'd called friend, so Smoke had heard. Jesse had given Smoke a pistol back during the war, when Smoke was just a boy, trying to hold on to a hard-scrabble farm back in Missouri, while his daddy was off in the fighting. John Wesley Hardin was still in prison down in Texas. Earp had killed Curly Bill Brocius just last year. Sam Bass was rotting in the grave, as was Clay Allison. Mysterious Dave was still around, but Smoke had no quarrel with him. As far as he knew, Mysterious Dave was still down in Dodge City.

But someone had been sticking close to his backtrail for two days now, and Smoke was getting a little curious as to who he, or they, might be.

He thought he was in Wyoming, but he wasn't sure. If he was, what was left of Fort Bridger would be off to the west some few miles. Smoke didn't know if there was anything left of the old post and wasn't that interested in checking it out.

But he would like to know who was trailing him. And why.

He was heading up toward the Green, to a little valley where a friend of his raised cattle, good cattle, and he'd written Smoke, telling him of the bulls he had for sale. The railroads had tracks all over the country now — well, almost — and getting the bulls back to his ranch would be no problem; a short drive on either end of a rail trip. Smoke could have taken the train most of the way, but with Sally gone back East to visit her family, the kids in school in Europe, Smoke had felt that old faithful tug of the High Lonesome and decided to saddle up and ride the distance.

He began seeing familiar landmarks and knew he was in the Cedar Mountains. In a couple of days, barring any difficulties, he'd cross the Blacks Fork and then pick up the Green River and follow it all the way to his friend's ranch.

He found a little spring bubbling out of the earth, a spot of graze for the horses around it, and made an early camp. It was still cold, but the snow was gone — at least for the present — and Smoke had killed a couple of rabbits and needed to get them on a spit, cooking.

He stripped saddle and pack from the horses and watched them roll and snort and kick and shake, then settle down for a bit of grazing. Smoke gathered up twigs to get his fire going, then laid on heavier wood and made himself a spit. He got the rabbits cooking, filled his coffee pot with cold spring water right at the mouth and fixed his coffee in the blackened old pot.

The horses abruptly stopped grazing and lifted their heads, ears pricked up. Smoke picked up his rifle and eared the hammer back.

He heard the sounds of hooves, coming from the north. Then the call. "Halloo the fire! I'm friendly and I got my own grub so's I won't be eatin' none of yourn. The twilight gets lonesome without conversation. All right to come in?"

"Come on," Smoke called.

The man looked to be in his sixties—late sixties—but he was spry and Smoke figured him to be a man of the mountains. Just a tad too young to have been a part of the heyday of mountain men, but nevertheless a man who'd probably spent his life in the High Lonesome. Smoke had been halfway raised by mountain men, and he knew the mark it left on a man. He had it himself.

"Light and sit," Smoke told him.

"Obliged. Let me tend to my animals and then I'll join you by the fire. My good horse here got hisself all tangled up in some of that goddamned barbed wire a couple of days ago. I got to put some salve on the cuts. The devil's own doin's, that's what that stuff is."

A lot of cowboys called barbed wire the devil's hatband. It was used, but many despised it.

"Name's Lute," the old man said.

"Pleased," Smoke said.

Lute looked under his horse at him and smiled when Smoke did not offer his name. "I got to call you somethin', boy."

"I'll answer to just about anything."

Lute chuckled and carefully rubbed salve on the healing

cuts inflicted by the devil's hatband. "I come in from the west. Smelled your fire and cut north. I didn't want you to think I was part of that bunch that's comin' up behind you."

"I knew I was being followed."

"I'm sure you did. You appear to be a mighty careful man. You got the mark on you, son. I think you've spent some time in the high country."

"For a fact."

"Thought so. Brands a man deep. The burn don't never come out. I come into the Lonesome back in '39. Me and old Preacher was partners for years."

"I knew him. He still alive?"

"Yep. Gettin' fat and sassy in his old age. Him and a bunch of other old mountain men got 'em a place up in the mountains. Them old coots just sit and rock and tell lies all the damn day. Mountain Men and old gunfighters. I might go there myself some day. When all the fire gets burned out in me and there ain't nothin' but ashes left."

"This bunch that's on my trail: how many?"

" 'Ppears to be a goodly bunch, boy. I bellied down on a rise and watched 'em. They ridin' like men with a mission. Hardcases, I'd say. You wanted by the law?"

"Not that I know of." Smoke rummaged around and found another cup. He poured the scalding coffee and passed a cup to Lute, who had finished doctoring his horse and had sat down by the fire.

"Much obliged to you, boy." He warmed his hands on the hot tin cup, waiting a moment for the coffee to become drinkable. His eyes took in Smoke's guns. "Don't see a rig like yourn too often," he remarked.

"Not often. But it suits me." Smoke turned the rabbits to even the cooking.

"Jensen," Lute said the words softly. "I knowed it would come to me. Smoke Jensen."

"That's right."

"Ol' Preacher sort of jerked you up after your pa died back in '66 or '67."

"That he did. But he never mentioned anyone named Lute. I find that odd."

"Had to change my name after I killed a man down in civilization back in '55. I hate towns . . . hate the people in towns. They fearful people, afraid to go it alone. Bullies live in towns, too. It was a bully I opened up with my good knife."

Smoke smiled at Lute's words. He didn't agree with the man in the main, but part of what he said held some truth to it.

"They comin' after you, boy," Lute said. "Has to be you. Someone has hired them to kill you. I know you got enemies."

"Then why don't they come on and try to do the job?"

"Don't know. You and me, we'll ambush 'em in the mornin'. How 'bout it?"

Smoke shook his head. "Lute, they may or may not be after me. I don't know that for sure and neither do you. I'm tired of killing. I just want to live in peace."

The mountain man snorted. "Right nice thought, but it ain't never gonna happen. As long as you're alive, they's them that'll be wantin' to try you. I shouldn't have to be tellin' you this." He stood up. "I'll get my grub. Told you I wouldn't eat yourn."

The fire burned down to coals several times and each time one of the men would rouse from his blankets to place wood on the coals. The stars began to fade when Lute rolled out of his blankets and disappeared into the brush outside of camp to do his morning business. Smoke took the other side of the camp, then came back and put coffee on to boil and to lay slices of bacon in the frying pan.

"Smoke," Lute called. "You'll wanna see this."

Smoke climbed up the small hill and stood by the old

mountain man. About five miles away, below where they stood, Smoke could see a half dozen fires twinkling in the darkness. He took off his hat and scratched his head.

"It makes no sense. It's as if they want me to see them; they want me to know they're after me."

"Maybe they do, boy. You seen bear-baitin', ain't you?"

"Yes. It's a cruel sport. What about it?"

"Maybe they do want you to know, boy. Maybe it's a game to them."

Smoke thought about that. "A game? Lute, what do you know that you're not telling me. And don't hand me any more crap about you just happening up on my camp yesterday afternoon."

"Let's get some coffee and bacon. I'll level with you."

They ate and drank their coffee. Eating was serious business and they wouldn't talk until the food was gone and they'd settled back for a pipe or a hand-rolled and a cup of coffee.

"I come up on a buddy of mine about two weeks ago over yonder-ways on Badwater Crick. He'd just ridden the steam engine as fer as he could from Dodge City. Whilst he was in Dodge he overheard some talk about this German Count or Baron or something like that, name of Frederick von Hausen. He's some sort of world traveler and ad-venture seeker. He was in some saloon there and askin' who was the meanest, toughest man in the west. Somebody piped up and said Smoke Jensen."

He paused to stuff and light his pipe and Smoke said, "You've been looking for me since then?"

"I owe Preacher," was Lute's response.

"You knew who I was all along, then?"

"I was pretty sure it was you. Anyways, this Baron— whatever the hell that means—said he wanted to mount a party and come lookin' for you. He said it would be great sport to hunt you down and see just how tough you really was."

Smoke's coffee was cold in the cup and forgotten. He set

the cup down and rolled a cigarette. Finally he said, "Lute, you can't hunt a man down for sport like some animal!"

" 'Ppears he's doin' it, boy."

"Didn't the law try to stop him?"

"The law ain't got nothin' to do with it, Smoke. And them men with him ain't talkin' 'bout it. He's payin' 'em big money."

Smoke had never heard of such a thing, and his face mirrored his inner confusion. "It's got to be a joke, Lute."

"No joke, boy. They aim to hunt you down, run you until you can't go no further, and then kill you."

Smoke lit his cigarette and inhaled. "Well . . . I have no option but to go to the law with this."

Lute smiled. "And tell them what, boy? You ain't got no proof that anybody's doin' anything wrong. Think about it."

Smoke took his handroll down to the butt and tossed it into the fire before he spoke. He had been hunted before, certainly, by men who were after him in the heat of anger or for promise of a false bounty, but never for sport. Smoke was genuinely tired of all the killing. The west was being tamed; why in the hell didn't people leave him alone and let him live in peace?

"I'll not play their game, Lute. I'll head for the high lonesome; I know places there where not even you could find me. He can't keep these men on the payroll forever."

"He's worth millions, Smoke. And his family's worth more millions. He ain't never worked. He's a so-called professional ad-venturer; whatever the hell that means. And yeah, he can keep these randy ol' boys on the payroll forever, I reckon. Son, the more you run, the more ex-citin' the hunt is for them."

"That's the reason you suggested we ambush them."

"That's right. Might as well get the un-pleasantness done with."

Despite the situation facing him, Smoke had to chuckle at the old man's coldness. Preacher had been the same way;

18

mountain men were not known for their kind, loving attitudes toward anyone who might be planning to do them harm.

Smoke sighed. "I just can't do it, Lute. I just can't ambush a group of people who, so far, at least, have done me no harm. Don't you see that?"

Lute refilled his own cup, tossed the cold out of Smoke's, and filled it up. "No, I don't. But I ain't settled like you, neither. Tell me, would you have acted this way ten year ago? Or even last year?"

Smoke shook his head. "Probably not. Lute, the most famous gunfighters in all the west have killed no more than twenty or thirty men — at the most. Do you have any idea of the number of graves I've got on my backtrail?"

"I 'magine it's a right large number."

"Enough to populate a fair-sized town, and then some. And I'm tired of all the blood. I'm tired of all the killing. I'm tired of the looks people give me. I'm tired of being the most notorious gun in all the so-called wild west. Now, I haven't turned over a whole new leaf; I'll fight if I'm pushed to it, Lute." He told him of the young man back in the saloon. "I didn't want to draw on that kid, Lute. But I saw that he was working himself up into a frenzy to drag iron on me. And I wasn't going to die so that he could live. I just wish to God that people would leave me and Sally alone and let us raise our kids and our cattle and our horses. Goddamnit!" Smoke cursed and threw his tin cup, hot coffee and all, against a boulder. "Is that too much to ask of people?"

Old Lute smiled a sad moving of the lips. "You'll do what you have to do when the time comes to do it, boy. I see that writ all over you."

Smoke said nothing.

"And them down yonder by the fires," the old mountain man said. "They think that you're the fox and they's the hounds. Oh, they'll run you, boy. I can see that, too. You're gonna give them a long, hard run for their money.

19

But I know something that they don't: you ain't no fox. You're half great gray timber wolf and half puma. With some grizzly bar tossed in for spice. And when you get your fill of runnin', and turn to face them, you gonna chill 'em to the bone when you throw back your head and howl to the mountains."

# 3

He was a man who had never failed at anything. No matter what the cost, no matter the misery caused or the price in human life, he always succeeded.

Frederick von Hausen had so much money not even he knew the total of his wealth. The money he was paying the men who rode with him on this quest was an enormous sum to them, to von Hausen it didn't even amount to petty cash.

He was a handsome man; not even his constant sneer could take away from that. Tall and blond and muscular, he was highly educated at all the right schools in Europe. He was an expert swordsman, an expert shot with rifle or pistol. He wore a dueling scar on his cheek like a badge of honor.

Frederick stood by the fire on this cold morning and looked toward the north. This Smoke Jensen person was up there, not more than four or five miles away. Hausen smiled. All that claptrap and big scene back in that saloon in Dodge City had been staged for the benefit of others. Hausen had been planning this hunt for months. He had a small fortune in bets riding on his ability to hunt down and kill Jensen. He rubbed his hands together. He was looking forward to this.

Frederick von Hausen looked for his companions; they were just now rising stiffly from their blankets and moving around in their tents. The cook had been the first one up, and was now preparing breakfast, having first made coffee, a strong bitter brew that was not to von Hausen's liking. But the twenty-odd men he'd hired along the way seemed to enjoy the black poisonous brew.

The first to leave their tent was von Hausen's traveling companion, Marlene Ulbrich. Just as haughty and almost as rich as von Hausen, Marlene was blonde and beautiful and just as bloodthirsty as von Hausen. Gunter Balke and his fiancée, Maria Guhl, were the next ones up and moving about. They were followed by Hans Brodermann and his wife, Andrea. All reasonably young, in their early thirties, and all enormously wealthy, they all shared something else in common: they were easily bored, spoiled to the core, and considered everyone else on the face of the earth to be their inferior.

They had slaughtered the earth's animals in every country that would allow them entry—and that was most. If a day's hunt proved unproductive, they would shoot dogs or cats or people, if they felt they could get away with the latter bloodletting. And they always had before.

They were all dressed properly for the hunt and carried the most expensive weapons that could be handmade for them. And they all had spent weeks gathering the scum of the earth around them.

The twenty-odd men—odd in more ways than one—gathered in a quiet circle around the big fire, staying away from the aristocracy, as they had been instructed to do.

"How long do they figure on stretchin' this thing out?" Al Hayre asked, after noisily slurping at his coffee.

"They plan on makin' a springtime e-vent of it," Leo Grant told him.

"I ain't yet figured out just what it is we're supposed to do," Utah Bob said.

"Prod Jensen 'til he makes a fight of it," Larry Kelly told him. "But we'll stay back, out of range, if we can, 'til we push him clear into the Rockies."

"These people, do they not know Smoke's reputation?" Angel Cortez asked in soft tones.

"Jensen's reputation don't spell crap to them or to me," Tom Ritter said. "I don't believe nothin' I ever heard about that man. I think most of it is lies."

Pat Gilman looked across the dancing flames at Tom. "There ain't none of it lies, Tom. Smoke Jensen's a he-coon from 'way back. I seen some of his graveyards; and they's plenty more that I ain't seen."

Tom Ritter said a very ugly word.

John T. Matthey smiled. "You boys is all from Texas and Kansas and Arizona and New Mexico way. Me, I'm from Montana, like Montana Jess there. Pat there is from Colorado. He knows about Jensen, just like Utah Red do. Let me tell you this: they's gonna be some of us ain't gonna come back from this foolishness. Maybe a lot of us ain't comin' back. Them uppity, high-falutin' folk over yonder, them barons and counts and princes and their snooty women think this is gonna be a real fun game. It ain't gonna be no such of a thing. Right now Jensen is tryin' to figure out why we're trackin' him close. Today, tomorrow, the next day, he'll try to lose us. When we keep on comin', he's gonna turn mean. And boys, that is one man who was born with the bark on. That man has faced six, eight, ten men eyeball to eyeball and tooken lead and kept on his boots. When the gunsmoke cleared, Smoke Jensen was still standin'. Now, I ain't got no use for him; he's kilt several of my pards. But I got respect for him. And you boys better have some respect for him, too."

Von Hausen had been listening. He said, "Are you afraid of this penny-ante gunslinger, Mr. Matthey?"

"There ain't nothin' penny-ante about Jensen, Mr. Hausen. Wild Bill Hickok said Smoke Jensen was the fastest gun in all the west. Earp said he'd sooner be locked in a room full of mountain lions than face Jensen. Sam Bass was a pard of mine. He was offered thousands of dollars to kill Jensen. He threw the money back in the man's face. Billy the Kid said Smoke Jensen was like a God. I could go on and on namin' gunfighters who had better sense than brace Smoke Jensen. You don't know the man . . . I do. I've seen him work . . . you haven't. Now, you payin' us top wages to track and corner him. And I tooken your money and when I do that I ride for the brand. But don't none of you lowrate Jensen. That would be a fatal mistake."

"You say you know him," Hans said, strolling up. "What are his weak spots?"

"Mister, Smoke Jensen ain't got no weak spots. He's about two hundred and thirty pounds of pure poison when he's riled up. Got arms on him 'bout the size of an average man's upper leg. He fist-fought men that stood six, eight and outweighed him seventy-five-eighty pounds and stomped them into a bloody pulp. He'll fight you with guns, knives, or fists or clubs. It don't make a damn to Smoke Jensen. He's a man that don't bother nobody 'til you start messin' with him. Then he's gonna come at you lookin' like nine kinds of Hell. He was raised by mountain men during the day and suckled in the den by she-wolves at night. Don't never sell Smoke Jensen short."

"What an intriguing description," Marlene said, stepping closer to the fire. "You make him sound like something out of mythology."

"I don't know what that means, your ladyship," John T. Matthey said.

"Well, let me put it like this," Marlene said. "You make it sound as though this Smoke Jensen person cannot be killed."

"Oh, he can be killed, ma'am. He's a human bein'. But I know for a fact that he's been shot a half a dozen times with rifles and pistols and just kept on comin'. That ain't hearsay, ma'am. That's fact."

Marlene clapped her expensively gloved hands together. "Oh, I just love it, Frederick! This is going to be such an exciting hunt."

"Quite, my dear," von Hausen said. "Come, let's have some breakfast."


Lute had pulled out shortly after Smoke had told him to go on about his business. He wasn't going to ambush the crowd supposedly chasing him—not yet, anyway—they'd have to open fire on him. But he was going to try to lose them.

"I'll be around, boy," the old man had told him. "You might need some help further on up the trail."

"I'm going up north to buy bulls, Lute."

Lute grinned; what few teeth he had left were tobacco stained. "Shore you are, boy. I believe that. But them down yonder just might put a kink in your plans. See you, Smoke."

Smoke broke camp and headed north toward the Green. He smiled as he settled into the saddle. These folks wanted to see some country. He'd show them some country. He decided to leave his friend up in Central Wyoming out of this.

Lute had told him that von Hausen had been on his trail for over a month, able to move much faster because of the trains. He had so much wealth that if the train was full, he'd order up several more cars and hook on.

Smoke thought about that as he rode. Rock Springs was on the Union Pacific's transcontinental line. He wondered if von Hausen would have supplies waiting for him there? Smoke bet he would. Either there or at the town of Green River just to the west of Rock Springs. Smoke's smile toughened as he changed direction, heading southwest, into very tough country. He'd lose them in that area and then head for the little settlement he thought was still there at the old Fort Bridger site—if the Mormons hadn't burned it down again like they burned it and Fort Supply back in '57 or '58 during the Mormon War.

He lost the party trailing him by setting a grueling pace, once he discovered they had several women with them, all riding side-saddle. Smoke couldn't imagine the mentality of any woman who would have anything to do with something this foolish and bloodthirsty.

"He's got to be headin' toward Fort Bridger," Montana Jess told von Hausen.

"The terrain?" the German asked impatiently.

"It ain't high country, but it's rough country. And the army's still got a garrison there."

"They most certainly do not!" Hans said. "It was abandoned several years ago. I have information to that effect."

Montana shifted his chew and spat, looking at the man. "Your information is wrong. And here's something else: you call me a liar again, Brodermann, and I'll kill you!"

Gunter stepped between the gunfighter and the prince. Hans really was a prince from some German family who had more princes and princesses than they knew what to do with. "We are not accustomed to your ways and methods in the wild west, Mister Jess. Be patient with us."

Montana nodded his head. "Yeah," he said, then walked away.

Hans said, "I'll have to give that fellow a good thrashing before this expedition is through."

"He is certainly deserving of one," Hans' wife, Andrea said.

"And he smells bad, too," Marlene pointed out.

"The fort was reopened a couple of years back," John

26

T. told them. "What about the supplies up in Green River?"

"We can always resupply," Frederick said. "Let's pick up this man's trail and press on."

"What if he tells the army about us?" Marlene asked. "That man that our scout saw riding away from Smoke's camp the other morning might have told him about us?"

"It's possible," von Hausen admitted. "But we have done no wrong. Besides, all of us are in this country under diplomatic papers. We have immunity from any type of prosecution."

"Has that been tested in the wild west?" Gunter asked.

"You're forgetting I was trained in international law. It's been law in the United States since 1790," von Hausen replied. "Mount up."


"It's a pleasure to meet you, sir," the commanding officer at Fort Bridger said, adding with a smile, "I think. Have you eaten?"

"No. I've been pushing hard getting here."

"Trouble?"

"More than my share of it, I'm afraid."

"We'll discuss it over some food. Perhaps I can help."

"Von Hausen," the Colonel said, after the meal was over and they had settled back over coffee and cigars. "Damn little I can do—even if this rather . . . bizarre story is true. Not that I'm doubting your word, Mister Jensen," he was very quick to add. "But have the people following you actually done anything?"

"Not one hostile move, Colonel."

The colonel leaned forward. "Von Hausen is not an unknown name in Washington, Smoke. The von Hausen family have long been in diplomatic service. I'm sure the younger von Hausen is protected under international law."

"You want to explain that to me?"

27

The colonel spoke for several minutes. When he finished, Smoke sat his chair and stared at him.

"Do you mean that somebody protected under this dumb law can cold bloodedly kill anybody they like and there isn't a damn thing any lawman can do to them?"

"They can be expelled from the country."

Smoke shook his head in disbelief.

"But it works both ways, Smoke. The same law protects our diplomats in their country."

"That doesn't give a whole lot of comfort to a man in the grave, now, does it?"

The colonel smiled. "No. I'm afraid it doesn't. What will you do, Smoke?"

"Keep on traveling north. They'll get to see some wild country if they hang on my tracks."

"I remember you from fifteen years ago, Smoke. When you were no more than a boy who was quick with a gun. You would have handled this quite differently back then."

"I hope I never have to pull a gun in anger again, Colonel. But I'll only be pushed so far. No man will talk down to me, and no man will threaten the life of my wife or children, or me, and expect to live. And I don't give one tinker's damn about this so-called diplomatic immunity."

"Just between you and me, Smoke, this Frederick von Hausen has been expelled from several countries and told not to come back. He calls himself an international sportsman—as some have taken to using the word—but he's no sportsman. He's a cold-blooded killer. You haven't said anything about those with him, but I expect they're pretty much of the same caliber he is. Male and female. Did this old man tell you any of the names of those riding with von Hausen?"

"He knew some of them. J. T. Matthey, Tom Ritter, Utah Red, Cat Brown."

The colonel shook his head. "Bad ones. I've heard of them all. Guns for hire. After hearing those names I have

28

to conclude that the old man just might be right. Von Hausen is certainly up to something."

"He had to have planned this, Colonel. This isn't something von Hausen just came up with on the spur of the moment. And if that is the case, he's studied me."

"I would think so. Yes."

"So he can make a sport of tracking me down, hunting me, cornering me, and then killing me like some wild beast."

Smoke smiled, but the colonel noticed very quickly that it was not a pleasant curving of the lips. The colonel sat silently, waiting.

"I'm going to give this baron or count or whatever he is a chance to break off this hunt, Colonel. I might even take a few shots in my direction—providing they don't come too close. I'm going to do this because I'm tired of all the blood-letting. I'm going to let these people see some country, and some mighty rugged country too. But when I've had enough, I'll stand and fight. And when I decide to do that, Colonel, I won't be taking any prisoners for trial."

"You're telling me that you are going to commit murder," the colonel said stiffly.

"Call it anything you like. I'm a man who set out to visit a friend and fellow rancher to buy some bulls. That's all. Then I find myself being dogged by some European aristocrat and his friends who have hired about twenty-five of the most mangy bunch of men who ever sat a saddle. I am warned that this bunch plans to make a sport out of tracking and hunting and cornering and then killing me. I go to the army for help. The army tells me there is nothing that can be done because of some law that I never even heard of. Put yourself in my place, Colonel."

The army officer sat for a moment without speaking. He toyed with his coffee cup, then said, "Off the record, Smoke?"

29

Smoke nodded.

The colonel's eyes were bleak as he said, "When it comes time for you to make your stand, don't just wound anybody."

# 4

Smoke resupplied at the fort and pulled out early the next morning, telling the boys at the livery he was heading for a little town just north of the mouth of Hams Fork. He left the post and headed straight north, riding north until he came to Muddy Creek. He rode in the river bed for several miles, then left it and headed northwest, toward the Bear River Divide.

This was a land not for the faint-hearted, even in the early 1880's. Between Fort Bridger and north to Trapper's Point, as the mountain men used to call it, there were no towns and few settlers. The northern branch of Muddy Creek forked almost in the center of Bear River Divide. When Smoke reached the southernmost branch of the fork, with Medicine Butte far to the south of him, he made a lonely camp, cooked his supper, then carefully hid all traces of his fire and rode north for several more miles before making his night camp amid a jumble of rocks that gave him a good lookout and a secure site.

He was on the trail before dawn, picking his way north, utilizing all of his skills in making his way, leaving as few tracks as possible.

He tried to put himself inside the head of von Hausen. What would he do in a situation like this? For one thing he would not accept that his prey had gone north toward Hams Creek as Smoke had told the boys at the stable;

that would be a deliberate ruse. Von Hausen had some good trackers with him. The gunslingers might be no more than human trash, with little values and no morals, but some of them could track a snake across a rock. Von Hausen had enough salty ol' boys with him to split his forces. Yeah. He'd do that. He'd send men racing toward the north, then start working them south, from the old stage road at Hams Fork over to the Utah line.

"Good, Smoke," he muttered. "Very good move on your part. Now you've got people coming at you from two directions. Preacher would not be happy with this move."

Then he chuckled and turned his horse's head due east. When he came to the stagecoach road, he turned north and headed for what was called the Sublette Cutoff. The cutoff was developed as part of the Oregon Trail; a faster way to get to Oregon country.

As Smoke approached the little town at the cutoff, he circled and came around from the east. He stabled his horses at the livery and stood for a moment in the darkness of the huge barn, studying the horses at the hitchrail in front of the saloon.

"Those two horses over yonder," he asked the boy. "They local brands?"

"Naw," the lad replied. "They come in this mornin'. From the south. Hardcases, they look to me. Askin' questions about any strangers in town. You look familiar, mister. Are you famous, or something?"

Smoke smiled. "In a way that I did not choose," he told the boy, then gave him a silver dollar. "That's for you. Rub my horses down good and give them grain. Watch that Appaloosa; he'll kick the snot out of you if you aggravate him."

"I seen you on the cover of a book!" the boy said. "You're Smoke Jensen, the gunfighter. Jeepers! Smoke Jensen is standin' right here in front of me!"

32

"I'm Jensen. Does that little cafe over there serve up good meals?"

"Yes, sir. It's the best place in town to eat." He thought about that. "It's the *only* place in town to eat."

"Fine. I want me a meal, a bath and a shave, and I can't do any of that until I get those two gunhands over there in the saloon off my back."

"Is there gonna be a shoot-out?" the boy asked excitedly.

"I hope not. But there might be a pretty good fist-fight in a few minutes. Is there a back door to that saloon?"

"Yes, sir. You can duck around the side of this barn and come up from the north. That's a blind side."

"Fine. Now you keep still about me being in town for a few minutes. Then you can tell your friends. All right?"

"Anything you say, sir. Yes, sir."

"Where's the marshal?"

"Out of town chasin' a thief. Stole a horse and rode right through Mrs. MacKenney's wash. Took her drawers slap off the line. She ain't found 'em yet."

Smoke laughed at that. "Is there a jail?"

"Right over yonder." He pointed up the street. "Got four cells."

"I'll just need one. Do my horses right now, you hear?"

"Oh, yes, sir!"

Smoke stepped out the back of the livery and walked the alley to the edge of the small town. He crossed the street and cut back toward the saloon, taking the alley route. If his plan worked out, von Hausen was going to be plenty miffed. Smoke thought that might do the arrogant baron some good. Or count, or whatever he was. Smoke had a pretty good idea what he was, but that wasn't printable.

Smoke found the rear door to the saloon — easily done because of the mound of broken whiskey bottles and beer kegs — and slipped inside. He made his way through the gloom and peeked through a hole in the wall. He could tell the regular patrons because they were staying well away from the two trail-dusty, sweat-stained and unshaven men standing at the bar.

Smoke opened the door and stepped inside the barroom. He walked up to the bar and told the barkeep, "Beer."

Lou Kennedy and Pride Anderson glanced at each other. Both of them wore very startled looks on their ugly faces.

The mug of beer was placed in front of Smoke and he took a sip. Bootsteps sounded on the short boardwalk in front of the saloon. A young man hurried inside, sat down at a table, and whispered something to the men seated there. The men all took a quick glance at Smoke, their eyes wide.

The barkeep waddled over to the table and listened. He looked at Smoke and at the two men standing at the bar. "Bar's closed," he announced, and sat down at the table.

Smoke dropped his right hand down to the butt of his gun. "Before I kill a man, or in this case, two men, I like to know their names."

"Oh, Lord!" a farmer-type said. "Somebody call the law!"

"Shut up," a cowboy seated across the room said. "Remember me, Mister Smoke?" he asked. "I rode for you down on the Sugarloaf two, three years ago. Dusty Hill."

"Dusty. Sure. But you stay out of this. They got any friends in town?"

"I don't think so. I'll watch your back, Mr. Smoke."

"Good enough." Smoke moved closer to the pair of gunslingers.

"I'm Pride Anderson and this here's Lou Kennedy. And we ain't huntin' no trouble, Jensen."

"Then why have you and the rest of that pack of rabid

coyotes been crowdin' me for the past week?" He moved still closer.

"It's a free country, Smoke," Lou said. "A man can ride where he damn well pleases."

Smoke stepped well within swinging range. "A man can get hurt crowdin' another man. But I'm not going to hurt either one of you — very much." Smoke hit Lou smack in the mouth with a big fist. As Lou was stumbling across the room, Smoke jerked Pride's gunbelt down, the rig falling around his ankles. A split second later, Smoke had busted him square on the nose. Pride hollered as the blood and snot flew as he fell down, all tangled up in his gunbelt.

Smoke met Lou coming at him and hit him a left and right that glazed Lou's eyes and further bloodied his mouth. Smoke turned and hit Pride twice in the belly just as he was getting up, the blows sounding like a man hitting a watermelon with the flat side of an axe. Smoke caught a blow to the side of his head that probably hurt Lou's hand more than it did Smoke's noggin. But it did sting. Smoke waded in, both fists swinging and connecting, the blow driving the man to his knees. Smoke turned and Pride hit him, bloodying his mouth. Smoke backheeled him and sent the man crashing to the floor. Smoke stepped forward and grabbing the gunfighter by the back of the head, he brought a knee up into the man's face and Pride stretched out on the floor, his mouth a mess and his nose flattened.

Smoke turned just as Lou was getting up. He measured his blow and put one hard right fist onto the side of Lou's jaw. Lou's eyes rolled back while he was falling, until only the whites were showing. He hit the floor, out cold.

Smoke walked back to the bar and drank his beer down. He turned to face the crowd. "These two are part of a gang that's been hunting me . . . for sport. I should have killed them both. But maybe this way is better. Maybe when the others come into town, the sight of these two will change some minds. Dusty, will you and some of these other good citizens drag these two over to the jail, lock them down, and bring the key to me?"

"We'll shore do it," Dusty said.

"I'll be registering at the hotel and then I'll be having me a bath and a shave."

"I'll find you," Dusty said.

Smoke walked out the front door.

"Shoot!" one citizen said. "I was wantin' to see a good gunfight."

"If there had of been," Dusty said, grabbing hold of Lou's ankles, "if you'd blinked you'd a missed it."


Smoke took the key to the cell holding Lou and Pride and dropped it down an old unused well. He had registered at the hotel and after disposing of the cell key, he walked to the barber shop and told the man to get some hot water ready for a bath. After his bath, he had himself a shave and a haircut. Then he went to the cafe for something to eat.

Smoke was eating roast beef and boiled potatoes and gravy when the marshal walked in, all dusty and tired-looking. The marshal paused in the door, gave the crowded cafe a once-over, spotted him, walked to the table, and sat down.

"Coffee, Pat," he called to the waiter. "And a plate of food. I'm so hungry I could eat a skunk." He cut his eyes. "You got to be Smoke Jensen."

"That's right."

"Did you put those two beat-up lookin' characters into my jail?"

Smoke chewed for a moment. "Nope."

The marshal waited for a moment. "Well, if it wouldn't

36

be too much of a problem, would you mind telling me who did?"

"Some of your citizens. At my request."

"Both of them yahoos wants a doctor."

"I imagine they do. They were both in fairly poor condition the last time I saw them."

The marshal looked at him. "One of them tagged you at least one good lick."

"Yes, he did. The waiter said they had apple pie. Is it any good?"

"It's very good. I have it every day. It's the only kind of pie the damn cook knows how to bake. Mister Jensen, what the hell do you want me to do with those two gunslingers in my jail?" He lifted his coffee cup, blew, and took a sip.

"I imagine you'll be keeping them for awhile. I threw away the cell key."

The marshal choked on his coffee. "Damnit, man. I only had the one key for that cell."

"I know." Smoke smiled at him. "Don't worry. The man who'll be coming to get them has plenty of money. He'll pay for rebricking the rear wall, after you have someone jerk it out to set them loose."

Smoke was miles north of the settlement when Frederick von Hausen and his party arrived, looking for the two missing members. The German was not amused at what he found.

"I demand that you release those men immediately!" he told the marshal.

"I ain't got no charges against either of them," the marshal replied.

"Well . . . turn them loose!"

"I surely wish I could. They're eating the town's treasury outta money. Never seen two men who could eat that much."

"Release them!"

"I can't."

"You are straining my patience," von Hausen told the man. "First you tell me there are no charges against either man, then you tell me that you cannot free them. This is all very confusing."

"I can't open the damn door," the marshal said. "Smoke Jensen threw away the only key."

Von Hausen cussed.

The marshal waited until the German had stopped swearing. "He said you probably wouldn't see the humor in it."

"Get us outta here!" Lou hollered.

"Where is the nearest locksmith?" von Hausen asked, getting a grip on his temper.

"Lord, I don't know," the marshal said, scratching his head. "Denver, I reckon."

"My good man," Hans stepped in. "We must free these men. It is an injustice to keep them locked up when they have done no wrong."

The marshal looked at him. "You got any ideas?"

"We could get some dynamite and blow the wall," John T. suggested.

"The hell you will!" Pride bellowed.

While the manhunters were arguing among themselves, the marshal opened a drawer of his desk and pulled out a pile of old wanted posters. Several of the gunslingers hit the saddle and left town.

"Just as well. Didn't want to fool with them anyway," the marshal muttered.

Smoke was a good twenty miles north of the town, camped along the banks of Fontenelle Creek, drinking coffee and cooking his supper before a team of mules was found and a chain hooked to the bars of the cell.

Frederick von Hausen had to count out the money for jail repairs and put it in the marshal's hand before the townspeople would allow the wall to be pulled down.

"Now will you release my men?" the German asked.

"Take it down," the marshal said.

The big Missouri Reds strained but the wall would not budge.

"Damnit, do something!" von Hausen yelled.

"You wanna get out there and get in harness with them mules?" the marshal asked him.

"You are a very impudent fellow," von Hausen told him.

"And you're beginnin' to annoy me," the marshal replied. "And when I get annoyed, I tend to get testy. The second best thing you could do is shut your mouth. The first best thing you could do is go back to wherever the hell it is you come from."

"Pull, babies!" the mule's owner yelled and the wall finally came down in a cloud of dust.

Lou and Pride staggered out, both of them looking as though they had picked a fight with a tornado.

They told their stories to an incredulous von Hausen.

"He whipped both of you?" the German said.

"Incredible," Gunter said.

"I warned you about Jensen," John T. reminded them.

While the back of the jail was being demolished, the ladies in the group had been enjoying hot baths and the boys in the town had been enjoying them a whole lot more by peeking through holes in the fence back of the barber shop.

By the time the men had been released, it was late in the day and pointless to continue. Von Hausen and his party stayed at the small hotel while the gunslingers slept wherever they could.

When the morning dawned and the European community and their scummy entourage finally got underway, Smoke was riding along the Fontenelle, with Commissary Ridge to the west.

39

He'd had his fun, and now the game would turn serious, he guessed. He had insulted his majesty and his lordship, and the prince and their ladies, and the Germans would not take it lightly.

But Smoke was still not going to start tossing lead at this point. He just could not accept that this was going to turn lethal. He just couldn't. Those following him were going to have to show that they really intended to kill him before he turned and made his stand.

He hoped von Hausen would call it off.

Deep inside him, he knew the German would not.

# 5

"He's stopped tryin' to hide his trail," Gil Webb said. "That makes me wonder what he's up to."

Nat Reed nodded his head in agreement. He took off his hat and ran his fingers through his shaggy hair. "What you gonna do with all the money them crazy people is payin' us, Gil?"

"Spend it on women and booze," the man-hunter said simply and honestly.

They were waiting for the main party to catch up, taking a few minutes to rest.

"That's a lot of damn money to spend on women and whiskey."

"So what are you gonna do with your pay?"

Nat grinned. "Spend it on women and whiskey."

The men laughed.

"You ever been up in this part of the country, Nat?"

"Nope. I'm a plains and desert man, myself. That map we looked at the other day showed some hellacious mountains just a few miles north of here."

"Yeah. John T. and Utah and them other high-country boys is gonna have to take the point from here on out. I ain't got no idea where we are."

John T. sat his saddle and looked down at the clear tracks Smoke was leaving. His smile held no humor. "He's leadin' us straight into the wilderness. I got a hunch he's gonna take us into the big canyon country."

"What is that?" Gunter asked.

"A damn good place to stay out of," John T. told him. "Smoke was raised by mountain men, so he'll know the High Lonesome mighty well."

"The what?" Andrea asked.

"A place where it's hotter than hell and colder than ice. Where the winds blow all the time and they don't never blow. Places were you can crawl to the edge and look down for more 'un five thousand feet—straight down." (Only a slight exaggeration). "Wild lost rivers that don't go nowhere." (Actually they do). "They's still Injuns in there that ain't never seen a white man." (Probably true). "Unless it was a mountain man. Like Smoke Jensen."

"Has it been explored?" Gunter asked.

"Rivers been traveled on some. Mountain men and Injuns know it. And smoke Jensen."

"How big is this place?" von Hausen asked.

"Don't nobody know for sure. If that's where Jensen is takin' us, he'll find a good spot to stash his horses and start to give us pure-dee hell. Jim Bridger country. It's wild, people, and it gets wilder the further north you go. Any of you ever seen a lightnin' storm in the high-up? They're terrible. You claim to have studied him, von Hausen; but I bet you got most of your information from gossip and from them damn Penny Dreadful books. The same with you boys from the plains and the flats. So I'll tell you what Jensen is and ain't.

"He's a mountain man. He knows 'em, he ain't scared of 'em, and he can climb 'em. He's at home in the mountains. And when he makes his stand, it'll be in the mountains."

John T. paused to roll a cigarette and light up. "You see, people, this is just a game to him right now. He's havin' fun with us. If he was takin' this serious, why they'd be some of us layin' back yonder on the trail, dead

42

from ambush. You real sure you want to go on with this so-called sporting e-vent, von Hausen?"

"Of course, I do!"

"Just checkin'."

"Mount up and let's go," von Hausen said.

Smoke crossed and recrossed the Fontenelle several times, knowing that would slow up those behind him. He could have taken a much easier route, but he didn't want to make things easy for his pursuers. He was hoping — knowing it was a slim chance — that if he took them over the roughest terrain he could find, they might decide to call off the chase.

Maybe.

He was going to ride straight north, up through the Salt River Range, have some fun with them up in Jim Bridger country — maybe get them good and lost for a time — and then head up the Snake Range, through the Teton Range, and then over the Divide. If they were still after him, and had proved hostile, there he would make his stand.

He had considered talking to the German, but decided that probably wouldn't do a bit of good. He had thought about leaving them a note, stuck to a tree, warning them off. But von Hausen might decide that was a challenge and really put on the pressure. Smoke had never been in any situation quite like this one and didn't really know how to handle it.

His rancher friend was not expecting him — Smoke had told him he'd be up sometime in the spring or summer — so his friend would not be worried about him.

"Hell of a mess," Smoke muttered, and headed north.

"This is the goddamnest country I ever seen in my life,"

*What is now Yellowstone National Park

Marty Boswell griped. "The sun's out now and it's warm; tonight it'll be so damned cold a body's gotta jump up and down to keep his feet from freezin'."

"At least Jensen's just as colds," Paul Melham said.

"No, he ain't," John T. corrected. "He's used to it and come prepared. He can build him a lean-to and a soft bed outta sweet smellin' boughs near 'bouts as fast as you boys can unsaddle your horse."

"Why do you constantly try to discourage the men?" Marlene asked him.

"I ain't tryin' to discourage 'em. I just want the soft ones to quit and get long gone away from me 'fore we tangle with Jensen. I don't want nobody but hardcases with me when that hombre decides to fight."

"Am I a hardcase, John T.?" she asked teasingly.

"You-all are payin' the bulldog, your ladyship. I just don't want no little puppy dogs around me when push comes to shove."

"What do you have against Smoke Jensen, John T.?"

"I don't like him. He's too damn high and mighty to suit me. Somebody needs to slap him down a time or two."

"And you think you're that man?"

"I might be. I do think that all of us—if we get real lucky and work real careful—can put an end to Smoke Jensen."

"Oh, I assure you, John T., that we are going to most definitely do that. Frederick has never failed—*never.*"

He ain't never run up on the likes of Smoke Jensen, neither, John T. thought, but didn't put it into words.

Smoke figured he was at least two full days ahead of his hunters, and perhaps even three. He was going to have to re-supply, and discard some gear while adding things more practical if this game turned deadly, as he feared it would.

He knew of a tiny town located on the west side of the Salt River Range, not more than three or four miles from the Idaho border. He'd head there, but he'd do so carefully, and try to lose his pursuers—at least for a time.

Smoke headed out and put Salt River Pass behind him, then he cut west and stayed on the east side of the Salt River, leaving plenty of tracks. He rode across a rocky flat, then stopped and tore a blanket up and tied squares of cloth over his horses' hooves so they would not scar the rock, then doubled back to the river and stayed in it, as best he could, for several miles. He found another rocky flat and exited the river there.

He swung down from the saddle and spent some time working out his tracks. Satisfied, he mounted up and headed for the settlement. He had probably gained another day; if he was lucky, maybe two days.

He spent a night in a cold camp, not wanting to chance a fire, on the off chance his hunters had gained on him, and Smoke was in no mood for nonsense when he rode into the tiny town the next day, at mid-morning.

He told the man at the livery to rub his horses down good and give them all the grain they wanted to eat.

"Payable in ad-vance," the man said sourly.

Smoke looked at him for a moment through the coldest, most dangerous eyes the man had ever seen.

"It's for ever'body, mister," he spoke gently. "Boss's orders. I just work here."

Smoke smiled and handed the man some coins, including a little extra. "Have yourself a drink on me at day's end."

"I'll do it," the man said with a returning smile. "Thanks. They's beds over the saloon or you're welcome to bed down here. Beth's is our only cafe and she serves up some pretty good grub."

"I'll check it out. Much obliged."

"Ain't I seen you before, mister?"

"Never been here before in my life."

"Shore looks familiar," the man muttered, when Smoke had walked away. Then he stood still as a post as recognition struck him. "Good God!" he said. "And I got lippy with *him?*"

Smoke checked out the rooms over the saloon, saw fleas and various other crawling and hopping creatures on the dirty sheets, and decided he would sleep in the loft of the barn. He'd always liked the smell of hay.

"You mighty goddamn particular," the combination barkeep and desk clerk told him.

That did it. Smoke grabbed the man by the shirt, picked him up about a foot off the floor, and pinned him to the wall. "Would it too much of a problem for you to be civil?"

"You better put me down, mister. Tom Lilly runs this town, and he's a personal friend of mine."

"And you'll run tell him about this little incident and he'll do your fighting for you, right?"

"Something like that. And he'll clean your plow, drifter."

Smoke dragged him to the landing and threw him down the stairs. "Then go tell him, you weasel. I'll be having a drink at the bar. From the good bottle."

The man scrambled to his feet and ran out the front door. Smoke walked down the steps, rummaged around behind the bar until he found the good bottle of whiskey, and poured himself a drink. Although not much of a drinking man, the whiskey was smooth and felt good going down.

He fixed himself a sandwich from the fresh-laid out lunch selection and poured a cup of coffee, then walked to a table in the back of the room. He took off his coat and sat down. Slipping the hammer-thong from his Colts was something he did the instant his boots touched ground out of the stirrups.

The front door opened and the lippy barkeep entered,

followed by a huge bear of a man.

"There he is," the barkeep said, pointing Smoke out. Then he ran back behind the bar. "And that'll be fifty cents for that drink of good whiskey."

"Money's on the bar," Smoke told him.

The man lumbered over, stopping a few feet from the table. The floor had trembled as he moved. Smoke figured him to be about six feet six inches tall and weighing maybe two hundred and seventy-five pounds.

"My name's Tom Lilly," the big man rumbled.

Smoke took a bite from his sandwich and said nothing.

"Are you deaf!" Lilly hollered.

"I will be if you keep shouting," Smoke told him. "Quiet down, will you?"

The man looked shocked. "You really tellin' me what to do, cowboy?"

"Yes, as a matter of fact, I am. And you smell bad, too. Step back, before your breath contaminates the cheese."

Tom was so shocked he was momentarily speechless. Nobody ever spoke to him in such a manner. A few had challenged him, years back, and he had broken their heads, their backs, or just simply and quickly stomped them to death. He had run this town with an iron hand — or fist — for several years; now this drifter shows up and starts with the mouth.

Finally Tom found his voice. "You better enjoy that sandwich, drifter. 'Cause it's gonna be the last thing you'll ever eat except my fist."

Smoke shoved the square table with all his strength, one sharp corner catching Tom in the thigh and pushing through the cloth of the big man's trousers, tearing a gouge in his leg. Tom screamed in pain and grabbed at his bleeding leg just as Smoke came around the table, picking up a sturdy chair during his brief journey. Smoke brought the chair down on Tom's head, driving the man to his knees and destroying the chair.

Using what was left of the chair back as a club, Smoke proceeded to rain blows on the bully, the wood ringing like a blacksmith's hammer as Smoke bounced it against Tom's head.

A crowd began to gather, both inside the saloon and on the boardwalk in front.

When Smoke had beaten the man unconscious, he tossed the club to the floor and dragged Tom Lilly across the floor and to the now open door. He dragged him across the boardwalk and dumped him in the street.

The citizens, male and female, stood and applauded Smoke as he walked back inside the saloon. The barkeep stood rooted behind the bar, disbelief and fear in his eyes. "Don't kill me!" he finally squalled.

"He's been Tom Lilly's biggest supporter," a tired-looking man said. "But he's nothing. As soon as Tom's men come back from making their collections around the area, you're gonna be in real trouble, mister."

"Collections?" Smoke asked.

"They claim to be protecting us," a woman said, standing outside the saloon and speaking through the open door. No way a good woman would enter a saloon. "They showed up here about three years ago. Next thing we knew, our part-time marshal was dead and Tom and his bunch were running things."

"Several tried to intervene," a man said. "They come up dead or missing."

"How many in Tom's gang?" Smoke asked, knowing he had gotten himself into another situation.

"It varies. Anywhere from six to ten. Scum just seem to gather around the likes of Tom Lilly."

"Oh, my Lord!" a woman cried. "Tom's gettin' to his feet."

Smoke stepped out onto the boardwalk. By now, all had noticed the unusual way he wore his guns and pegged him as a gunfighter. The man from the livery stood on the fringe of the crowd and said nothing. But there was a big grin on his face.

With blood running down his face from the savage beating he'd just taken from Smoke, Tom Lilly staggered to his feet and swayed for a moment. "No man does this to me and lives," Tom snarled the words. Then he grabbed for his gun.

# 6

Smoke's draw was faster than the blink of an eye. He put a .44 slug into Tom's arm, the slug breaking the bully's elbow and rendering the arm useless. Tom screamed as the gun dropped back into leather. Smoke's draw had been so fast Tom had been unable to clear his holster.

"Jesus," a man said. He cut his eyes to Smoke. "Who in hell are you, mister?"

"A man who doesn't like bullies," Smoke told him.

"My arm's ruint!" Tom bellowed. "You done crippled me."

"You people do with him as you see fit," Smoke told the crowd. The whole town had turned out; about a hundred people, including the dogs and cats.

"My boys'll burn this damn town to the ground," Tom yelled. "They'll have their way with the women and kill the men. You people better wise up and run this drifter outta town and get me some medical help."

"We'll help you," a man said, uncoiling a length of rope he'd taken from his saddle.

"I'll be down the street at the cafe," Smoke said. He walked back into the saloon and got his coat and hat. He looked at the barkeep. "If you have any sense at all, you'd better take to the air and don't look back. The townspeople are gettin' ready to hang Tom Lilly and they just might decide to string you up, too."

"Who are you?" he stammered, his face sweat-shiny from fear.

"Smoke Jensen."

The barkeep gulped a couple of times then hit the back door at a run. Seconds later, the sounds of a galloping horse filled the cool air.

"Now wait a minute!" Tom Lilly yelled. "You people can't do this to me."

"Shut up, Tom," a woman told him. "Your days of bullying and killing are over."

Smoke walked over to Beth's Cafe and stepped inside.

"Get him up on that horse!" a man yelled, just as Smoke was closing the door. "Take him down to the hangin' tree."

"Goddamn you all to hellfire!" Tom screamed.

Smoke sat down by a front window and smiled at the lady behind the counter. "Coffee and a plate lunch," he said. "Or would you rather go down and see the hanging first?"

"Just as long as Tom Lilly does get hanged," she said. "He's got about seven pretty bad ol' boys due back in town right around noon. What are you going to do about them?"

"I'm not going to do anything," Smoke told her. "Unless they crowd me. I think the townspeople will handle them."

She brought him coffee. Smoke watched through the window as men armed with rifles began stationing themselves on roof tops.

"He ran the town through fear and intimidation," Beth said from the kitchen. "He threatened to do terrible things to the kids. He would take a child's pet and kill it with his bare hands, right in front of the children. He's raped more than one woman. Tom Lilly is a horrible man."

"Was," Smoke said, as he watched the crowd of people come walking back up the wide street, leading a riderless horse. "Tom Lilly is swinging in the wind now."

Beth placed his plate of food in front of him. "Got puddin' for dessert."

"Sounds good." Smoke ate slowly of the thick stew and hot, fresh-baked bread laden with sweet butter. When he had finished, Beth brought him a big bowl of pudding and he topped that off with more coffee.

Riders galloped into town just as Smoke was sugaring his coffee. He rolled a cigarette and watched the men rein up in front of the saloon.

"Lilly's men?" he asked.

"Yes. And a scummier bunch never sat a saddle."

"I don't think they'll ever sit another saddle," Smoke told her.

The words had hardly left his mouth before a dozen rifles smashed the mid-day air and seven bodies lay crumpled in the street, their blood staining the dirt.

"Town's yours again," Smoke said.


Smoke made his purchases that afternoon, and although the owner of the general store was curious about what the stranger bought, he asked no questions.

Smoke bought several hundred feet of rope, dynamite, caps, and fuses. He bought a rifle and several hundred rounds of .44's, then bought a sawed-off shotgun and several boxes of shells. He carried his purchases back to the livery and packed it very carefully.

"Thanks for not spreading my name around town," he told the liveryman.

"I figured you wanted it that way. You got people on your backtrail, Smoke?"

"Yes. A big bunch of them."

"They must be fools," the man said.

"I haven't figured out exactly what they are, to tell the truth. I'm trying to avoid a fight, and they just keep on coming at me."

"I think," the liveryman said drily, after seeing Smoke's purchases, "them folks comin' up behind you are gonna be awful sorry when they do catch up with you."

Smoke had a long, hot bath—figuring this might be the last chance he'd have to take one for some time—and then a shave. He ate an early supper at the cafe but heard no mention of Tom Lilly nor his gang among the townspeople. It was a closed chapter in their lives and probably would never be discussed outside the home. There are an awful lot of people buried in unmarked graves throughout the west.

Smoke went to bed shortly after dark and was up long before dawn. The liveryman had his quarters in the big barn and had coffee boiling when Smoke climbed down from the loft.

"I ain't fitten for nothin' 'til I have my coffee," the liveryman said. "Some folks say I'm plumb grouchy. I figured you for a coffee-drinkin' man, too."

"You figured right. What's between here and the Montana line?"

"Damn little. Couple of old tradin' posts is all."

"That's what I thought." Smoke sipped his coffee and took a bite of the cold biscuit with a piece of salt meat in it the liveryman had offered. That meant that von Hausen would have to carry a lot of supplies with him, for once they passed this little settlement, there was nothing for a lot of long hard miles.

"You got a wicked look in your eyes," the liveryman said.

"I got wicked thoughts in my head," Smoke replied with a smile.

The liveryman went off to get the coffee pot and Smoke took that quiet time to think. The Tetons had been explored a half dozen times by the government, the last one being only a couple of years back. Settlers were now coming into that area, entering by way of the Gros Ventre River and Teton Pass. What the liveryman didn't know was that two little villages were already established in that area; there might be more but if so, Smoke hadn't heard of them. But once past the junction of the two narrow roads, just south of Pacific Creek, there was nothing except wilderness until you got up into Montana. And Smoke doubted that von Hausen and company had ever seen wilderness like where he was leading them.

"Tell the people in this town that while they might think they owe me, don't refuse any type of service to this bunch that'll be coming along the next day or two. They're a bad bunch, so don't cross them."

"I understand, Smoke."

"Be sure you do." He shook hands with the man and saddled up. "See you around, partner," he said from the saddle.

"See you around, Smoke."

Smoke rode out into the cold early morning air and headed north.

Angel Cortez picked up Smoke's trail on the west side of Salt River. Some rocks had been disturbed and that was enough to put the Mexican on the trail. Satisfied he had the right trail, Angel rode back to the main party and told them the news.

"Excellent!" von Hausen said.

"I know where he's goin', now," John T. said. "Little settlement just a few miles north of here. Tom Lilly's town, so I been told."

Utah Red spat a stream of tobacco juice. "I bet it ain't if Jensen rode through there."

"No bets there," John T. said, picking up the reins. "We'll soon find out."

The townspeople heeded Smoke's warning, but they didn't like it and made that very clear by having every man and woman in the town armed when von Hausen and party rode in. It made for quite a show of force.

54

"He's been here," John T. said glumly. "Don't nobody make any quick moves or act hostile. Smoke's done shoved some steel up these folks' backbone and they gonna be quick on the shoot. You boys understand all that?"

They understood, and so did von Hausen and his party of adventurers.

"We'll have us a bite to eat, conduct our business quietly, and we shall be gone in one hour," von Hausen instructed.

"Probably be gone sooner than that," Leo Grant told him. "They's a closed sign in the cafe winder." He looked at the abundance of sawed-off shotguns in the hands of grim-faced men and shuddered. He'd seen men cut in two with those things. Sickenin' sight.

"Saloon's closed, too," Nat Reed observed. "I think that we'd just better tend to our business as quickly as possible and ride on."

"I concur," Gunter Balke said. "What say you, Frederick?"

"Yes. From the looks of things, this Tom Lilly, and I would assume his men too, are no longer around."

"Oh, they're around," John T. said. "Six feet under."

"Yonder's the hangin' tree," Cosgrove said softly. "With the rope still on it."

"Makes my throat hurt just lookin' at it," Paul Melham said. "I got an idea: why don't the most of us just ride on through and we'll be waitin' for y'all outside of town? This is a stacked deck if I ever seen one. They's men on rooftops with rifles, too."

"Boss?" John T. looked at von Hausen.

"Yes. Good idea. Ride on. You men leading the pack animals stay to help load."

Von Hausen's stomach muscles knotted up when he led his group into the general store. There were men all around the store, all armed with sawed-off shotguns.

"We mean no harm to anyone," Gunter said. "We just

want to resupply and we'll be gone within the hour."

"Fine," the owner of the general store said. "But you gonna find this mighty expensive shoppin'."

Marlene looked at a freshly printed sign and smiled. Beans: $4.00 a lb. Taters: $6.00 a lb. Sugar: $15.00 a lb. Coffee: $20.00 a lb. And so on.

Von Hausen found the whole thing humorous and laughed when she pointed out the sign to him. "Obviously a depressed area, my dear. Let them have their fun. Spread our wealth among the colonials, so to speak. It's good public relations, you know."

They bought their supplies, paid for them, and were gone in thirty minutes. At the edge of town, Bob Hogan pointed out a row of fresh-dug graves, the mounds still muddy. "Smoke Jensen came through," was all he had to say.

Frederick glanced at Hans and arched an eyebrow. "Formidable opponent," he said, and rode on.

Ol' Preacher talked about this country, and took Smoke through it when he was just a boy. The old mountain man told Smoke all about the rendezvous he'd attended in the Snake River country back in the early '30's. The event was held close to where three Wyoming rivers meet: the Snake, Greys, and Salt.

Smoke rode deeper into the High Lonesome, memories of Ol' Preacher all around him. It seemed to Smoke that his friend and mentor was guiding him on.

After leaving the settlement, Smoke had angled over, crossed the Salt River Range, and followed the Greys up. He was not far from where the old mountain man, William Sublette, had reached a particularly beautiful and lonesome place and named it Jackson Hole, after another mountain man and close friend, David Jackson. Preacher had told him that was back in '29, long before the damn settlers started coming in and civilizing everything they touched.

Five decades later, there were still damn few settlers in the area, but those hardy ones who had come, had stayed. The valley where Smoke was heading was approximately forty-eight miles long and about six to eight miles wide, with mountains pushing thousands of feet into the sky all around it and in it.

Smoke was going to test those following him. He was going to give them a little taste of what was in store for them if they persisted in hunting him clear up into the High Lonesome of northwest Wyoming, where the peaks pushed two-and-a-half miles into the sky and one misstep meant death.

Here in the hole is where he'd find out if those on his backtrail really meant to kill him. For if that was true, he would leave some of them to be buried among the Aspen, Englemann spruce, Douglas fir and lodgepole pine. And where the mountain men used to join the wolves in their howling, lending their voices to the ever-sighing winds of the High Lonesome.

# 7

"Magnificent country," Gunter said, riding in a valley between the towering mountains.

"Some of us will enjoy it for eternity, I think," Angel said.

The words had hardly left his mouth when John T. called for a halt. Frederick rode up to the point. "What's the matter?" the German asked.

John T. pointed to a strange design of rocks in the middle of the trail. "That's the matter."

"What does it mean?"

"That's the Blackfoot sign for warning. Tellin' us not to come any further."

"Oh!" Marlene said, riding up. "Will we get to shoot some red wild Indians?"

"No Injun put that there, your ladyship," John T. told her. "Smoke Jensen done that."

"How do you know that?" Hans asked.

"See that little squirmly lookin' thing off to one side? That's the sign for smoke. He's tellin' us that from here on, the game is over."

"Good, good!" Frederick said. "He's throwing down the glove." He dismounted and with his boots, kicked the strange assemblage of rocks apart.

"How will Smoke know we've picked up his challenge?" Gunter asked.

" 'Cause he's watchin' us right now," John T. said. "Bet on it."

The howl of a wolf touched them, the quivering call echoing all around them.

Montana Jess looked at John T. "And there he is."

"Yep. And there he is," John T. said.

Frederick looked all around him. The silence of the deep timber was all he could feel and see. "Jensen!" he called. "Smoke Jensen! Your time has come to die. Not by a faster gun, but by a man who is much more intelligent than you. You'll see, Jensen. You'll see."

Jerry Watkins glanced at Mike Hunt. The two gunmen from West Texas shrugged their shoulders. They'd heard brags before.

Von Hausen took his rifle from his specially-made saddle boot. "Well, come on!" he said impatiently. "Our quarry is challenging us to hunt him. So, let's hunt him."

John T. looked down from his saddle. "You want us in on this?"

"No," von Hausen said. "We're just going to toy with him a bit this time."

"Uh-huh," John T. said. He swung down from the saddle and led his horse away.

Von Hausen and the others loaded up and took the caps from the telescopic sights. Von Hausen grinned. "We'll have some fun with him now." He levered in a round and started blasting at the quiet of the woods.

The others in his party followed suit and between the six of them put about eighty rounds into the woods, the slugs howling off rocks, scaring the birds, scarring the trees, and ruining the peacefulness of the hole.

"All right," Smoke said, and lifted his Winchester .44-.40 he'd bought back at the settlement. "Now we know." His first round tore the saddle horn off of von Hausen's horse and sent the animal bucking and snorting in fear. His second slug tore up the earth at von Hausen's feet and put the German nobleman on the ground. His third slug howled wickedly off a boulder and just missed—as was his intention—Gunter's head. He hit the ground and hugged it.

The women—who had never been under fire—shrieked and ran for cover.

Hans gallantly stood his ground. He raised his rifle to fire at the puffs of gunsmoke coming from above him and Smoke put a round between the man's boots, showering and stinging his ankles with rocks. Hans hit the ground and sprawled out quite unaristocratically.

Smoke shifted positions immediately, vanishing silently as a great gray wolf back into the thick timber.

John T., cold-blooded killer that he was, had taken cover—just like the rest of his crew—before the echo of the first shot had died away. John T. had the general location of Smoke spotted, but damned if he was going to expose himself to Smoke's deadly fire. Not yet. They had plenty of time.

"Swine!" von Hausen said, getting to his knees and brushing himself off. He shook both his fists at the wilderness. *"Arschloch!"*

"Wonder what that means?" Ford asked his buddy Cosgrove.

"I don't know. But it sure sounds nasty."

"Are you ladies all right?" Gunter called to the women, huddling behind a huge boulder.

"Yes. We're quite all right," Andrea returned the call. "That man really must be of terribly low quality to fire on women, don't you think?"

The fact that she fired first at Smoke apparently never entered her mind.

Cat Brown and Paul Melham exchanged glances, Cat saying, "That's a strange way of lookin' at it."

"Ain't it the truth. Women start shootin' at me, I'm damn sure gonna return the fire."

"Break up into groups," von Hausen ordered the gunfighters. "Five groups. The first group to corner Smoke Jensen and lead me to him gets an additional five thousand

60

dollars. We start the hunt first thing in the morning. John T., find us a suitable place to make camp."

"We break up into groups of five," John T. said. "One group stays with the Germans and we'll switch around ever' day so's ever'body can get the same chance at the additional money." He rolled him a cigarette. "Damn sure beats the hell out of killin' homesteaders. I think," he added.

Smoke had worked his way back to his horses and was gone, vanishing back into the rugged wilderness. He rode through the harsh and unforgiving terrain with the ease of a man who was comfortable with the elements; at home with them. The mountains, the desert, the swamps . . . they are neither for nor against a man. They are neutral. But if one is too survive, that person must understand what he is up against and work with his surroundings, never against them.

Smoke understood that. Probably the men of the west riding with the Germans knew it too. He doubted any of the others did. And eventually, he would use that lack of knowledge and their natural arrogance to work against them.

He could have easily killed von Hausen and the others a few moments ago. But he did not want to kill anymore. He wanted to dissuade them from this stupid hunt.

He wondered if that was possible?

He didn't think so, but he had to try.

Briscoe killed a deer and the meat was cooking as the night began closing in around the hunting party in the Tetons. The hunters were very quiet, each with their own thoughts in this harsh land. Miles away from them, in a very carefully selected spot, Smoke sat before his own small fire—which he would soon extinguish for safety's sake—and cooked his supper and boiled his coffee. It had been years since he'd been in this country, but all the trails and creeks and rushing mountain streams and cul-de-sacs were mapped in his mind.

He was camped between Hunt Mountain and Prospectors Mountain. To the west lay Fossil Mountain, the east, Phelps Lake. Below him were the hunters. He could actually see their fires, when he stepped out of the rocks which concealed his camp.

"Vain, silly people," Smoke muttered to the night. "Leading others to their death if they keep this up."

A wolf howled in the night, and Smoke smiled. He could commiserate with the wolf; knew just how the animal felt. Knew how it felt to be hunted for no real reason. He knew the wolf posed no real threat to mankind; never had and never would, if people would just give it room to hunt and exist. But Smoke knew that much of humankind was timid and selfish; much of what was left were just like those hunting him: the types of people who wanted to kill for the sake of blood-letting alone, enjoying seeing their prey suffer. Smoke had no use for those types. None at all.

Ol' Preacher had told him, long ago, that if God hadn't wanted all the critters of the forests and plains and swamps and deserts to exist side by side with man, the Almighty wouldn't have put them here. Preacher had said that if given the chance, nearly all the critters would leave man alone, if man would just take the time to understand them. Indians felt the same way. But most men were too impatient, and would not take the time to really understand the value of those who share the earth.

Smoke recalled Ol' Preacher's words: "One of these days, boy, after we're dead and gone and has become a part of the wind and the sky and earth, man is gonna look around him and say: I wonder what happened to the wolf, the puma, the bear, the deer, the beaver, the jaybird, and the eagle. I miss them. What happened? And most will be too gawddamn stupid to understand that *they* was what happened. Bloodthirsty for the kill. Arrogant and unfeelin' for God's lesser creatures. Sometimes I wonder just who is God's lesser creatures. Us, or the animals. Animals don't kill for sport, just man. Animals don't kill 'ceptin' for food to eat or to protect young'uns or territory. Hell's fire, Smoke, I've personal seen babies that wandered off from their tipis that was taken in by wolves and kept alive until they was found. And that's the truth. You'll see it yourself as we travel this land, you and me. I have to laugh when I hear folks say wolves is savage creatures. Not unless you mess with 'em they ain't. But don't we humans turn savage if somebody messes with us? We damn shore do. It's a mighty strange and hypocritical world we live in, boy. We humans expect more out of animals than we do out of our own kind. And that's stupid, boy. Stupid and arrogant."

The wolf howled again. Its voice was beautiful in the night. Somewhere close to the wolf, a puma coughed a warning to stay out of its territory. An owl hunted in the darkness.

"Stay with us," Smoke muttered as he put out the fire. "Stay with us. We need you a lot more than you need us."

Smoke put out his fire and wrapped up in his blankets; but sleep was elusive on this night. He wrestled with his thoughts. He knew he should take the fight to those hunting him. Knew that with just one night's deadly work he could so demoralize those man-hunters that many of those left would pull out, their hearts and minds numbed with fear.

So why didn't he?

Because he was tired of the killing. He didn't want to spill any more blood. It was just that simple. He wished he could shout to the world: Smoke Jensen wants no more.

Wants no more?

When did he ever want the killings? Sure, he had taken the fight to many people over the years. But only after they had done a harm to him or those he loved.

So what made this situation any different from any of the others? What had he done to any of those people hunting him?

The answer was that he had done nothing to any of them.

So why all the reluctance on his part?

He tried to convince himself as he turned in his blankets that it was because of the women with the group.

But he knew that held little truth. From what he had seen so far the women were just as savage and blood-thirsty as their male counterparts. They certainly hadn't shown any hesitation to fire their weapons. He had seen that evidenced this afternoon.

The bottom line was that he was sick of all the killing. But there was an addendum to that.

Those hunting Smoke seemed determined to kill him.

So where did that leave him? What options did he have? Sleep finally took him as he was thinking: No options.


Al Hayre and his group looked at the silent timber and the towering mountains that loomed all around them. They could feel eyes on them; sensed that Jensen was watching them. It was an uncomfortable feeling knowing that he could see them but they couldn't see him.

"I don't like this," a bounty hunter known only as Gary said.

"You got any better ideas on how to flush him out?" Utah Red asked.

Gary sat his saddle and shut his mouth, a glum expression on his face.

"That's what I figured," Utah said. He looked around him. "Where the hell is Cosgrove?"

The wind sighed off the mountains and through the lushness of the unspoiled wilderness, the cold breeze teasing the men, as if to say: I know.

"Well, hell!" Al Hayre said, twisting in the saddle and looking around him. "He was right behind me a minute ago."

"Somethin' movin' in the timber," Gary said, pointing. "Right over there."

The men dismounted and ground-reined their horses,

taking their rifles from the saddle boots and fanning out, moving toward the timber.

Cosgrove's horse walked out of the timber, dragging its reins and trying to graze.

"Rope's gone from the saddle," Angel Cortez said.

"What the hell does that mean?" Gary asked.

No one replied. No one knew.

As the men drew nearer, muffled sounds came from the gloom of the timber and the thick underbrush.

"Somethin' kickin' in there," Utah said. "High up, 'bout twenty foot off the ground. See it?"

"Si," Angel said. "But I don't know what it is—it does not look human."

Utah was the first to enter the timber from the valley. He pulled up short. "Hell, it's Cosgrove. He's all trussed up and hangin' from a limb. Cosgrove," Utah yelled, "what in the hell are you doin' up there?"

But Cosgrove couldn't answer. One of his socks was stuck in his mouth and tied in place with Cosgrove's own bandana. He was swinging from his own rope. His guns were missing from their holsters.

The man-hunter was lowered to the ground. The dirty sock was pulled from his mouth. Cosgrove coughed and spat and cussed for a full minute.

"Son of a bitch trussed me up like a side of beef," Cosgrove said. "He was sittin' on a tree limb and jerked me off like I wasn't no more than a baby. I didn't get to holler or nothin' 'fore he whapped me up side the head with a club. I wasn't out no more'un a couple of minutes. He's got to be close. Took my guns, too. Damn!"

"Don't bet on him being close," Utah said. "He's probably cleared out of this area and huntin' some of the others."

He was wrong. Smoke was less than fifty yards away, flat on his belly under some brush, listening and watching.

"The man must move like a ghost," Angel said, nervously looking around him.

"Knock off that ghost business," Utah said. "He puts his

pants on the same way we all do. He just got lucky, that's all." But Utah didn't sound too convincing.

"He gave me a message to tell y'all," Cosgrove said. "He said he was tired of this business and to leave him alone. If we keep pushin', he's gonna start killin'. And when he starts, he's gonna do it right; that there wasn't none of us gonna leave the High Lonesome alive. He said that no amount of money was worth our lives. And to think about that."

"Jensen had you and didn't kill you," Utah said, thinking: That ain't-like him. If what I'm thinkin' is true? . . .

Angel looked around him, at the silent timber and the towering mountains, thrusting their snow-capped peaks into the skies. The clouds were low this day, the hint of rain or snow in the air. "I do not like this place," the Mexican gunfighter said.

"This place is just a place," Utah said. "The place ain't what we got to worry about. It's Smoke Jensen we got to watch out for."

"Smoke Jensen is this place," Angel said. "He is of the mountains." Angel sniffed a couple of times.

"You smell somethin'?" Gary asked.

"Yes. Death."

# 8

Marlene Ulbrich sat her horse and stared at the dark timber. Her horse had just pricked up its ears and she was instantly alert. She was an excellent horsewoman, and knew to trust her animal's instincts. She saw something move. It looked like a man. She lifted her rifle and fired. The others in her team were at her side within seconds.

"What did you see?" Hans asked.

"A man. Right there by that lightning-marked tree."

Smoke had hit the ground the instant he saw the woman lift her rifle. The slug had missed him by several feet; but the act had confirmed his suspicions that the women in the group were just as dangerous as the men. Maybe more so. He had rolled back into the timber, leaped to his now-moccasined feet, and made his way deeper into the thickness of nature.

With a sinking feeling in his stomach, he now knew he had no choice in the matter. He was not going to run and run and run in the hopes they would give up; that would do nothing except delay the inevitable. Those hunting him were set on killing him, so he had to fight with the same callousness they were exhibiting.

He would let the man he'd strung up give his warning to the others. If they still chased him after hearing that . . . Smoke would do what a man had to do, and let the chips fall.

* * *

"Anybody want to leave?" von Hausen faced the group. No one spoke or moved.

"Very well," von Hausen said. "We shall commence the search at first light. John T., put out guards. Jensen will surely attack the encampment in some fashion this night. We've got to be ready for him."

"Yes, sir. You men get your slickers. It's gonna rain," John T. told them, after looking up at the leaden skies. And the advantage is gonna be Jensen's, he thought, but did not say it aloud.

"I am sure I hit him," Marlene said. "You know, I seldom miss a shot."

"Perhaps he's wounded," Gunter said.

"There was no sign of blood," Hans said. "And I inspected the area carefully. If he is wounded, it's slight."

"Jensen'd pay no more attention to a flesh wound than he would a mosquito bite," John T. muttered to Utah.

"You goin' all the way with this, John?" Utah asked.

"Until either me or Smoke Jensen is dead," the gunfighter said. "It's personal."

"Thought it might be. He kill a friend of yourn?"

Utah grunted. "He's killed about a *dozen* friends of mine. And about a dozen friends of yours and a dozen friends of every man here. But I know something them royal folks over yonder don't, Utah, and you keep it to yourself, all right?"

"If you say so."

"I put it all together just this morning, after the news about Cosgrove. I had me a hunch all along, and that just sewed it up in my mind."

"What?" Utah moved closer. He had a hunch he knew.

"Jensen don't wanna kill no more, Utah. I think he's run out of nerve."

"But I been hearin' you tellin' them counts and dukes and such that . . ."

68

"I know what I been tellin' them. I been doin' that deliberate, tryin' to get them skittish. I want Jensen myself, Utah. I want him bad."

"I see what you mean. I had the same feelin' this mornin'."

"Think about it. Jensen's probably gonna slip into camp and scare the drawers offen them ladies. But he ain't gonna kill, Utah. He ain't got it in him no more. He's all burned out. If Tom Lilly had faced Jensen last year, Jensen would have shot him without blinkin'. That rummy from the town told us that Jensen shot Tom in the arm. In the arm! That ain't the Smoke Jensen I been hearin' songs sung about and books writ about and stories bein' told. You see what I mean?"

"You right, John T." He grinned in the lightly falling mist. "You gonna be famous, John T. I can see it now. The man who kilt Smoke Jensen."

"That's right. I want you boys to just stand back when we corner him. I want him, Utah. Me. Understood?"

"You got it, John T. He's all yourn."

Maria did not stir at the slight bumping sound in the night. The bumping sound was Smoke laying the butt of a .44 against Gunter's head. Hard. She did not even stir when the lightly falling rain and the cold winds entered through the slit in the back of their tent. What did get her full attention was when a hard hand clamped over her mouth and another hand grabbed her by her long blonde hair and jerked her halfway out of the blankets.

Her wide open and frightened eyes looked into the coldest, meanest eyes she thought she had ever seen in her life.

"I'm Jensen," the big man said in a whisper. "You didn't pull out after I roped and trussed-up and warned your hired skunk today, so I thought I'd pay you a visit and tell you personally. No, your man's not dead. I just conked him on the noggin. He'll have a headache, but nothing else when he wakes up. But if you continue to chase me, he will be dead. Do you understand that, lady?"

She nodded her head.

Outside, the sky rumbled darkly with deep thunder and the rain picked up.

Smoke looked through the very dim light at the badly frightened woman. Gunter snored in his Smoke-induced unconsciousness. "I want to be left alone, lady. That's all I want. You people leave these mountains now. Do it tomorrow. . . first thing. I don't want to see any of you women hurt. But if you keep on chasing me, odds are you'll get hurt. You understand?"

She nodded her head.

Smoke turned her head with the biggest and hardest and roughest hands she had ever felt in her life. She looked at his guns. He had two in holsters, and two stuck down in his gunbelt. "Now what you'll do, lady, is this: I'm leaving. You're going to count to one hundred and then you can squall and holler all you want to. But if you start screaming before that real slow hundred count is over, I'm going to turn around and fill this tent so full of lead there isn't a chance you won't catch at least one slug. Do you understand all that?"

Again, she nodded her head.

Smoke lowered her head back to the silk pillows and pulled the covers up to her eyes. "Goodbye, your ladyship. I really hope I never see you again."

Then he was gone, moving silently through the rainy night.

Maria lay in her warm blankets and dutifully counted to one hundred. Then she started bellowing like a lost calf in a hail storm.

The camp was filled with men in various stages of dress and undress.

"Smoke Jensen!" Maria screamed. "He was in my tent. He manhandled me and hit Gunter on the head." Then she lost all her expensive finishing school training. "Five thousand dollars to the man who kills that son of a bitch!"

The night erupted in gunfire, with nobody hitting anything except raindrops. But in the two minutes that Smoke had been gone, he had covered a lot of ground, far out of range of even the best rifle made. He had not heard Maria's offer for his head. An hour later, Smoke had dried off, changed clothes, and was snug in his lean-to.

He had built a hat-sized fire, boiled his coffee and fried some bacon, and then put out the fire. He leaned back amid the sweet-smelling boughs that lined the ground under his ground sheet and blankets.

He chuckled. If he hadn't been mistaken, Princess Maria had been so scared she had peed in her expensive drawers.

The morning brought with it a mountain downpour. There was no way anybody was leaving camp in all this fury. Gunter was nursing a headache to go with the lump on the side of his head and Maria was still cussing, furious because a damn commoner had dared put his filthy hands on her.

"You was right, John T.," Utah said. "Jensen could have kilt a dozen of us last night. He's lost it."

John T. nodded his head in agreement. "But it shore shook them noblepeople up, didn't it. Even ol' ramrod-up-the-butt von Hausen is lookin' at Jensen in a different light. We got it made, Utah. Got it made, man!"

But John T. was wrong about von Hausen's different attitude.

"Nothing that Jensen has done so far agrees with all the talk about him," von Hausen told his group. "The man could have demoralized the camp last night. He could have killed a dozen men. He didn't. Why?"

Gunter shook his head and grimaced at the pain.

Hans shrugged his shoulders.

Maria cussed.

"He hasn't lost his nerve, if that's what you're thinking,"

Marlene said. "That took a lot of cold nerve to come into an armed camp."

"Oh, no," Frederick said. "He still has plenty of courage. But he *can't kill anymore!*"

That got everybody's attention.

"Add it up. That chap we met on the trail several days back. He told us about that young hooligan in that saloon back south that braced Smoke. According to what the drifter heard, Smoke refused to be goaded into fighting him; actually walked away from the young hoodlum. A gambler killed the loud-mouth moments later. And that thug, Tom Lilly. That old drunk said Smoke shot him in the *arm*. Smoke Jensen never shot anybody in the arm in his life. He fired at us the other day. But did he? I think not. He was shooting all around us. But not at us. He roped Cosgrove but didn't even hurt him. Smoke Jensen can no longer kill. The game now becomes ever so much more interesting."

"How do you mean, Frederick?" Marlene asked.

"We press him. Push him. Force him to stand and fight. And then we can all have a good laugh at his expense as we watch him stand helplessly, unable to kill. That will truly be a moment for posterity. The great legendary Smoke Jensen, unable to use his guns, reduced to tears." His laugh was triumphal.

"This calls for champagne," Hans said. "I believe we can safely open one of the few bottles we brought for this occasion."

"But of course!" von Hausen said, his voice full of good cheer. "But we must save at least one bottle to drink over Smoke Jensen's body while Hans takes pictures of the event. Your camera equipment is intact; it stood the journey well, Hans?"

"Oh, yes. We shall have our pictures, Frederick. I assure you of that."

* * *

Smoke took advantage of the furious storm to break camp and move north. He moved carefully, taking his time, and rode up to just south of Jenny Lake. It took him two days to make those few miles. The yellow arrowleaf balsamroot blossoms were just opening and, when he crossed the little valley, he seemed to be moving through a living sea of yellow and green. He made little effort to hide his tracks. He had heard the gunfire after he'd left the woman's tent, and knew his words had been wasted. And it had saddened him. Von Hausen and his people were not going to quit. They were going to continue pushing him, pressing him, until he would be forced to start shedding blood.

Their blood, not his.

Smoke caught his supper from the lake and after eating, moved his camp back into the rocks where he was protected from prying eyes, the wind, and bullets.

The next morning he found a secluded and well-protected place for his horses, with plenty of water and graze. He rigged a pack for himself and chose the weapons he would take that day—and they were formidable ones. He stuck a packet of crackers into his pack and set out, skirting the meadow he'd crossed and staying in the timber as much as possible as he back-tracked to the trail he'd used coming in.

There was no point in kidding himself any longer. He had run out of options; run out of ways to try to convince those chasing him to give it up. Those coming after him were not going to quit. This was going to be a fight to the finish so, he concluded, let us get on with it.

At the trail, he rigged a swing trap using a limber limb, a length of rope, and a stake set off the trail. Someone was going to have a very messed-up face when the horse triggered the rope placed close to the ground. Further on up the trail he rigged a deadfall employing the same methods. Then he carefully chose a defensive position and waited for the action to start.

\* \* \*

Nick was at the point, riding slowly, scanning the terrain ahead of him. Jensen had left plenty of sign to follow, so there was a need to look at the ground only occasionally. His horse's hoof hit the rope and the limb sprang forward. Nick took the full force of the green limb in the face, slapping him out of the saddle, smashing his mouth and nose, and knocking him unconscious. He was still out, sprawled on the ground, when Pat Gilman found him.

"Hold it up!" Pat shouted, swinging down from the saddle. "John T. Up here, Nick's down."

"He ain't dead," John T. said, kneeling down beside the bloody Nick. "But his face is some messed up. Lost some teeth and busted his nose for sure." But Jensen isn't killing, he thought. We'll all take some bumps and bruises, but that's a damn sight better than taking a bullet.

"Oh, I say now," Hans said, riding up and looking at the bloody Nick, sitting up and bathing his face with a wet cloth. "This isn't playing fair at all. The man obviously is no sportsman."

John T. glanced up at the man, thinking: and none of you is playin' with a full deck, either. I never met no people like you in all my days. You're all nuts! If Jensen hadn't run his string out, you'd all see that this here ain't no damn game.

"Can he ride?" von Hausen asked.

"Yeah," John T. told him. "Just as soon as he comes to his senses. He took a pretty good lick in the face."

"I'll get the medical kit," Gunter said, waving to a man leading a pack horse.

"Scout on ahead," von Hausen told a gunfighter from Nevada. "And keep your eyes open for more booby traps."

The hired gun nodded and moved out. He was soon lost from sight in the lush wilderness. The brush and timber and undergrowth was so thick a horses' hooves could not be heard more than a few yards away.

John T. stood up from his squat and met the eyes of Frederick von Hausen.

He knows, John T. thought.

He knows, Frederick von Hausen thought.

The man from Nevada accidentally missed the deadfall when he left the trail and rode for a few hundred yards in the timber. He was riding with his rifle across the saddle horn. He turned and got back on the trail. The trail wound around a jumble of huge boulders. The man from Nevada pulled up short and tight when he saw Smoke Jensen standing in the trail right in front of him, his right hand hovering near the butt of a pistol.

"I tried to warn you the best I could," Smoke said. "But none of you would listen."

The man from Nevada stared at Jensen. His mouth was cotton-dry.

"None of you can say I didn't try," Smoke said.

"Now what?" the man from Nevada managed get his tongue to working.

"Make your play, gunfighter."

"I ain't got a chance thisaway."

"That's your problem. You're chasing me, not the other way around."

The man from Nevada suddenly turned his horse, jerked up his rifle and eared the hammer back. Smoke let him get the hammer back before he drew. He shot the man one time, the slug striking the man from Nevada just under the armpit, right side, and blowing out the other side. The gun-slinger tumbled from the saddle, dead before he hit the ground.

Smoke vanished back behind the boulders and picked up his rifle. "Come on," he muttered to the winds. "All bets are off now."

# 9

Everybody was in the saddle and moving as the sounds of the single shot filtered faintly to them. John T.'s horse triggered the deadfall and the logs came crashing down, blocking the trail behind him and putting several horses into a panic. They bucked and snorted and tossed Gunter to the ground, knocking the wind from the man. Briscoe's horse reared up and the gunfighter fought to regain control. His horse's hooves slammed against the flank of the horse Marlene was riding. Her horse jumped in fear and Marlene's butt hit the ground. She squalled in shock and sprawled quite unladylike in the hoof-churned mud. She said a lot of very ugly words, in several languages.

John. T. left the saddle in a flying dive when he spotted the body of the man from Nevada. A slug whined wickedly just as he left the saddle. If he had waited another second, his brains would have been splattered against a tree.

So much for Jensen losing his nerve, John T. thought, as he hugged the ground.

Smoke's second shot tore the saddle horn off and the horse bolted in fear. Leo Grant came riding up and Smoke sighted him in and fired just as Leo turned in the saddle, the .44-.40 slug taking him high in his left arm. Leo screamed in pain but managed to stay in the saddle and jump his horse into the timber.

Smoke had lost the element of surprise and knew it. He grabbed up his pack and ran into the timber behind the jumbled mass of boulders.

"Stay back!" John T. yelled down the trail. "Stay back and get down. Get off those horses and get into the timber."

"Oh, damn!" Leo moaned. "I think my wing's busted. Jesus, it hurts."

"Quit complainin'," John T. told him. "You'll live."

"Is Matt dead?" Utah called, crawling through the brush.

"Near as I can tell, he is," John T. returned the call. "Leastwise he ain't movin' and they's an awful lot of blood on the ground."

"Damn!" Utah said. "Guess we was both wrong about Jensen."

"Yeah. Von Hausen had the same idea, I'm thinkin'. We all misjudged Jensen."

Smoke had moved back into the timber for a ways, then cut south, making his way through the timber silently and coming up in back of the group.

Larry Kelly turned to glance nervously at his back trail and his eyes widened in shock and fear. Smoke Jensen was standing in the center of the trail.

"Oh, no," he said, just as Smoke lifted his rifle and pulled the trigger.

The slug took Larry dead center in his stomach with the same effects as a blow with a sledgehammer. The force of it doubled him over and dropped him to the trail, screaming as the pain surged through him, white-hot fingers that seemed to touch every nerve in the man.

Smoke jumped to the other side of the trail and vanished. But he didn't vanish for long.

A stick of dynamite, tied to a short length of broken off limb came sputtering through the air.

"Goddamn!" Valdes yelled. "That's *dynamite!*" Then he hit the ground and said a prayer. It was said very quickly.

The dynamite exploded and horses went running in blind panic in all directions. The pack animals ran into the timber, losing their packs and sending supplies scattering everywhere. Another stick of dynamite came hissing through the air and landed near Maria. When it blew the concussion lifted her off the ground and sent her tumbling down the hill. She landed in a creek, banged her head on a rock, and came up sputtering and yelling.

Nat Reed tried to cross the trail to get a shot at Smoke and a bullet burned his face, taking a chunk of meat out of his cheek. Thinking he was more seriously wounded, Nat bellied down on the ground and started hollering that he was dying.

The wilderness became silent; no more dynamite was thrown, no more shots. But the people of the von Hausen party did not move from their cover for several minutes. With the exception of Maria. She had crawled from the icy waters of the creek to lay huddling, trembling, and sobbing behind a large rock.

"He's gone," John T. announced, his voice reaching those sprawled on the ground, crouched behind trees, and hiding in the bushes. John T. stood up and walked over to Larry Kelly who lay on the ground, his legs drawn up and both hands holding onto his .44-.40 punctured belly.

"Help me!" the gun-for-hire said.

"You know there ain't nothin' nobody can do," John T. told him. "We'll build a fire and make you comfortable, Larry. That's about it."

Larry started weeping.

Even von Hausen was shaken by the suddenness and the viciousness of the attack. He sat on a rock and willed himself to be calm.

Gunter slipped and slid and stumbled down the bank toward Maria. Halfway there he lost his footing and rolled the rest of the way, landing on his ass in the cold waters of the creek.

Gunter said a few very vulgar words.

"Assemble," von Hausen said. "Let's see how much damage was done."

"One dead, one dyin', and two wounded," John T. told him.

"I don't wanna die!" Kelly screamed.

"You shoulda thought of that 'fore you signed on," Utah told him. "That's the problem with you young squirts. You don't consider that a bullet might have your name on it."

"Go to hell!" Kelly yelled at him.

"I'll be right behind you, boy," the older gun-for-hire told him.

The cook, Walt, was walking around gathering up what supplies he could find and muttering to himself. An old gunfighter who had given it up years back, Walt no longer carried a gun on him.

"What the hell are you mumbling about?" Hans asked the man.

"You told me this was a huntin' trip," Walt snapped at him. "You didn't tell me 'til we was five hundred miles gone that it was a *man*-huntin' trip."

"You find that repugnant?" von Hausen asked from his seat on the rock.

"I don't know what that means," Walt replied, a sack of flour in his hands. "But I think you're all about half nuts—or better—chasin' after Smoke Jensen. Ifn you'd asked me from the start I woulda told you Jensen is pure poison. You'd be better off stickin' your arm in a sackful of rattlers."

"Keep your opinions to yourself," Gunter panted the words, as he shoved Maria over the top of the bank. "Just cook."

"I'll do that," Walt said. He tossed the sack of flour to

Gil Webb.

"What the hell do you want me to do with this?" Gil asked.

Walt suggested a couple of things.


Smoke left the trail and headed west, between Jenny Lake and Leigh Lake. Miles behind him, Larry Kelly and the man from Nevada were buried in shallow graves, the mounds covered with rocks to keep the scavengers from digging up and eating the bodies.

"Suggestions?" von Hausen said to John T.

"We ain't got nothin' to use as leverage to make him come to us," John T. said. "If you wanna go on, all we can do is keep chasin' him."

"I shall press on to the last man," von Hausen told him. "Will the men stay?"

"There ain't nobody talkin' about quittin'.'"

"Mount the men."

Marlene fell back to ride beside old Walt—when the trail permitted that. "Did you know this Preacher person who raised Smoke Jensen?"

"I knew of him." The cook didn't like the women any better than he liked Von Hausen, Gunter, or Hans. If anything, he liked them less. Women didn't have no business out here in the wilderness, shootin' and chasin' a human bein' like he was some kind of animal.

"What was he like—that you know of."

How could I tell you somethin' about him that I didn't know, you ninny? Walt thought. "Tough as rawhide and wild as the wind. He taught Smoke well. Give this hunt up, missy. You're headin' for grief if you don't. Smoke's done showed you how he fights. And if you think he'll spare you 'cause you're a woman, you're flat wrong. You start shootin' at him, he'll put lead in you just as fast as he would a man."

"Frederick will never quit," she said with a toss of her head. "This is the ultimate challenge for him, and for us."

"Well, you couldn't have picked a prettier place to be buried, Missy."

"You can't believe that Smoke Jensen is going to win this, do you? That is ludicrous!"

"I don't know what that means, Missy. But I do know this: Smoke cut down your party some yesterday. Tomorrow or the next day he'll whittle it down by two or three more, all the while leading us north, always north, higher and higher into the mountains. And I'll bet you a dollar that when we get to the north of this lake, Jensen will have cut west." He smiled.

"Why are you smiling and what significance does the direction have?"

"I'm smilin' 'cause Jensen is smarter than you folks; only the whole lot of you don't have enough sense to see it. You're all a bunch of arrogant fools. The direction means that if we follow his trail, we'll soon be out of food and the only tradin' post open to us is on the east side of Jackson Lake. Jensen will be on the west side, headin' straight north. That'll give him two/three days, at least, to get ready for us up yonder in the wilderness."

Marlene left the old cook's side, in a huff because of his words. "Arrogant, indeed!" she said. She rode straight to Von Hausen and told him what the cook had said.

"I know," von Hausen said. "I've been looking at maps—such as they are. He's right about that. What the old fool thinks of me, or us, is of no concern at all. And there is the head of the lake," he said, pointing. "We'll rest here for a time. I have to think."

Von Hausen walked back to the cook, gathering up a few men along the way. "Walt, you and these men take the pack horses and head up to the trading post on this little creek or river or whatever it is. We'll rendezvous here on the Snake." He looked at the old cook. "Marlene tells me you think we're all on a fool's mission."

"That's right, your lordship on high." There was no backup in Walt. None. He'd lived too long and seen the varmint too many times to back up from any man.

Von Hausen laughed at him. "And she also tells me that you think we are all arrogant and not nearly as intelligent as Smoke Jensen."

"Tattlin' little thing, ain't she? That's right. I shore said it. And meant every word of it."

"Old man, if you were younger, I'll give you a thrashing for saying those things about us."

Walt stared at him and smiled slowly. "No, you wouldn't, Baron von Hausen. And you won't do it now, neither. But if you want to test your mettle, Baron, you just let me get my rig outta my pack and we'll have us a showdown right here and now."

John T. had walked up, standing off to the side. He was slowly shaking his head at von Hausen, warning him off.

Frederick smiled, then laughed. He patted Walt on the shoulder. "Perhaps later, Walt. Not now. We need you to cook for us." He walked away, John T. following him.

"Don't never take up no challenge on fast gunnin' out here, Baron," John T. told him. "Walt Webster's no man to fool with. That old man's still poison with a short gun. He's laid men a-plenty in their graves over the years."

"Why . . . the man must be seventy years old!"

"That don't make no difference. Not out here. His daddy was a mountain man. Come out here to Washington or Oregon Territory in 1810 or so. Married him a French lady that had something to do with the North West Company. Walt was raised by Injuns and mountain men and the like. He was a fast gun before it become a household word. And he'll kill you, Baron. Don't crowd that old man."

* * *

Smoke cooked his supper of fresh caught fish and fried potatoes, then he leaned back against his saddle and enjoyed a pot of coffee just as the sun was going down. It had been three days since he'd ambushed von Hausen's party and Smoke lay in a little valley just north of Ranger Peak. He was under no illusions; knew that von Hausen was somewhere behind him, probably a day or day and a half. He'd climbed a high peak a couple of days back and picked them up through field glasses. Least he thought it was them. At that distance they were no more than dots, even magnified.

He'd follow the Snake into the Red Mountains and wait for his pursuers to come to him. There might be a few people up in that area, since Smoke had heard talk about the federal government making it some sort of park a few years back. Called it Yellowstone. But Smoke didn't figure there would be too many folks around. If there were some sightseers and gawkers, he'll tell them to get the hell out of the way, there was about to be a shooting war.

Smoke was letting his fire burn down to coals in the pit he'd dug. He'd wake up occasionally to add twigs and such to the coals, in order to keep it going through the cool night.

Smoke poured his pot empty and leaned back, trying to figure out what month it was. After some ruminations, the closest he could come was maybe the latter part of March or the first part of April.

He sipped the hot strong brew and frowned. Had it been that long? Yes. Von Hausen and his bunch had been on his backtrail for weeks, worrying at him, nipping at his heels like some small dog, and he was growing very weary of it. It was just a damned nuisance.

Smoke had stopped worrying about any moral aspects of his situation, as he had started calling it in his mind. He'd done everything he could to end it without killing. So much for good intentions.

He smiled as the face of his wife entered his mind. He wondered if Sally was enjoying her vacation back east. He sure hoped she was having more fun than he was.

# 10

The more Smoke thought about people being in the park area—although it was still early and the nights were cold—the more he decided against following the Snake into the area. He abruptly cut east, crossed a road that had not been here the last time Smoke was in the area, and headed for the Continental Divide. The point he was looking for was just east of Pacific Creek. He crossed the Divide and then cut due north when he reached the Yellowstone River.

One thing about it, Smoke thought with a faint smile, he was sure giving those behind him a chance to see some wild and beautiful country. Although he doubted that few, if any, among his pursuers would take the time or have the mental capability to appreciate the view.

Smoke made his camp in a long, narrow valley sandwiched by low hills, the high peaks behind them. He'd killed a deer before entering the park boundaries and spent a day jerking some meat. He wanted to have something in his pockets to eat on in case he got cut off from his horses and supplies.

He took a very quick bath in a creek, in waters that almost turned him blue. But he got most of the dirt and all the fleas off him by using strong soap. He was shaking with cold by the time he dried off and climbed into clean dry longhandles and dressed in brown shirt and jeans. He put his boots and spurs away and stayed with high-top moccasins, his britches tucked inside and laced up.

He caught some fish and broiled them over a low fire. He was out of beans and flour and lard; but, he thought, smiling, von Hausen's group had probably resupplied at the post down by Jackson Lake and they would have plenty. He'd have to see about stealing some of their supplies some night. And maybe doing some headhunting while he was at it.

He'd cross the Yellowstone tomorrow, and once he crossed Monument Creek, he'd be in the big lonesome once more. There he'd start the fireworks.


"He crossed the road," Montana Jess said, riding back to the main party. "He's headin' for the Divide."

"Why, for God's sake?" Hans blurted. "I thought he was going to take us into this park area?"

"He is," John T. told him. "But he don't want to get amongst a bunch of visitors when he opens this dance. He's probably waitin' for us 'tween the Beaverdam and the Monument. And it'll take us a good week to get over there."

Ol' Walt smiled with deadly humor. And he's runnin' you yahoos out of supplies, too, the cook thought. You folks just ain't yet figured out that you're up agin a professional.

Ol' Walt had given a lot of thought to just pullin' out some night and leavin' these blood-crazy people. But he wanted to stick it out and see the final outcome. He figured it was gonna be right interestin'.

"Take the point, Utah," John T. told the man. "Jensen ain't makin' any effort to hide his tracks."

That became very apparent the next day when Utah gave a whoop and the party came on a gallop.

"Those are *mine!*" Andrea shrieked, looking at a pair of bloomers hanging from a tree limb by the trail. "I lost them when the packhorses bolted and scattered the supplies." She snatched the bloomers from the limb and stuffed them in her saddlebags, her face crimson. "The nerve of that man," she fumed. "The gall of that . . . that . . . *heathen*."

"Jensen has a very strange sense of humor," Gunter remarked. "Especially when one considers he does not have that much longer to live."

Walt shook his head at that remark. These people still hadn't got it through their noggins that Jensen wasn't plannin' on dyin'. Jensen was plannin' on killin' *them*.

Walt met the dark and serious eyes of Angel Cortez. The Mexican gunfighter knows, the cook thought. He knows just how deadly this business is. Of all of them here, Angel'll be the one to hold back and maybe come out of this alive. Angel had told him the only reason he came along was that he'd been buddyin' with Valdes and the outlaw had convinced him to come along. He had nothing against Smoke Jensen and had yet to fire upon the elusive Smoke.

Angel nodded his head and smiled at Walt. The two men reached a silent understanding.

They swung back into the saddle and pulled out, both of them hanging back at the rear of the column.

"These people," Angel said, "I think they are playing a fool's game."

"I know they are," Walt told him.

"I have tried to convince my compadre, Valdes, that what we are doing is the same as hunting a panther in his own territory while armed with no more than a stick. He does not see it that way. I think Valdes will die in this terrible wilderness."

"If his lordship up yonder don't call this fool thing off, they's gonna be a lot of people die up here," Walt said.

"Do you think Jensen would harm the women?"

"I don't know. I don't think so. No decent man wants to harm a female. And Jensen is a decent man. I think he'll do everything in his power not to harm them. He might turn them female manhunters over his knee and wallop the beJesus out of their backsides. Lord knows they sure need it."

Angel grinned. "Now to witness that would be worth the ride, I think."

Walt chuckled. "Shore would be some caterwaulin' goin' on, for a fact."

"Why can't the men we ride with see that Jensen is goading us on? He is deliberately leading us into another ambush. He is going to whittle us down one by one. You see it, I see it, why not the others?"

"Them blue-bloods up yonder is too damned arrogant to see anything past the end of their noses. The rest of these outlaws and gunslicks . . . well, all they can see is big money danglin' in front of them."

"And the reputation of being among the men who killed Smoke Jensen," Angel added.

"True. But what they're gonna get, Angel, is nothin' but a very cold and lonely grave."

"Is there such a thing as a grave that is not cold and lonely, senor?"


Smoke had laid down a trail that a one-eyed, city slicker could follow. And he was waiting for his pursuers. He had chosen his spot well, and only after careful scouting. He had a mountain pass at his back, a pass that he had found only after very carefully searching the area. Inside the pass, there was a small valley hollowed out by millions of years of winds and rains and slides. There was water for his horses and good graze for four or five days. He would move his horses into the green pocket when he spotted his hunters coming across a dusty plain some five miles in the distance. The area being chosen with just that thought in mind. Unless of course they moved through at night. But Smoke didn't think any of them would be willing to take that chance. He'd probably still be able to smell the dust. Unless it rained, he thought with a warrior's grim humor.

Now he was ready to get this show on the road. He had some bulls to buy before the summer was over and he was anxious to get back to the Sugarloaf . . . and Sally.

The gunfighters and man-hunters traveling with von Hausen and party knew this was too easy; knew Smoke was setting them up. But none of them really knew this country. Only John T. and Utah had ever even been in this area, and maybe Montana Jess—except for Walt Webster, and the old cook had told only Angel about his knowledge of the wilderness. The two of them had become good friends on the long ride north. Valdes had begun to shun Angel, preferring instead the dubious company of the other gunslingers.

Angel had taken it philosophically with only a very Latin shrug of his shoulders. "He is a greedy man, that Valdes. And that is something I have told him to his face more times than once. It makes him ver' angry. But he knows better than to draw on me."

"You pretty good with that iron, huh, boy?" Walt asked.

"I am quick enough. But I have never started a fight in my life. Well . . . only one. A vaquero down in New Mexico Territory tried to take my girl from me one night. He called me many bad names. I invited him to step outside. He stepped. He called me more bad names and went for his pistol. I was faster. Now I can never go back to New Mexico Territory."

"And the girl?"

Angel smiled. "She married and now has two babies. I think she had forgotten about me before I had left the county."

Walt nodded. "Monument Crick is just ahead, Angel. 'Bout five more miles. We'll be off this plateau soon as we cross the crick."

"And? . . ."

"That's when Jensen will open this dance."

Mountains loomed up in front of the party. Von Hausen halted the parade and consulted a map. "Monument Creek," he said. He turned his head and looked at the mesa to his right. He started cussing.

The others followed his gaze. Scratched into the side of the millions-year-old rock formation, in huge letters, was this message: STRAIGHT ACROSS THE CREEK, PEOPLE. The initials S.J. followed that.

"That arrogant *bastard!*" von Hausen said.

Walt and Angel exchanged glances.

John T. smiled as he took off his hat and scratched his head. They'd have to split up and ride cautious from here on in, riding with rifles across the saddle horn. Jensen was through playin' games. He moved his horse forward, reining in by the still cussing Baron von Hausen.

"You're doin' 'xactly what he wants you to do," John T. told the German. "Losin' your temper."

Von Hausen glared at the gunfighter for a long moment, then slowly began calming himself. He nodded his head in agreement. "You're right, of course. Absolutely correct. Now is not the time to lose one's composure. Not with the quarry so close. We'll camp here for the night, John T. Put out guards."

"Yes, sir."

Von Hausen walked to where Walt was setting up the cook tent. "How are the supplies holding out?"

"Somebody better start killin' some deer," Walt told him. "The larder is gettin' mighty low."

"Is the shooting of animals permitted in a national park?" von Hausen asked.

Walt looked at him and smiled. "Now that is a right interestin' question to ask, your nobleship. Here you done chased a man about five hundred miles tryin' to kill him for sport, and now here you stand, worryin' about whether it's against the law to shoot a deer in a park. You are the beatin'est fellow I believe I have ever seen."

"I see nothing unusual about it," von Hausen said stiffly. "Nothing unusual at all. I have always considered myself a law-abiding man."

Walt blinked a couple of times at that. He stared at the man to see if von Hausen was having fun with him. The German's face was serious. "Do tell?" he finally said. "Well, now, that's plumb admirable of you. Yes, sir. Shore is."

"Thank you," von Hausen said. He wheeled about and marched away.

"Angel," Walt said. "That feller can act as crazy as a damn lizard on a hot rock."

"Si," the Mexican said. "But really he is just as sane as you or I. He is a man who has always gotten his way, I think. And a man who has no regard for the lives of others . . . those who work for him, and those who he hunts."

Walt nodded his head. "Let's get the beans to cookin'. I'll make a good bait of biscuits, too. We'll feed 'em right tonight. For some of them, this just might be the last supper they ever get."

Von Hausen and his party rode all the next day. The only sign they saw of Smoke were the stone arrows he placed along the trail, so von Hausen would be sure to see them. The more miles they put behind them, the madder von Hausen got. Every time von Hausen saw another stone arrow it set him off into fits of cussing.

They stopped for the night at a spring near the base of a towering mountain. Pat Gilman brought von Hausen a note he'd found under a small rock near the spring. Then the gunfighter got out of the way.

THOUGHT YOU MIGHT CAMP HERE. WATER'S

91

GOOD. HOW'S YOUR SUPPLIES HOLDING OUT, VON HAUSEN? It was signed S.J.

Von Hausen threw the note on the ground and jumped up and down on it, cussing and screaming like a madman. He stomped the note into muddy shreds.

Panting for breath, his chest heaving, von Hausen screamed, "Tomorrow, Jensen dies." He pointed a finger at Utah. "You find him, Utah. When you do, report back to me immediately. We will launch a frontal assault." He stomped off.

Briscoe said, "I ain't real sure what that means,"

Walt cut his eyes to the gunfighter. "It means that some of you won't be comin' back, Briscoe."

"Aw, shut up!" Briscoe told him. He looked at Angel. "What are you, now, the cook's helper?"

"Si," the Mexican said. "You have some objections to that?"

"Then I tell you now, your pay will be the same as the cook's," Gunter said.

"That is quite all right with me," Angel replied. "I will sleep much better at night." He took off his gunbelt and stowed it in his saddle bags.

Valdes walked over to his friend. "I cannot believe you are actually doing this, amigo. You are too good with a gun to make biscuits and stew."

"What we are doing is wrong, Valdes. Smoke Jensen does not deserve to be hunted down like a rabid animal. I say to you in friendship, give up this madness."

Valdes stared at him. "I never thought you would lose your nerve, Angel. You are a coward. You are no longer my friend. Go to hell!"

Valdes gave his friend an obscene gesture and walked away.

"Forget it," Walt said. "He wasn't never much of a friend to do something like that. Money's cloudin' his eyes. I tell you this for a fact, Angel: you and me'll 'bout be the only ones ridin' out of this mess."

Angel's good humor surfaced with a small smile. "But we will have callouses on our hands from all the grave digging, no?"

Walt chuckled. "But less cookin' and washin' up dishes, right?"

The rough humor was infectious and soon both men were laughing as they set up the cook tent.

"Sounds like a gaggle of old women. I think they both done lost their brains," Tom Ritter said, listening to the men crack jokes and laugh.

"Or found 'em," Leo Grant said, trying to ease his shot-up left arm into a less painful position in the sling.

"Now just what the hell does that mean?" Gary asked, a sour expression on his unshaved face. "Are you turnin' yellow on us, too?"

John T. stepped quickly between the two men, just as Leo was dropping his hand to the butt of his .45. "Stand easy, boys. Look at it this way: with Angel out of the picture, they's that much more money to be spread around. Think about that 'fore you start pluggin' each other."

Gary looked at the mountains looming around him, then nodded his head and returned his gaze to John T. "What the hell is a frontal as-sault, John T.?"

"Somethin' that we're not gonna do," the gunfighter told him. "Von Hausen will cool down by mornin'. He's just mad right now, that's all. You boys get you some coffee and settle down. We might just bring this hunt to a close by this time tomorrow."

"And when we do, we'll be pocket heavy with money, won't we?" Leo stated with a grin.

"Damn right! And Jensen will be *dead*."

# 11

Utah Red sensed more than heard movement behind him and to his right. He twisted in the saddle just as the rope settled around him and jerked him from his horse. Utah hit the ground hard, knocking the wind from him. He struggled to free himself of the loop and managed to slip loose and was reaching for his guns when a hard fist connected solidly against the side of his jaw. The blow knocked him sprawling. His guns fell from leather.

Cursing, Utah scrambled to his boots and swung a big fist at his attacker's head. Smoke ducked the blow and planted a left, then a right in Utah's gut. Gasping for breath, Utah stumbled away, trying to suck air back into his lungs. Smoke pressed him hard, with left's and right's that bloodied Utah's mouth and smashed his nose flat.

Utah made a dive for his guns, sliding belly-down on the rocks and the dirt. Smoke gave him a foot in the face that slowed his slide and further bloodied his mouth.

Reaching down, Smoke jerked the man to his boots and walloped him on the side of his face with a big right fist. The clubbing blow knocked Utah to his knees. The last thing Utah remembered before he lost consciousness was his daddy's warning that if the boy didn't straighten up, he'd never amount to a thing.

Pride Anderson and Lou Kennedy untied the ropes that held Utah belly-down across his saddle. They noticed that Utah's guns were gone, short guns and rifle. When they laid him on the ground, on his back, both of them grimaced at the mess that was once Utah's face.

"Jensen shore whupped the snot outta him," Walt said, walking up with a pan of water and a cloth. "He's out of it for a week, at least."

The party had stopped for their nooning and Utah had decided to scout on ahead for signs of Jensen. He found much more than he bargained for.

"Teeth knocked out, nose busted, both eyes swelled shut," Pride said. "I ain't seen but a couple of men whupped this bad in all my life."

Marlene stood away from the growing circle of men, a worried look on her face and in her eyes. Nothing was turning out the way they'd planned. This was supposed to had been a fun trip: hunt down and shoot a western gunslinger, celebrate with a bottle of champagne, and return to Europe to boast about it among their limited circle of friends.

But none of them had taken into consideration that the men of the American west—who had helped tame the country—didn't like to be hunted down. None of them had planned on their quarry fighting back so savagely. Marlene didn't think Smoke Jensen was really in the spirit of things; he certainly wasn't playing fair.

"I can't feel that he's got any ribs busted," Pride said, standing over the conscious and moaning Utah Red. "But he's sure out of it. I guess Jensen took his guns."

"I'll check his saddlebags," Bob Hogan said, walking to Utah's horse. "I know he's got a bottle in there. He could use a drink, I reckon."

Seconds later Bob screamed out a shriek that chilled all in the camp. They whirled to look at the man. A rattlesnake was wound around his right arm, the big fanged mouth striking at his face again and again. Marlene and Maria and Andrea started screaming and the men stood around helplessly. There was nothing they could do. The big rattler presented no target with its writhing and striking.

Bob fell backward to the ground, his face blackened and swelling from the venom. His hands were clenched into fists of pain and his throat was too swollen to allow sound to push through. He kicked and jerked a couple of times and then lay still as the massive injection of poison killed him stone dead.

The women had turned away, weeping and sickened by the sight.

"What kind of man would think to do something like *that?*" Gunter questioned. His face was pale, his hands shaking, and he wanted to throw up.

"A man like Smoke Jensen," Walt said bluntly. "One of you boys kill that rattler and somebody get the shovels. Angel, get a blanket to wrap Bob up in. I'll go get the Good Book outta my gear."

Von Hausen's legs were trembling so badly he had to sit down on a log and try to regain his composure. He was in mild shock, sweating profusely. He clenched his hands into fists to still the trembling. He had never seen anything like this in all his years. He tried to put himself into the mind of Smoke Jensen. He could not. But it never occurred to him to call off the hunt.

Less than a half mile away, Smoke sat on the ground and ate jerky for his lunch while he thumbed the cartridges out of Utah's gunbelt and put them in a small sack.

Finding the rattlesnake and sticking it into Utah's saddlebags had been a nice touch, Smoke thought. He bet it sure got everyone's attention. He picked up his pack and rifle and moved out. He was smiling.

"Be interestin' to see what the Baron does now," Walt said to Angel.

"Yes. Utah is out for a good three or four days—his face is so swollen he can't open his eyes—and Bob is dead. That's three dead and two wounded and nobody has yet to get a clear shot at Jensen. A smart man would give this up."

"You don't see any of these man-hunters and so-called gunslingers pullin' out, do you?"

"No."

"That tells you how smart they are right there."

John T. walked over to von Hausen, who was sitting in a camp chair in front of his tent, drinking coffee. He looked up at John T. and shook his head.

"Barbaric act on Jensen's part."

"Yes, sir."

"I wonder how long he had that snake?"

"He probably just caught it and come up with the idea. The snake got away 'fore anyone could shoot it."

"Wonderful," von Hausen said sarcastically.

"Hole's dug and Bob's ready for plantin'. Walt's gonna read words over him."

"The ladies are still quite distraught. They won't be attending. Andrea had to take to her bed."

"Sorry to hear that, Baron."

"I'll get my jacket and be right with you. I'll join you at the services."

At the gravesite, John T. noticed that both Angel and Walt were wearing white handkerchiefs tied around their upper arm. "What the hell's all that about?"

"We want Jensen to know we ain't huntin' him," Walt told him. Just in case he decides to attend the services, he added silently.

John T. shook his head in disgust.

The entire camp—except for the ladies—gathered

around the grave and Walt read from the Bible. The body was dumped in the hole and Walt closed his Bible. Just as two men picked up shovels and started covering Bob, a sputtering stick of dynamite landed in the center of the camp with a thud—about a hundred yards from the burial site.

"What was that?" Montana asked.

The dynamite blew and the horses tore loose their picket pins and went galloping in all directions. One of them ran behind Gunter and Maria's tent, a rope tangling around the horse's neck and bringing the tent down and taking it with him. Maria was in the middle of a sponge bath one second and standing smooth out in the open the next second, frozen in wide-eyed, open-mouthed shock for all to see. And she had a lot for the men to see.

It didn't take her long to find her voice and let out a shriek that probably echoed around the mountains for days. Then she fainted.

Smoke was busy setting the other big tents on fire. He touched the flame to a very short fuse and let another stick of dynamite fly just as the men—minus Walt and Angel who had the good sense to jump behind the mound of earth at the gravesite—came running toward the dust-swirled camp grounds.

"Get down!" John T. bellowed, seeing the dynamite come sputtering through the dust.

This stick of dynamite took out the cook tent, ruined the pot of beans and demolished the dutch oven.

"Crap!" Walt said. "I wish he hadn't a done that."

"Least he saved the coffee pot," Angel said.

No sooner had the words left his mouth before Smoke's .44-.40 barked twice and the coffee pot got punctured.

Andrea and Marlene came staggering out of what was left of their burning tents, in various stages of undress, both of them coughing and choking, hair all disheveled and looking like sisters of Medusa.

Smoke couldn't see because of all the dust and billowing smoke from the fires he'd started so he chose that time to haul his ashes out of there. He hit the timber running and slipped away. But he was very curious about the two men he'd spotted at the gravesite with white handkerchiefs tied around their arm. And neither one of them had been wearing guns. One of them looked like the old gunfighter, Walt Webster, and the other was a Mexican. Maybe he had two allies in camp?

The tents were gone and most of their contents went up with them. The women had been hustled off — after Maria was revived and a robe draped over her — and positioned safely behind a jumble of rocks, under guard.

"One big coffee pot left," Walt said. "The cook pot's busted. The oven's bent plumb outta shape and broke besides. The big skillet ain't got no handle. They's flour and beans and lard all over the damn place."

Men were out looking for and rounding up their horses. They never did find the horse that took Maria's tent with it, but they did find what was left of the tent.

Von Hausen found his camp chair, sat down in it, and the chair collapsed, sending the Baron sprawling on his butt in the dirt. He picked himself up with as much dignity as he could muster, and brushed off the dirt from his riding breeches.

"How far are we from civilization?" he asked through clenched teeth.

"There's a tradin' post up on the Shoshone," Montana said. "That'd be north and east of us. As the crow flies, about thirty miles or so."

"Could you get there?" Gunter asked.

"Oh, yeah. Best way to go would be to stay on the south side of Eagle Peak, then crost the north end of the Absaroka Range and hit either Eagle or Kitty

Creek. Follow that on up to the Shoshone."

"And that would take how long?" Hans asked.

"Days. Some of that is mighty rough country."

Von Hausen tossed a small sack to the man. "There is more than ample funds to re-supply and to hire more men—if you can find them. We're going to fall back to that plateau we crossed several miles back and set up a defensive position. That's where we'll be. Assign men to go with him, John T." He looked toward the north. "I shall not leave this wilderness until I have spat upon your grave, Smoke Jensen. I swear that."

Smoke didn't figure von Hausen would be sending anyone after him—if he could get anyone to come after him—so he returned to his camp and set about fixing supper. He wanted all fires out by dark, just in case.

He'd grabbed up a side of bacon and a sack of potatoes in the jumble of supplies he'd rooted through before getting down to business at the camp, and now planned on having a hot meal and a pot of coffee. But first he saw to his horses and found them looking fat and sleek and contented.

Smoke fixed his supper, drank a pot of coffee, and then rolled up in his blankets. He went to sleep with a smile on his face.

John T. assigned four guards to a shift, the shift to be changed every two hours so no one would get sleepy and let Jensen slip into this new camp. John T. still planned to kill Smoke, but he had to admit that his admiration for the man had grown over the long weeks of tracking him. Smoke Jensen was every bit the warrior rumors made him out to be. That was one hell of a daring move, coming into their camp in daylight and blowing things up and setting tents on fire. Man could move like a Injun, for sure. But he had to have a weak spot. John T. would find it. He was sure of that.

"Keep a sharp eye out, boys," he called across the elevated flat to the guards. "And keep in mind that Jensen can move like a damn ghost."

At that moment, Frederick, Hans, and Gunter were making a pact that they would carry out this campaign down to the last man. Smoke Jensen would die, or they would all die trying.

"It's now a matter of honor," Gunter said. "If we fail in this hunt, we'll be ridiculed back home. I won't have that."

"Nor will I," Hans agreed.

Von Hausen nodded his head in agreement. "We may possess all the money in the world, but if we are stripped of our honor, we would have nothing. We must go on with this hunt. And we must be victorious."

"I have spoken with the women," Gunter said. "They are also in agreement that this sporting event must continue. They have been humiliated and they are very angry."

"The mood of the men?" von Hausen asked.

"John T. is testing the waters now, so to speak," Hans informed him.

"Work's hard enough to get for men like us," John T. said offhandedly to a small group of gunslingers. "Times are changin' all around us. I just can't see turnin' my back on no good-payin' job like this one."

"I ain't about to give up this here hunt," Pat Gilman said. "We stand to make more money doin' this than we could make in five years doin' anything else."

"Count me in," Ford said.

"And, me," Al Hayre echoed.

"Montana and them with him told me that they was in all the way," John T. said. "Lemme go talk with the others."

Tom Ritter and Gil Webb and Marty Boswell were in. So were Pride Anderson, Lou Kennedy, Cat Brown, Paul Melham and Nat Reed. Utah Red mumbled that he'd done swore on his mother's tintype to kill Smoke Jensen; wanted to torture him first. Make it last a long time. Ford, Jerry Watkins, Mike Hunt, and Nick were in all the way.

"They're in," John T. reported to his bosses. "For the money and because their pride's been hurt."

"Excellent," von Hausen said, and smiled for the first time since Smoke's attack that day. "Montana said he could probably round up three or four more men. He thought he knew where there was a long-range shooter. I wanted Mike Savage, but he's somewhere down in Arizona Territory at this time. Montana said the man he had in mind was better. We'll see."

"All this waitin' is just givin' Jensen more time to dig in and plan," John T. pointed out.

Von Hausen brushed that aside. "It can't be helped. We've got to be resupplied if this expedition is to continue with any hope of success. Look at it this way: There is no way Jensen can get to us up here on this flat. We have an excellent view in all directions and a fine field of fire. And the supplies will afford us some much-needed creature comforts. We have to keep the ladies in mind, John T."

John T. nodded. "Whatever you say, boss. I sent a couple of the men south to see if they could kill a deer or elk so we'll have a change from beans and hardtack."

"Excellent. I wish them a successful hunt."

After John T. had walked away from the group, von Hausen rubbed his hands together and smiled, a cruel glint in his eyes. "I feel better now. We've had our setbacks, but that is to be expected in any campaign. I feel that we've ironed out the kinks and learned some hard but

102

valuable lessons. I think that from this point on, success is inevitable. Let's drink to it, gentlemen. To the death of Smoke Jensen!"

# 12

Smoke had watched the camp on the flats through long-lenses and decided that now was a dandy time to pull out. He returned to his own camp, packed up his gear, and pulled out, heading straight north. He crossed the Beaverdam, keeping on the west side of Atkins Peak. He spent a couple of days camped along the Columbine and then once more headed north. After crossing the Clear, he pointed his horse's nose northeast and headed up toward the northern end of the Absaroka Range, recalling a camp he and Preacher had made between the Lamar River and Miller Creek, up near Saddle Mountain. He spent a couple of days there then headed west, for the Mirror Plateau; from there, he'd take his followers into canyon country and see how they liked that. He had a strong hunch that some of them would spend eternity there.

Montana returned with the supplies and five new men. "This is all I could round up on short notice, boss," he told von Hausen. "But they're good boys and they'll stick it out to the end. Roy Drum, Mack Saxton, Ray Harvey, Tony Addison, and this here is Don Langston. If he can see it, he can hit it with a rifle."

Von Hausen was impatient. Smoke had had days to

hide his trail. There had been no sign of him, so all concluded he had pulled out. He voiced that shared opinion with Montana and the new men.

"Don't fret none," Montana said. "Roy's the best tracker in this part of the country. We'll find Smoke. Roy's got a personal reason to find him."

"Oh?" von Hausen looked at the man.

"Killed my uncle 'bout ten year ago over in Utah. I hate Smoke Jensen."

"What did your uncle do to provoke Jensen?" Gunter asked.

"That don't make no nevermind. Jensen killed him, and I'm gonna spit on Smoke Jensen's body. That's all that matters."

"Get packed up. We pull out at first light."

The trail was cold, but Roy knew his business. He found Smoke's trail and stayed on it. When Smoke crossed Cold Creek and turned more east than north, Roy pulled up and scratched his head. "This don't make no sense. I think he's leadin' us on a fool's chase."

"What do you mean?" Hans asked.

"He's just killin' time. Just wanderin' to wear us out. If I was gonna make me a stand up here, I'd do it in the canyon country. I think if we head north, we'll pick up his trail after he crosses the Lamar. He'll be headin' west, over the plateau. Bet on it."

"We'd save how many days if you're correct?" Gunter asked.

"Week, maybe more 'un that."

"John T.?" von Hausen asked.

"I'm with Roy. Let's try it."

"Lead the way, Roy," von Hausen ordered.

Smoke didn't know if his aimless wanderings would fool those behind him for very long. It really didn't make much difference; the situation had to be settled sooner or later.

He had made an early camp after killing a deer. He had

skinned it out and was roasting a steak when he heard a rider coming. He reached for his rifle.

"Hello, the camp!" came the shout. "We're government surveyors."

"Come on in," Smoke called through early twilight. "I've got food if you've got coffee."

"That we have, sir. My, but that venison does smell good."

There were four of them, all dressed like eastern dudes on an outing. But they were friendly and not heavily armed.

Smoke pointed to the meat on the spit. "Help yourselves. I've plenty more to cook when that is gone."

"Say, this is very kind of you. I thought we had provisioned ourselves adequately. But I'm afraid we stayed out a bit longer than we should have. By the way, I'm Charles Knudson. This is Harold Bailey, Morris Robertson, and Perry Willard."

"Pleased," Smoke said.

The men fell to eating and with a smile, Smoke cut another hefty chunk off the hanging deer and fitted it on a fresh spit.

"Haven't eaten since last evening," one of the government men said, coming up for air. "And would you believe that we haven't even seen so much as a rabbit this day?"

"I can believe it," Smoke said. "I've been there a time or two myself."

Charles took a break to rest his jaws and said, "Sightseeing, sir?"

"In a manner of speaking."

"Unusual arrangement of pistols, sir," Perry said. "I don't think I've ever seen a rig quite like yours."

"Not too many of them around. I like it for a crossdraw. You boys aren't from the west, are you?"

"Why . . . no. As a matter of fact, we're not," Charles replied. "What gave us away?"

"Nothing in particular. I just guessed."

Smoke let them eat in peace for a moment, then asked, "Not that it's any of my business, but what direction did you men come in from?"

"From the north," Harold said. "We've been working up near Tower Falls." He looked puzzled. "Why would it not be any of your business? It was a perfectly harmless thing to ask?"

"Out here, boys, it's sometimes not healthy to ask too many questions about a man's back trail."

"Ahhh!" Charles said. "I see. The person to whom the question is directed might be a road agent?"

"Something like that." Smoke fixed his plate and poured a cup of coffee.

"Would it offend you if I inquired as to your name, sir?" Morris asked.

Smoke smiled. The young men all looked to be about the same age. Early twenties at best. "My name is Jensen. People call me Smoke."

The young men stopped eating as if on command. They froze. Smoke went right on eating his supper and sipping his coffee. Finally he lifted his eyes and looked at them. "Eat, eat, boys. Your supper's getting cold." He smiled again. "I don't bite, boys, and I've never shot a man who wasn't trying to do me harm. So relax."

"I . . . ah . . . thought you would be a much older man," Harold said when he finally found his voice.

"We've read all the books about you and we saw the play about you in New York City our senior year in college," Morris said. "Did you really ride with Jesse James?"

"Nope. Only met the man one time. I was just a boy during the war when Jesse and his bunch stopped by the farm and I gave them a poke of food. He give me a pistol; Navy .36 it was, and an extra cylinder. That's the only time I ever saw him."

"You've killed a . . . ah . . . uh . . ." Perry stopped, an embarrassed look on his face.

"A lot of men," Smoke finished it for him. "Yes. I have. First white men I killed was down in Rico, just west of the Needle Mountains. Back in '69 or '70. Me and a mountain man name of Preacher was riding over to Pagosa Springs to find the men who killed my father. A man by the name of Pike and a buddy of his—I never did know his name—braced me in the trading post. They were a little slow on the draw."

"You killed both of them?"

"Yes."

"And since then?" Charles asked softly.

"Long bloody years. I changed my name for several years. Married and had children. But trouble came my way and I faced it. I'm Smoke Jensen and if people don't like it they can go to hell."

"Mind another question, sir?" Harold asked.

"Go right ahead."

"I—we—heard that you were a successful rancher over in Colorado."

"That's correct. My wife and I own a spread we call the Sugarloaf."

"Yet . . . here you are in the middle of the wilderness. The first national park in America. There are no cattle here, Mister Jensen."

"No. But there is plenty of cover here, and no people to get hurt when the lead starts flying. I've got about twenty-five or thirty hardcases on my backtrail, led by a crazy European Baron name of Frederick von Hausen. They plan on killing me . . . for sport."

All four young men stared at Smoke, disbelief in their eyes. Morris broke the silence. "They plan on *killing* you, sir?"

"Yeah. It's a sporting event, according to them. Track me down, corner me, kill me, and then go home and boast about it, I suppose."

"Have, uh, they found? . . ." He shook his head and frowned. "Well, it's quite obvious they haven't found you. You're still alive."

"Oh, they've found me a couple of times. I killed three or four of them, beat the crap out of one, and nicked two or three more. I blew up their camp last week. I suspect von Hausen has sent for more men. He seems to be a very determined man."

"You *killed* three or four, sir?" Charles said.

"Yeah. I could have killed them all when I Injuned into their camp one night and laid down a warning to one of the women in the bunch. But I didn't."

"They have *ladies* with them?" Perry was horrified at just the thought.

"I don't think they're ladies. That'd be stretching the point some. But they're definitely female."

"And this bunch of hooligans . . . they are here, in the park?"

"Oh, yeah. I blew their camp up down on the Monument, then hauled my ashes after I watched several men head out to re-supply. Probably at that trading post up on the Shoshone. But they're coming after me. So you boys rest easy here tonight, and I'll fill you full of deer meat for breakfast and then you best be on your way 'fore the lead starts flying."

"But we can't have anything like that going on here!" Charles said. "Good heavens, sir. This is a national park. We have many visitors every year. Many come just to see Old Faithful erupt."

"Old what?" Smoke asked.

"Old Faithful. It's a geyser just north of Shoshone Basin. It was named by the Washburn-Langford-Doane expedition back in '70 because it spouts so faithfully."

"Valley of the Roaring Clouds," Smoke said. "That's what Preacher says the Indians called it. Sure. I know what you're talking about now." He smiled a very wicked smile. "That thing still go off regular?"

"Certainly does. Every 65 to 70 minutes."

"Do tell? That's interesting. A man could get badly burned if he got caught out in that stuff, now couldn't he?"

"Oh, yes, sir. Badly burned. That is extremely hot water coming out of the earth."

"Might work," Smoke muttered.

"I beg your pardon?" Perry asked.

"Nothing of importance," Smoke told him. "You boys getting enough to eat?"

"Oh, plenty, sir. Mister Jensen," Charles said, "I must report this deadly game to the superintendent. You understand my position?"

"Sure. Go right ahead. I imagine it'll take you boys three or four days to get to him—after you've re-supplied at your base camp—then three of four days to get back here. But I'll be long gone by that time. Then what will you do?"

The young government surveyors looked at each other. "The important thing, I believe, Mister Jensen, is what will you do?"

"Survive," Smoke told him.


"There they are," Roy said, pointing to the now familiar tracks of Smoke's horses. "He's headin' for the canyons."

"Will there be many people there?" Hans asked. "Sightseers?"

Roy shook his head. "Doubtful. It's too early in the season. 'Sides, this place is about three thousand square miles. Take a lot of gawkers to fill that up. We'll find a place to corner and kill him." He lifted the reins and moved out.

"How long will Smoke keep this up, you wonder?" Angel questioned.

"He's kept it up longer than I thought he would," Walt replied. "I reckon he's hopin' they'll give it up and go on back home. When he does decide to make his stand, Angel, it's gonna be a terrible sight to behold."

"That rattlesnake business told me that," Angel said soberly. "I do not ever wish to see another sight like that."

"I 'spect Jensen's got tricks up his sleeve that'll equal it," the old gunfighter said, as the two men rode along, bringing up the rear of the column.

Angel shuddered. "What in God's name could be worse than that?"

"Jensen'll think of something. Bet your boots on it. He ain't even got mad yet."

"I have a brother in Chihuahua. He is a lawyer. I think I will visit him when this is over."

"Least you'll be able to visit, son. That's more'un them thirty-odd fools up ahead of us'll be able to do. And them three gettin' stiff in the ground behind us."

Smoke found the canyon area along the Yellowstone River completely void of human life. And he had never seen a more perfect place for an ambush.

He carefully scouted out the area where he'd chosen to raise some hell, locating a retreat route that wound down to the river, and selected a place in the narrow pass to plant dynamite. He'd light the fuse on his way out and block the pass, forcing those behind him to detour miles before being able to ford the river. By that time, he'd have chosen another place of ambush and would be lying in deadly wait.

He picketed his horses close to the narrow, torturously twisting pass, near water and graze, and moved into position just at dusk, about half a mile from the river and high above it. He awakened long before dawn and built a tiny fire to boil his coffee. He put out the fire as soon as he had warmed his hands and boiled his coffee. His breakfast was jerky and hardtack. He had already sighted in his .44-.40 for long-range shooting and fixed in his mind the landmarks he'd chosen for distance markers along his approach to the area. Now he waited.

Two riders appeared. Smoke lifted his field glasses and adjusted them for distance. He recognized one rider by his shirt and the horse. He did not think he'd ever seen the second man before. So that meant von Hausen had recruited more man-hunters. Smoke wondered where in the hell he'd found them up here and how many he'd hired?

He put those thoughts out of his head and concentrated on staying alive. The point men were still much too far away for any kind of accurate shooting when they reined up, obviously wary and suspecting an ambush. That told Smoke the men weren't entirely stupid. That left greedy and rather foolish.

More men rode up. Smoke lifted his binoculars and pulled in von Hausen and more men than he'd seen previously. "Come on," he muttered. "Come on. Let's get this going."

He was facing east, and the sun was bright. He did not want to risk any reflection from the lenses of the field glasses, so he cased them and settled back, rifle in hand, and waited. The point men rode closer. He saw one of them point to the ground, spotting Smoke's tracks. The other one twisted in the saddle, calling back to the others and pumping his clenched fist up and down in the military signal to come on.

"Yeah," Smoke muttered. "You do that."

The point men passed the first landmark Smoke had fixed in his mind. Smoke lifted the rifle and jacked back the hammer on the .44-.40, sighting one of the riders in. He took up slack on the trigger and the rifle boomed, jarring his shoulder. Cosgrove was knocked from his horse as the big slug struck him dead center in his chest.

Smoke levered in another round and squeezed the trigger. But he shot high and blew the second man's hat off.

The winds caught the hat and sent it sailing. Smoke waited.

"Cosgrove's had it," Roy said, reaching the column. "Jensen shot him right through the heart."

"Goddamnit!" Ford cussed. "Me and Cos buddied all over the west together." Before anyone could stop him, Ford had spurred his horse and was racing up the trail. He shucked his rifle out of the boot just as he passed his ex-partner in crime, stone dead on the rocks beside the trail.

Smoke led the rider in the sights and let him come on. He could hear Ford cussing and hollering in his rage. "Come on," Smoke muttered. "I want you close enough so maybe your horse will come this way and I can see if you've got anything to eat in your saddlebags."

Ford was less than a hundred yards from Smoke's position when Smoke pulled the trigger. The bullet caught Ford in the center of his chest and Ford joined his buddy on the trail. He hit the ground and did not move. His horse kept right on going. Smoke jumped down into the rocks and grabbed the horse's trailing reins, talking to the spooked animal, calming it down.

He found some salt meat and biscuits wrapped in a clean cloth and nothing else of value. He stripped saddle and bridle from the animal and turned it loose. Then Smoke climbed back into position and had breakfast . . . compliments of Frederick von Hausen.

# 13

Von Hausen studied Smoke's position through binoculars, studying every angle carefully. Finally, with a curse and a shake of his head, he cased his field glasses and returned to where his group had gathered.

"Whatever else the man may be, he knows tactics," von Hausen said. "He could hold off an army from his position. It would take several days to get to one end or the other of this canyon then find a way through and work our way behind him. If we split our people and try to trap him in there, he'd know it because of the damned flats on both sides of us, and the high ground to our rear. To charge him would be suicide. It's a standoff." He looked around him. "Where is Langston?"

"Trying to work his way out to get a shot at Jensen," John T. told him.

Von Hausen had decided, several days back, that the sporting aspects of this hunt could go to hell. Just kill Jensen, he told his people.

"Where is he leading us?" von Hausen asked. "Or is he leading us anywhere? The man doesn't think like anyone I ever knew. He's unpredictable. In every war there are plans, tried and true, that are followed by both sides. This man is a . . . a savage. I can't work out what he is going to do from one day to the next."

"Do we make camp here?" Walt asked. "I gotta know so's I can start cookin'."

A single shot rang out. Von Hausen ran to the rocks, the others right behind him. Don Langston lay sprawled on his back below them, his fancy inlaid rifle shining in the sunlight, on the rocks some twenty feet from the body. Langston had been shot right between the eyes.

Walt shifted his chewing tobacco and spat. "I'd say he got a mite too close. I'll go put the beans on."

"Hey, Baron!" the shout came across the rocky flats. "How about you and me settling this?"

"What do you mean, Jensen?" von Hausen yelled.

"Just what I said. You and me, pretty-boy. Stand up, bareknuckle fight. The best man wins."

"Marquess of Queensberry rules?"

Smoke's laughter was taunting. "Anyway you want it, Baron. We'll hold it in Denver."

*"Denver!"* von Hausen shouted.

"That's right—Denver. In front of a crowd at a ring. I'm not going to take a chance out here on one of your rabid skunks shooting me after I beat your face in."

"I wouldn't recommend it," Utah Red said. He was now able to see out of both eyes, but his face was lumpy and still mottled with bruises.

"Oh, I could take him in a ring," von Hausen boasted. "It might be fun."

"How about it?" Smoke shouted.

"I think not, Jensen. You can't run forever."

"Hell, I'm not running now, von Horse-face. Why don't you come on across and get me."

Von Hausen's face reddened at the slur upon his name. "You, sir, are no gentleman."

Smoke told von Hausen what he thought about the German's ancestry.

Obviously, Walt concluded, he don't think much of it.

"You are a foul, stupid man, Jensen," von Hausen hurled the words.

"But I'm a better man than you, von Hose-nose," Smoke called. "I don't need an army to do my fighting."

Frederick touched his nose. *Hose-nose!* "Fill that area with lead!" he shouted.

The men fired, but it was done half-heartedly. The distance was just too great to hope for any damage.

After the firing had ceased, von Hausen called, "How about that, Jensen?"

Silence was his reply.

"You don't suppose we got him with a ricochet?" Cat Brown questioned.

"We wouldn't be that lucky," Pat Gilman said. "He's just playin' 'possum, hopin' one of us will go over there to check it out."

"Hold your positions," von Hausen said. "We've already lost three this day."

"Ford died 'cause he was stupid," Mike Hunt said. "You can't lose your control when fightin' a man like Jensen. Ford better be a lesson to us all."

"Agreed," von Hausen said.

The group waited, all bunched up, for almost half an hour. An explosion jarred the area, followed by a dust cloud drifting up out of the rocks.

"Now what the hell? . . ." Gary muttered.

"I betcha he blew the pass," John T. said. "And I betcha it's the only pass for miles, north or south. Time we work around over there it's gonna be another cold trail."

"I'll find it," Roy said. "I told you all: I aim to kill that man."

"Collect the bodies," von Hausen said wearily. "Get your Bible, Walt."


"Now let me get this straight," the superintendent of the park said to the four young surveyors. "Smoke Jensen—*the* Smoke Jensen, the most famous gunfighter in all the world—is here in this park?"

"That is correct, sir," Charles told him. "He shared his food with us."

"He was a very nice man, I thought," Morris said.

"Smoke Jensen . . . was a very nice man?"

"Yes, sir. Much younger than any of us thought. I would say he is in his mid-thirties."

"That's about right. And people are hunting him? To kill him. In *my* park?"

"Yes, sir. Quite a large gang, I understand. Led by someone named Baron Frederick von Hausen."

"Von Hausen. I'm not familiar with the name. A Baron, you say?"

"Yes, sir."

"Who are the men with him?"

"Bounty-hunters, professional killers. Men of very low quality," Perry said.

"Quite," Charles added.

"Well, this cannot be allowed to continue," the superintendent said. "I'll get word to the army. They'll do something about it. This is federal land, after all."


After crossing the Yellowstone, Smoke headed north, into the Washburn Range. He knew he had bought himself a day, maybe a day and a half; no more than that. He was out of supplies, except for a little coffee, and he was living off the land, just as he and Preacher had done during those early years. But Smoke, like most western men, was a coffee-drinking man, and he wasn't going to be out of coffee for very long. He could live off of fish and rabbits and berries, but damned if he was going to be denied coffee.

On the second day after fording the Yellowstone, he spotted a thin plume of smoke in the distance and headed for it. He rode up to the camp, stopping a respectable distance from it, and eyeballed those in the camp who were, by now, eyeballing him.

The three men and three women were dressed in some sort of safari clothes; Smoke thought that was the right description for it. The women dressed just like the men, in britches and high-top, lace-up boots. He'd never seen hats like they were wearing. Looked like a gourd hollowed out. Funniest looking things he'd ever seen.

"Hello, the camp," Smoke called. "I'll approach with your permission."

"Why, of course. Come right in, sir," a rather plump man returned the call.

Smoke rode in and dismounted. He loosened the cinch strap on the horses and picketed them on graze.

The men and women—none of whom were armed—quickly noticed Smoke's guns. One of the women thought the stranger moved like a great predator cat. And my, what a ruggedly handsome man. She fanned herself at his approach.

They were scientists, Smoke was told. Gilbert, Carol, Robert, Paula, Thomas, and Blanche. Anthropologists and some other names that sounded to Smoke like they were clearing their throats. He didn't have the foggiest idea what they meant.

"Share our lunch with us?" Robert asked.

"I'd be obliged. I ran out of supplies several days ago."

"You poor man!" Blanche said. "You must be starved."

"Oh, no," Smoke told her, "I've been living off the land." He smiled at her. My word, what a handsome man, she thought. "No reason for anybody to go hungry in this land of bounty, ma'am. You just have to know something about surviving out here. The only bad thing is running out of coffee."

"Well, we have plenty of that," Thomas said.

Something popped in the timber and suddenly the stranger was on his feet from his kneeling by the fire and he had a gun in his hand. His draw had been so smooth and so fast none of the scientists were aware of it. It just seemed to appear in his hand.

All did notice, however, how hard and tight his face had become, and how cold were his eyes.

"One of our mules," Paula said quickly.

Smoke nodded and walked to the edge of the small clearing. He could see mules and horses picketed. "Pull them in closer," he said, returning to the fire and the coffee pot. "You got your picket line too far away from camp. There are folks out here who'd steal from you. The west has tamed somewhat, but not that much. Move it right over there." He pointed. "You see anybody trying to steal your livestock, shoot 'em."

"*Shoot* them?" Gilbert said.

"Yes. You do have weapons, don't you?"

"We have a rifle and a shotgun," Thomas said. "And Robert has a sidearm."

"That's good. Keep them close by." He walked to his packhorse and returned with two gunbelts he'd taken from bounty-hunters in von Hausen"s party. "Here," he said, handing the guns and leather to Gilbert. "I'm gettin' loaded down with weapons. I'll give you folks a .44 carbine, too."

"This is very generous of you, sir," Gilbert said. "Let us pay you for these fine weapons. We're out here on a government grant."

Smoke shook his head. "The people I took them from don't need them any longer."

"You're a lawman?" Blanche asked.

"No, ma'am. Those guns belonged to some ol' boys who were chasing me. They caught up with me." He looked at her confused expression and smiled, transforming his entire face, taking years from him. "I'm not an outlaw, if that's what you're thinking. I'm a rancher from down in Colorado. My wife is the former Sally Reynolds of New Hampshire."

"How marvelous!" Paula said. "The banking family. Very old and respected name." She closed her mouth and looked at the others in her group. "Then you must be? . . . It was in all the newspapers . . . Some thought it was so scandalous . . . For her to marry a . . . Oh, my God!"

"Yes, ma'am. I'm Smoke Jensen."

The women got all flustered and the men got all nervous. Smoke sipped his coffee. Too weak for his taste. But he wasn't about to complain.

"I read in the newspapers before we left that Sally was home visiting friends and family," Carol said. "Her parents are still in Europe, are they not?"

"Yes, ma'am. With our children. Look here, what do you call those hats y'all are wearing?"

"Pith," Robert said.

Smoke almost spilled his coffee. He blurted, "I beg your pardon, sir?"

"Pith helmets," Paula said. "They're quite the rage for any type of expedition into the wilderness."

"If you say so," Smoke mumbled.

Thomas said, "These guns you just gave us . . . the men chasing you gave them up voluntarily?"

"They did after I shot them."

Blanche sat down on a log. "Were they severely wounded?"

"About as severe as you can get," Smoke said, spearing a piece of bacon from the skillet. "They sure weren't in any condition to complain about it."

"You turned the thugs over to the law?"

"No. Their buddies buried them."

Carol sat down beside Blanche and both women started fanning themselves vigorously.

"You . . . *killed* them?" Gilbert asked.

"I sure did." Then Smoke explained, in detail, about those chasing him. While he was explaining, he spotted the coffee can and made a fresh pot of coffee. Stuff that was drinkable. Cowboy coffee. "I just can't seem to convince that crazy German to leave me alone. He's about to make me mad."

Robert poured a cup of the fresh brew and took a sip. His eyes bugged out as he bravely swallowed it. He sat the cup down.

"How . . . many men do you have chasing you?" Gilbert asked.

"Oh, I don't know. Twenty-five or thirty, I suppose. I killed three more the other day, over on the Yellowstone. They just keep coming at me and I just keep whittling them down. I'm goin' to have to make a stand of it somewhere, I reckon. But I don't want to see any innocent people get hurt."

"I don't think there is anyone else in the park this time of year," Thomas said. "We did see some young men a couple of weeks ago. Government surveyors."

"I ran into them. Nice bunch of boys. They said they were going to tell the superintendent about the men after me. But by the time he gets word out and the army, or U.S. Marshals get in, this fracas will be over."

"You are very . . . well, *cavalier* about this matter, Mister Jensen," Carol said.

"No point in getting all worked up about it." Smoke nibbled on a biscuit. "I'll just handle it my way."

"But there are *thirty* gunmen chasing you!" Blanche said.

Smoke shrugged. "More or less. And I assure you it'll be less in a day or two. I faced eighteen men in the streets of a town on the Uncompahgre some years back. I was just out of my teens. I left all eighteen belly down in the dirt."

"Eighteen!" Robert said. "You killed eighteen men by yourself?"

"Sure did. They got lead in me, I won't deny that. Almost killed me. But I was still standing when the dust cleared . . . sort of. I was on my knees in the street but I was still alive."

"Where was the law?" Paula asked.

Smoke tapped the butt of a Colt. "Right there, ma'am.

The law is good for handling lost horses and finding run-away kids and the like. It's good to see the law walking the street and tipping their hats to ladies. Makes everybody feel good. All secure and such as that. But there are some things that a man has to handle personal. If he's been pushed to the end of the line and can't get any relief and if he's capable and has the where-with-all. I'm capable and I damn sure have the where-with-all."

Smoke rolled a cigarette and poured another cup of coffee.

"Then you are a follower of Kropotkin?" Thomas asked.

"Who?"

"A Russian anarchist. A revolutionary."

"No, sir. I'm just a man who believes in saddling his own horses and stomping on his own snakes. I'm all for law and order. We have us a fine sheriff back home. I voted for him. But I also believe there are people out there in society who don't give a damn for anybody's rights or wishes or privileges. Now if the law is around when those types break the rules, that's fine; let the law handle it. But there are others in society who would have me run away from this situation with my tail tucked between my legs and go crying to the law about those chasing me. I don't believe in that. I believe that if a man can't or won't follow even the simplest rules of conduct, or abide by the simplest of moral codes . . . get rid of him. Sooner or later, somebody is going to have to do it. Why not now, before that person can bring more grief to innocents?"

"For the simple reason that as human beings they deserve a second chance; a chance to redeem themselves," Gilbert said.

"Fine. But do they deserve a tenth chance, or a twentieth?" Smoke countered. "When does society say that's enough and dispose of them? And how many more innocent, law-abiding people have to suffer all types of losses

122

and indignities and injuries and even face death and die—sometimes horribly—before those criminals are either put away for life or hanged? Their victims often don't get a second chance at life. Why the hell should the criminal have more rights than the victim? That type of thinking doesn't make any sense to me."

The scientists looked at one another.

"I set out from my ranch to buy some bulls from a friend of mine in Central Wyoming," Smoke said. "That's all. Just a simple legal business transaction between two men. Suddenly I find myself being tracked and hunted by a gang of nuts. Then I learn that they plan on using me like some poor animal; cornered and killed for sport. I went to the Army with it. I was told they couldn't do anything about it. Well, fine. But I can sure do something about it. I can kill every no-count scummy bastard—excuse my language, ladies—that's coming up the trail after me. And that is exactly what I intend to do."

# 14

The anthropologists re-supplied Smoke and wished him well on his journey. Then they quickly packed up their equipment and beat it back to park headquarters as fast as they could lope their mules.

Smoke headed north, toward one of the strangest sights he had ever seen in all his life: the dead forest. Old Preacher used to tell a story about Jim Bridger, when someone asked him if it was true about the stone trees. Preacher said Bridger told the person, "That's pee-trification. Head to the Yellowstone and you'll see pee-trified trees a-growin', with peetrified birds on 'em a-singin' peetrified songs."

Preacher swore it was true. However, Preacher said he never could find them peetrified flowers a-bloomin' in colors of crystal that Bridger said he saw. "Bridger wasn't above tellin' a lie ever' now and then," Preacher admitted.

Smoke didn't make any effort to hide his tracks. The government—or somebody—had cut a nature trail through the park and he stayed on it. It was easier on his horses and on him. He crossed Tower Creek and followed the trail as it curved westward. Near as he could remember, the twenty-five or thirty square miles of stone trees were only a few miles further, most on a ridge.

The scientists in the pith helmets back yonder had

told Smoke that the stone trees were millions of years old, buried alive by volcanic ash. Since Smoke had never seen a volcano—and really didn't want to see one, not up close—he really didn't have an opinion on it one way or the other.

He pulled up short this time, just as he had the other times he'd looked upon the strangeness of the stone forest. It was eerie, and very quiet. Many of the trees here had not fallen, but stood like silent sentinels over their fallen comrades.

Smoke did not enter the silent dead forest at this point. He rode on, staying with the trail for several miles. When he did decide to enter the stone forest, he made his trail clear for a time. Then he tied sacking around his horses' hooves and led them out of the stone forest to a small cul-de-sac with graze and water. He blocked the entrance with brush and logs and slipped back into the stillness of the stone forest, taking with him only what supplies he could comfortably carry in a small pack on his back.

He hiked back to Specimen Ridge and chose his site carefully; one that gave him a commanding view of all that lay in front of him. since he had ridden up, no small feat for his horses, von Hausen and party would be coming up the same trail—he hoped. Smoke would be shooting downhill, so that would be tricky, but nothing that he couldn't overcome with the good sights on the .44-.40.

Now all he had to do was wait and hope that von Hausen and company took the bait.

Roy Drum halted the parade in the valley that Smoke overlooked from his spot on the small mountain that held the stone trees.

"What's the matter?" von Hausen asked.

"I don't like it," the tracker said. "Jensen went right

up that big ridge yonder with them dead stone trees. It's like he wanted us to see his tracks."

"Hell, man!" John T. said. "He ain't tried to hide his tracks in a hundred miles."

"Well, that's a fact," Roy admitted.

Von Hausen began scanning the ridge with his long lenses. After several minutes of searching, he cased the binoculars, hung them on his saddle horn, and picked up the reins. "Let's go. The ridge is void of life."

"Gary, take the point," John T. said. "Might be a good idea if we walked our horses up. That's a steep climb. Wouldn't do to have a horse break a leg now."

"You're right," von Hausen said, and swung from the saddle to help the ladies down. A true gentleman.

Smoke lay flat on his belly behind a huge stone stump of what had been redwood, millions of years back. He had measured the distance between stone stumps and trees from where he now lay to the crest of the ridge. He had ample brush to help along the way and in addition, a cut in the earth several feet deep that led to the crest and curved with one wall facing those below him.

Gary paused to catch his breath and it was his last one. Smoke's .44-.40 boomed and Gary went down.

"Goddamnit!" Roy yelled, diving for cover. "I knowed it was a trap."

Al Hayre exposed part of his body from behind a stone and Smoke drilled him clean through the shoulder. Al dropped his rifle and began a fast roll down the ridge toward the valley below, hollering and yelling and cussing until his head hit a rock and shut him up.

Smoke slung his pack and rolled to another, better protected area, angling toward the cut. Pride Anderson stepped out from cover and dropped to one knee and fired, the slug howling off stone and sending chips into Smoke's face. Smoke wiped off the blood and moved to the other side of the huge fallen tree, slipping behind a mass of brush and stone. Pride made the mistake of trying for a second shot at Smoke. He would never get another shot at anything.

Smoke quick-sighted him in and pulled the trigger. Pride took the .44-.40 slug in the center of his forehead. The force of the bullet snapped his head back and Pride tumbled, rolling lifeless down the ridge.

Smoke sent several rawhide bound sticks of dynamite down the ridge and everybody hit the earth. Everybody except Smoke. He scrambled for the cut and ran to the top of the ridge just as the dynamite blew. Once again, horses panicked and ran off down the hill.

Smoke found him a good spot behind a small stand of trees on the crest, punched more cartridges into his rifle then chewed on a biscuit and waited.

"A couple of you men work your way over to the timber in that direction," von Hausen ordered. "Two more to that side," He pointed. "Try to box him in."

"You'll never do it, your majesty," Walt said, safely behind a petrified log.

Smoke had pulled away from the ridge and worked his way some two hundred yards back from the crest. It put him that much closer to his horses and in better cover should von Hausen order men to attempt to flank him.

On the hill, Andrea and Marlene and Maria looked with horror and disgust in their eyes—more disgust than horror—at the smear of blood and hair and brains that Pride had left on the side of a stone stump.

"Al's stirring down there," Angel said, sitting beside Walt behind the huge log.

"If he's smart, he'll find his horse and get the hell gone from here."

"One arm's hanging limp by his side," Angel said. "He looks sort of confused."

"Busted his head on the way down. There's another walkin' wounded for us to tend to. We're gonna look like a hospital 'fore this trip gets over."

Marty Boswell's daddy had always told him he had

sawdust for brains. Marty got tired of listening to his daddy and shot him dead one day back in Nebraska. Smoke proved Marty's daddy wrong when Marty stuck his ugly face out from behind a large rock for a look-see. He had some brains. But they were now several feet behind the gunslinger, on the ground, due to the impacting of a .44-.40 slug with Marty's head.

Gil Webb wisely decided not to move from his position.

Smoke said to hell with it and made his way back to his horses. He was saddled up and riding out ten minutes later. Gil Webb left his hidey-hole only after long moments of silence had passed. He made his way carefully to Smoke's last position, checking out all possibilities along the way. He found where Smoke had left the ridge, his moccasin-clad feet digging into the soft earth, heading for the timber behind the ridge. Gil motioned for the two men on the other flank to check it out, then called down the ridge for the others to stay put. Of course, von Hausen and those in his immediate party ignored that.

The men scrambled up the ridge to squat panting beside a stone tree. "Marty?" von Hausen asked.

"Dead. Jensen put one right in the center of his forehead."

"That's three dead and one wounded," Hans said. "I don't know how badly wounded Hayre is."

"He's out of it," Cat Brown said, coming over the crest of the ridge. "Hit high and pretty hard. He wants his money and wants to get gone from this fight."

Von Hausen nodded his head. "Pay him off, Gunter. Wounded as he is he'd be of no further use to us. He'd only be a hindrance. Have Walt and Angel tend to his wounds and then send him on his way."

Gunter was gone back down the steep hill.

"He's gone," came the shout from the timber. "Headin' west."

Von Hausen paced the distance between Smoke's last defensive position over to where Marty lay dead, a hole in his head. Von Hausen reluctantly admitted—to himself—that Smoke was one of the best marksman he had ever seen.

"What type of weapon is he using?" he asked John T.

".44-.40. It's got an extra rear sight for better accuracy. Jensen's good," he grudgingly conceded.

The German looked at the gunfighter. "That's like saying trains run on tracks. I measured the distance. Smoke made this shot from two hundred and ten paces."

John T. whistled softly. "That's some shootin'."

"To say the least," von Hausen added very drily. "Have the men dig some graves, John T."

"Yes, sir. And have Walt fetch his Bible?"

"Yes. This is becoming a routine."

Smoke rode west. He put a few miles behind him, knowing that by the time von Hausen and party rounded up their horses, buried their dead, and tended to the wounded, it would be dark. There would be no further pursuit this day.

He stopped long enough to fix his supper and boil his coffee, then moved on another couple of miles before finding a good spot to spend the night. He was up and moving before dawn, pushing west. He was not all that familiar with this region. Years back, he and Preacher had cut north at the stone trees and headed up into Montana. Preacher had told him about the western part of this region, but Smoke had not personally seen it.

He cut southwest, heading for the Gallatin Range. As he rode, he added up how many people—approximately—von Hausen had left. As close as he could figure it, he still had about twenty-five people after him, including the women, and he damn sure wasn't going to discount them.

His horses began acting skittish, eyes all walled around and ears pricked up. Smoke reined up and listened. And he didn't like what he heard. This was grizzly country and it was spring, with the mother grizzlies out of the den with cubs. A big grizzly can be as much as seven feet tall and weigh close to a thousand pounds. Smoke heard the huffing sound of a grizzly, and the whining of cubs, and the sounds were close. And he also smelled fresh blood. That probably meant that the grizzly had killed a fresh dropped elk calf and would be awfully irritated at anything that interrupted her meal.

Smoke left the trail and moved east for about a mile, getting away from the grizzly and her cubs—if any—and her meal. Smoke had enough to worry about without the added danger of a grizzly bear.

When his horses had calmed down, he cut west and once more picked up the trail. Although a bear steak would taste nice, there was no way Smoke would kill a mother with cubs. Preacher had instilled in Smoke a deep love and respect for the land and the animals that lived there. Should he kill a bear, there was no way he could come close to using the meat, and no one around to give it to. Smoke had never killed any type of animal for the so-called sport of killing, and never would. He had nothing but contempt for those who killed without need.

There was another reason that humans should be extremely careful in grizzly country: a grizzly can run up to thirty miles an hour; no way a human being could out-race one. But grizzlies, because of their bulk and long straight claws, seldom climb, even as cubs.

Ol' Preacher had told Smoke that there was only two kinds of trees in grizzly country: them that he could climb and them that he couldn't.

Smoke hoped that von Hausen and his party didn't run into a grizzly. Those stupid people would make no effort to avoid contact. They'd just shoot it.

Smoke rode for several days, sometimes making an effort to conceal his tracks, but oftentimes not. He crossed Panther Creek, Indian Creek, and made camp at the north end of Grizzly Lake. Roaring Mountain was somewhere off to his east, he believed, as was Obsidian Cliff, an outcrop of black volcanic glass that was used by various Indian tribes over the centuries for arrow-points. Geyser Basin was to his south. Hot ground, Preacher had told him. Burn your feet, so said Preacher.

That afternoon, before the sun went down and Smoke could still see to write, he scoured the area until he found a large flat rock. Using a small rock, he scratched out a message. Before he left the next morning, he carefully placed the rock in the center of the trail. There was no way von Hausen could miss it if he came this way.

Then he left the trail and headed on over toward Solfatora Creek. He had another ambush to set up.

"Some of the men are grumbling," John T. informed von Hausen. " 'Bout half of them want to quit."

"We discussed this last evening, John T.," von Hausen said. "Among the six of us." He tossed the man a small leather sack filled with gold coins. "Several thousand dollars in there, John T. Spread that out among the men. That should make them happy. And tell them there will be a thousand dollar bonus for every man who finishes this."

"They'll stay after this," John T. said.

"The great unwashed," Gunter said after John T. had left. "They are the same all over the world." He opened a container of caviar and spread a bit on a cracker. He smiled, but there was a worried look in his eyes.

The next morning, Pat Gilman was riding point. He came up on the flat rock in the trail and read the words. He felt his guts churn and another part of his anatomy tighten up. He yelled for John T.

131

John T. sat his saddle and read the words scratched on the big flat rock.

I HAVE RUN OUT OF PATIENCE. FROM THIS POINT ON THERE WILL BE NO COMING BACK FOR ANY OF YOU IF YOU FOLLOW ME. THIS IS MY FINAL WARNING.

Von Hausen read the scratchings. He turned to the men. "Anybody want to quit?"

No one did. They all had big money in their eyes. It was easy to forget those men lying lonely in cold graves on the trail behind them when their pockets were jingling with gold coins and big money waiting at the end of the line. What they should have realized, but didn't, was that only death awaited them at the end of this line.

"How are the supplies holding out, Walt?" Hans asked.

"If we can kill a deer every other day or so we'll be all right. As far as eatin' goes. I 'spect if Jensen keeps thinnin' the culls out like he's been doin', we'll have plenty."

"I really wish you would stop that kind of talk," Gunter said.

"You wanna fire me and Angel? You say the word and we'll damn sure leave right now."

"Settle down, old man. You're entitled to your opinion. Relieve Pat at the point, Briscoe."

One minute off the trail, following the hoof-prints of Smoke's horses, a shotgun roared.

"Down!" Hans shouted, as he left the saddle.

They all waited, crouched in the early summer foliage that grew thick and lush in the darkness of the timber. But no more shots were heard.

"Jensen!" von Hausen yelled. "Jensen!"

He received no reply.

"Smoke Jensen!" von Hausen tried again. "Stand and fight like a man, damn you!"

"He wouldn't be fightin' us with no shotgun," Montana Red said, after a moment of deep woods silence. "You 'member we come up missin' the shotgun that night he attacked the camp and figured it got burned up or blowed up. He musta tooken it and rigged an ambush."

"Check it out, Nick," John T. ordered. "And goddamnit, be careful."

The man with the busted mouth and nose—he wheezed like a steam engine when he talked—was back in a few minutes. "Jensen's long gone. He rigged a booby trap with the shotgun. You better come look at this." He cut his eyes to von Hausen. "But not the wimmen, sir."

Smoke had secured the express gun in the fork of a tree, about head high, then cocked the triggers, pulling the cord taut, that was attached to a cord from the triggers to a trip wire. The loads of buckshot had hit Briscoe in the neck and face, completely blowing off his head. It was a very ugly scene.

Hans took one look and barfed all over the place.

Walt strolled up, shifted his tobacco and spat. The old gunfighter said, "I reckon we can scratch that one off the supper list, Angel."

# 15

Briscoe was buried in the deep timber—minus his head. They couldn't find enough of it to bother with scooping up. The hunters rode on a few very careful miles before making camp for the evening. When they made camp, the bounty hunters and outlaws each sat apart from one another, saying little or nothing. Briscoe's death—more the way it happened than the thug's demise—had deeply affected them all.

All had heard the stories that when pushed to his limits, Smoke Jensen was a ruthless man, who would fight like a cornered puma, stopping at nothing. The events of earlier today had damn sure proved that gossip out.

Hans sat with Gunter. The women were in their tents. Von Hausen was talking with John T. and Roy Drum. "Gunter," Hans said.

His friend cut his eyes.

"Is going on worth it?" Hans was the first among the three to say the words.

"By now, every gambler from Monte Carlo to New York City knows of this hunt and is taking bets," Gunter spoke softly. "If we left now, we would return home in disgrace. Yes. I've been giving it some thought. We have to press on. As we discussed before, it is a matter of honor. Are you really having second thoughts?"

"Yes. My God, Gunter, how many dead men have we

left behind us. Nine? Ten? Heaven forgive me I can't even remember!"

Gunter chuckled and patted his friend on the arm. "Well, let's just hope that God has a sense of humor, Hans."

"*He* might. Smoke Jensen doesn't."

Smoke softly whistled part of a tune he'd once heard played at a concert he and Sally had attended in San Francisco. Pretty piece. Something by Brahms, he thought. Or maybe Wagner. Whatever. It was a pretty piece of music.

He was waiting in thick underbrush, behind a fallen tree, just off the bank of a fast-moving creek. He had angled down into the Central Plateau. Not too many large mountains in this part of the range, but plenty of hills and marshes and excellent ambush sites. Smoke was cold-minded now. He had issued his final warning. If von Hausen chose to ignore it—that was too bad for them. Smoke intended to empty every saddle he saw that he knew an outlaw sat in. Or a nutty European sportsman—so called.

It was almost a shame to do it, Smoke thought. None of those following him seemed to have any imagination; they just stayed on his trail and pushed blindly ahead. Smoke picked his ambush spots several days apart, having observed through binoculars that those behind him would be cautious for a day or so when approaching a likely spot, but would become careless on the third or fourth day out.

They just never seemed to learn.

Like now, he thought, as he heard the sounds of riders approaching from the west. He eared back the hammer on his .44-.40, thinking: von Hausen and party damn sure made good time this trip. He wasn't expecting them until late that afternoon or the next day.

135

He gently let the hammer down when he saw that this bunch was not von Hausen's hunters. It was the army. Smoke lay behind the log, in the brush, and listened to the men gripe.

"Top Soldier," a slick-sleeve private said to a sergeant major. "What are we gonna do with this von Hausen when we find him?"

"Order him from the park, MacBride."

"And Jensen?"

"He ain't done nothin'. Now, when we spot Jensen, just stand easy, men. Don't make any sudden moves. Don't do nothin' to rile him."

Smoke stood up. "Afternoon, troops," he called.

The army patrol stopped in the creek. The top soldier forded on across and waved his men on. He reined up and dismounted. "Loosen 'em up and let 'em blow, men." He turned to face Smoke. "Would you be Smoke Jensen?"

"I am."

"I'm Sergeant Major Murphy. I got orders to say this, as silly as it sounds. Are you aware of a large group of men, and some ladies, following you with hostile intent?"

"I am quite aware of them, Top Soldier. I've emptied about ten or so saddles over the past month or so. I was waiting for them here."

"So I see. Well, the hunt is over, Mister Jensen. You are now under the protection of the United States Army."

"It's going to be interesting to hear what von Hausen has to say about that, Top."

"They will be escorted from the park and ordered to leave the country, Mister Jensen. Those American citizens with them will be placed under arrest—if you press charges."

"They'll just lie for one another and nothing will be

136

accomplished by my doing that, Top. And you know it."

"That is probably very true, Mister Jensen. But I was under orders to inform you of that."

"I have so been informed. You men got here awful quick."

"We were here. We're an advance party checking out likely places to build the park headquarters."

"I killed a deer this morning, Top. It's strung up over there. Why don't you boys cut you a steak and we'll have an early supper."

"Music to my ears, Mister Jensen. Mighty pretty music."

"Just Smoke, Top Soldier. Just Smoke."

While the steaks were sizzling, being cooked in what skillets the six man patrol had and the rest on sticks held over a fire, MacBride asked, "How long has this crazy damn game been going on, Smoke?"

"Too long, Top. As close as I can figure it—you know how you lose time out there—about two months."

*"Two months!"* a young soldier said. "How come you let it go on so long, Mister Jensen? I mean, with your reputation and all, why didn't you? . . ." He shut his mouth after a dirty look from Murphy.

"I didn't want to start the killing, and I didn't want it to go on. But they just kept pressing me, harder and harder. I finally knew that I had no choice in the matter. So I did what I felt I had to do."

"Nobody at all is blamin' you, Smoke," Top Soldier said. "Them people you run into all talked real nice about you. And you also got some powerful friends in government that jumped on this situation like a monkey to a banana."

Smoke nodded his head. He just didn't feel good with the situation. The six-man patrol could easily be shot to pieces by von Hausen and his men. Murphy was a grizzled old veteran of countless Indian wars—and probably the Civil War. But the rest were just kids. He put his worries into words.

"You think they'd dare fire on the U.S. Army, Smoke?" the Top Soldier asked.

"Without hesitation, Top. Von Hausen has promised these men all sorts of big money. They're not going to let it go without a fight."

Murphy lowered his voice. "Johnny over there, the single-striper, he's in his second hitch. He's a good one with more than enough battle experience. The rest . . ." He shrugged his shoulders. "They ain't been tested under fire."

"Yet," Smoke added.

"Somehow I knew you were gonna say that," Murphy said mournfully.


Montana Jess was riding point with the tracker, Roy Drum, when they reined up about two hundred yards from the fast-moving creek. They'd both been smelling wood smoke for about a mile, and were moving very cautiously. They dismounted and slipped through the timber to the west bank of the creek.

Montana Jess cussed under his breath. "Cavalry. And yonder's Smoke's horses. See 'em?"

"Yeah," Drum whispered. "I think we got us a problem, Montana. Let's get back to von Hausen."

"It might be a problem," the Baron admitted. The hunting party had stopped about two miles from the creek. "Does the U.S. Army have arrest powers?"

"They might in here," John T. said. "This bein' a national park and all."

"How big a patrol is it?" Leo Grant asked. His left arm was healing and he had limited use of it; he no longer had to use the sling.

"Six," Drum replied.

"What are you thinking, Leo?" von Hausen asked.

The gunfighter shrugged his shoulders. "Take 'em out," he said simply. "It sure wouldn't be no big deal. Injun up and blow 'em straight to hell."

"Now just wait a damned minute here!" Walt protested. "I ain't havin' no part of killin' government troops."

"Nor me," Angel said. "You boys better think about what you're about to do."

"Aw, shut your traps," Paul Melham said. "Who gives a damn about a bunch of soldier boys? I say we go for the money."

"I'm with you," Lou Kennedy said. "I ain't about to turn my back on more money than I could make in five years hasslin' homesteaders and the like."

"I'll stay," Gil Webb said. "I got warrants on me in half a dozen states and territories. I ain't about to ride in no army camp and let them arrest me."

The rest of the bounty hunters and gunslingers quickly fell in line. That left Walt and Angel looking down the muzzles of a dozen guns.

"You shoot us," Walt said, thinking very quickly, "you got no surprise left, 'cause them shots will carry to the soldier boys . . . and Jensen."

"Tie them up and leave them here," von Hausen ordered. "We'll dispose of them once we've killed the soldiers and hanged Jensen."

"Yeah. I like that idea. Hang 'im slow," Utah Red said. "I wanna see him die real slow and hard. We'll put his feet in the fire first. Make him scream."

"They'll be none of that!" von Hausen said sharply. "We'll hang him properly after we try him for the murders of those men we buried along the trail."

Walt shook his head in disgust.

"Now, I like that!" Tony Addison said. "Real legal-like. I wish somebody had brought some pitcher-takin' machinery. I'd like to have me a pitcher of Smoke Jensen swingin'."

Marlene smiled. "Oh, but we do have photographic equipment. The newest and very best. And it's packed very carefully."

The women had long miles back discarded their riding costumes and side-saddles. They were all dressed in riding breeches and rode astride, and all of them carried side-arms.

"Tie them up," von Hausen said, pointing to Walt and Angel. "Leave them here and picket the horses. We'll move out on foot as soon as this camp is secured. Take your spurs off and anything else that might make a noise."

Walt and Angel were trussed up and dumped on the ground. Cat Brown stood over Walt and grinned at the old gunfighter. "I'm gonna personal kill you, Webster. I been tired of your mouth for weeks. I'm gonna gutshoot you and listen to you squall."

"That's about your speed, punk," Walt told him, defiance in his eyes.

Cat kicked the man in the belly and laughed at him.

"Move out," von Hausen ordered. "When we reach the creek, I'll go up to the bank alone and give the patrol a shout. When they stand up, open fire. Knock a leg out from under Jensen. We want him alive. Remember that. *Alive!*"

The hunting party was just out of sight when Angel said. "I am blessed with teeth that are ver' strong, Walt. If my brain was as strong as my teeth I would not be in this situation, I am thinking. Let me scoot around and I will go to work on your bonds."

"I'm glad one of us still has his choppers," Walt said. "I lost most of mine years back."

Smoke had led his horses to new graze, about two hundred and fifty yards from the camp, he picketed

140

them behind a huge tangle of brush and thorns; it wasn't done deliberately, that was where the best graze was. He was walking back to the camp when he heard the shout. He recognized the voice and knew instantly that something was very wrong. Von Hausen wouldn't just walk up to an Army camp knowing by now that the word had spread about what he was doing.

Smoke ran toward the camp to warn the men when the first volley of shots thundered in the mid-morning air. A stray bullet whanged off a rock and slammed into his leg, knocking him sprawling. He grabbed his leg at the wound to keep any blood from leaking to the ground and crawled into a thicket. Inside the tangle, he turned and with a leafy branch on the ground brushed out any sign of his entry and rearranged the brush at the opening. It might work, he thought. They would see his horses gone and just might assume that he'd never been in the camp, or had already departed.

If they didn't search too diligently, if they were anxious to get gone after the killing ambush of Army troops, if his horses didn't whinny and give away their position . . .

A lot of ifs.

"Finish him," von Hausen said, pointing to the top soldier, who was gut shot and glaring at him through bright, pain-filled eyes.

Marlene coldly, and with a strange expression of excitement on her face, shot the sergeant major in the head.

"Help me," a young soldier pleaded.

"Why, certainly," von Hausen said. He lifted his pistol and shot him between the eyes.

"Damnit!" Roy Drum said. "Jensen's gone. Both of his horses is gone. He must have pulled out just after we seen them this morning."

"That's right," Montana Jess said. "Jensen's hoss was

141

saddled. I 'member now."

"We'll pick up his trail," von Hausen said. "He can't have gone far. It's been no more than two hours. Scatter the supplies. The Army lives on hardtack. Leave it. I have no taste for that horrible ration."

"What about the bodies?" John T. asked.

"Leave them where they lie. The bears will have them eaten by this time tomorrow."

"Their horses?"

"Leave them. We don't want to be seen riding a horse wearing an Army brand. Let's get back to camp and get on Jensen's trail. Quickly, men. Move!"

When the last man had splashed across the creek, Smoke rolled out of his hiding place and limped to the death camp. He quickly checked the bodies. They were all dead. Cussing under his breath, he tied a bandana around the wound on his leg and then grabbed as much of the scattered equipment as he dared take the time to do so. Then, gritting his teeth against the pain, he limped as quickly as he could to his horses. Ten minutes later he was in the saddle and gone, staying off the trail and weaving through the timber, heading for the high country. He would heat a knife point and dig the lead out later. Right now, he had to put some distance between himself and the death camp.

"Goddamnit!" von Hausen yelled, looking at the ropes on the ground. "They've escaped. I thought you said the men were tied securely?"

"They was!" John T. said. "I checked 'em personal. They was trussed up like pigs."

"Angel Cortez has teeth like a beaver," Valdes said. "He used to win bets in bars by bending coins between his teeth. But they cannot have gone far."

"John T.," von Hausen said. "Assign men to track down and kill Walt and Angel. Get in the saddle, men. We've got to get on Jensen's trail."

142

Marlene smiled. She had seen through von Hausen's plan. The men could not back off now. They had to kill Jensen if it meant dying to the last person. They would all—to a man—hang if caught for the killing of the troops. She trembled with excitement. There was no thrill on earth like that of killing a man. Nothing compared to it. Nothing.

She wondered how it would feel to slip the noose around Smoke Jensen's neck.

# 16

Smoke rode hard for several miles, then stopped to let his horses blow. He quickly built a small fire, ripped his jeans around the bullet wound, and took a look at it. The slug had lost some of its power when it struck the leg, but still had enough punch to tear a hole. He felt all around the wound and could feel the slug buried just beneath the skin. He took the hot sterilized blade and slipped the point under the skin, digging around and popping the slug out, his face dripping with sweat from the cauterization of the wound. That would have to do it. If the wound felt infected by morning, he'd cut it open, pour gunpowder in, and burn out the infection. He'd done it before, so he wasn't looking forward to a repeat performance. It wasn't pleasant, but it worked.

He swung back into the saddle and headed out. He was going to the temporary headquarters of the park superintendent. Von Hausen and his people could not afford to let anyone live. For their plans to succeed, anyone who knew they were in the park had to die. And Smoke was sure that by now, the surveyors, the scientists, and the superintendent and his staff knew about von Hausen. They had to be warned.

Smoke pointed his horse's nose toward the temporary headquarters of the superintendent. He had a hell of a ride ahead of him.

"You know where the home of the man who runs this place is located?" Angel asked.

"North. Up near the Montana line. And von Hausen knows it, too."

"I heard them talking, too, my friend."

The men had stopped to rest their horses and to make plans. "We for sure got men comin' after us, Angel," Walt said. "He can't afford to have us get free and bump our gums."

"We'll ride on until we find just the right spot," Angel said. "Then we will take some of the pressure off of Mister Smoke Jensen, si, amigo?"

Walt grinned. "Right, my friend."

The men swung into their saddles and headed north.

"We got to be careful with Ol' Walt and Angel," Mack Saxton said, when they had stopped to rest their horses. "That old man's a pistolero from way back."

"He ain't nothin'," Lou Kennedy said. "I used to think he was, 'til he started takin' Jensen's side in this. He's just a wore out old man is all he is."

"An old rattler'll kill you just as quick as a young one," Mack said. "And Angel ain't no one to fool with neither."

"He's just a damn greaser is all," Nat Reed said. "Full of beans and hot air. I'll take him."

Mack walked away to relieve himself in the bushes, thinking: Get us all killed is what you'll do. Angel Cortez is a bad man to fool with.

Smoke pushed his horses hard. He had the entire Washburn Plateau to travel before he reached the superintendent's quarters. And he knew he also had to deal with those behind him at some point along the way. He had to take some of the pressure off.

Smoke made a cold camp that night, not wanting to risk a fire, and was stiff and sore when he rolled out of his blankets the next morning. It was dark as a bat's cave so he couldn't look at his leg. He'd do that later; but when he touched the area around the wound, the leg was not hot with infection. He saddled up and headed north.

"He ain't makin' no effort to hide his tracks," Roy Drum said. "And he's headin' straight north."

"To the park headquarters," John T. said. "If he reaches there . . ." He let that trail off.

"It won't make any difference," von Hausen said. "We can leave no one behind. No one. Man, woman, or child who knows we were in the park." He looked at the men. "It has to be that way. We'll all hang if word gets out about the soldiers. Do it my way, and you'll all be rich men. I promise you that." He looked up at the leaden sky. "What is wrong with this wretched place? It's supposed to be summer, but the temperature seems to be falling and those clouds look like *snow* clouds."

"They probably are," Drum told him. "This is Yellowstone, Baron. Hell, it's liable to snow in July."

"But the vegetation is out and blooming," Hans said.

"It ain't gonna freeze hard enough to kill this stuff," Drum told him. "It's liable to be seventy-five degrees tomorrow. Let's go find Jensen today and finish this." He stepped into the saddle.

The temperature continued to drop during the day. Winter was not yet ready to completely lift its hand from the Yellowstone. It began to spit snow and the women began to complain (the men would have started it first but that was not the manly thing to do).

146

Von Hausen decided to stop for the night, although it was only mid-afternoon.

Smoke kept going, not pushing his horses as hard as the days behind him, but at a steady, mile-eating pace. He smelled the woodsmoke before he could see it through the snowfall. He dismounted and slipped through the foliage, strange now in green and white. He pulled up short with a smile on his lips. Then he went back to get his horses.

"Hello, the camp," he called.

"Mister Jensen!" Charles Knudson called. "My word, didn't the Army find you?"

"No. I found them." He dismounted and stripped his horses of their burden and rubbed them down before he thought to see to himself. Warming his hands by the fire, he explained what had happened.

"All . . . dead?" Gilbert the scientist asked. "The patrol has been murdered?"

"Yes." Smoke poured a cup of coffee and drank it down. It was the first he'd had in several days. It was still too damn weak. "Where is the superintendent?"

"Gone to Washington for a few weeks. My God!" Harold said, noticing the bloody bandana tied around Smoke's leg. "You've hurt yourself."

"They shot me. It's all right. I dug the bullet out and cauterized the wound. I just keep the bandana on to hold the bandage in place."

Paula stood up. "Please go over to the lean-to and sit down, Mister Jensen. Among other things, I am a trained nurse. Gilbert, get the first aid kit. And take off your pants, Mister Jensen."

Smoke stopped at that. "I got some extra jeans, ma'am. I'll just open the tear in this and let you . . ."

"Take off your damn pants!" she yelled.

"Yes, ma'am," Smoke said, and shucked out of his moccasins and jeans behind the blanket someone had rigged for privacy.

147

"I can see no sign of infection," Carol said, after applying some sort of medicine on the healing wound and rebandaging it. "But that knife must have been awfully hot. There are burn scars all around the entry point."

"Very hot, ma'am. But it still beat fillin' it up with gunpowder and burning out the infection."

She sighed. "I wish people would stop that practice. Gunpowder is not the most sanitary substance around."

"But it works," Smoke said.

Smoke gathered the group around him in the rapidly diminishing snowfall. It had dusted the land but would be gone shortly after sunup. "We've got problems, people. Big problems. Alone, I could shake those behind me and get out and tell the law about what happened to the Army patrol. But if I do that, you people will die. Von Hausen and his scummy bunch have to kill anybody that knows they were in the park. And that's all of you . . ."

"But the superintendent knows," Perry said.

"His word against twenty-five. Actually," Smoke continued, "von Hausen is playing a fool's game. I'm the only one who any defense lawyer would probably allow on the stand. You people have never seen him in here. But von Hausen and those with him are scared; they're not thinking rationally. So that means you're all in danger. Now I don't know whether von Hausen is still coming at me through this snow, or not. I'd guess not. But they will be at first light. Bet on it. And they're only about six or seven hours behind. We've got to come up with a plan for staying alive. And we don't have much time to do it."

"Run for it?" Charles suggested.

"We're not fighters, Mister Jensen," Gilbert said. "None of us here have ever fired a shot in anger at anything. None of us have combat experience. But if you say we stand and fight, we will."

Smoke thought about that for a moment, then shook

his head. "No. You people have to get out. I've got to buy you some time to get clear and get to the army. Are there any troops still in the park?"

"About half a dozen up at White Mountain. They're Army engineers. I don't even know whether they have guns."

"They're armed," Smoke said. "There are still hostiles in the area. I want you people up and ready to go at first light. Head for White Mountain. Connect with the Army, and get the hell gone for the nearest town that has wires. Get a telegram off to Washington and let them know what's happened in here and what is happening."

"Where will you make your stand?" Morris asked.

"Up the trail somewhere. I'll know it when I see it."

"More coffee, Mister Jensen?" Thomas asked.

"Only if I can make a fresh pot."

"I'll have tea," Gilbert said quickly.


"Their horses is gettin' tired," Mack said, looking down at the tracks left by Walt and Angel. "And them tracks is fresh. We're closin' in, boys."

"I want Ol' Walt," Lou said. "I want that old bastard lookin' at me when I drop him."

"This ain't gonna be no stand up and draw thing, Lou," Mack told him. "Our orders is to kill them both the best and quickest way we can."

"Hell with orders. I want to see what kind of stuff that old coot has."

"You do that," Mack said, "and he just might be the one standin' over you when it's done."

Lou sneered and cussed as he swung back into the saddle. "No way, Mack. No way. We got about an hour of daylight left. Let's go."

"Come up lame," Walt said, stripping the saddle and bridle from his horse and patting it on the rump. "I felt it when he hurt hisself back yonder on them rocks. Built a fire, Angel, let's have us some coffee and bacon. I 'spect them that's doggin' us will be along right shortly. I'll have me another horse right after dark."

Angel grinned and began gathering up firewood while Walt rigged a shelter-half for them in the timber. Walt had strapped on his guns and tied them down. He spun the cylinders, checking the loads.

Angel was thinking: I'd not want to mess with that old man. He knew Walt had given up gunfighting simply because he was tired of the killing, tired of the blood, tired of having to prove himself against every two-bit punk that came along. But he was still snake-quick and a dead shot. And now he was ready to go again. Walt Webster was a living legend. Not in Smoke's class, but close. Real close.

The two men drank their coffee and ate the bacon, then moved back into the timber, after building the fire up. It could not be missed by anyone coming up in the fading light.

"Lou Kennedy was always bragging about how he could take you any day, Walt," Angel said.

"He's a loud-mouthed tinhorn," the old gunfighter said. "All bluster and no brains."

"What will you do if he calls you out?"

"Walk out and shoot him dead."

"I will have a rifle on the others should that be the way it happens."

"Obliged. Here they come."

"It's a trap," Mack said, spotting the fire. "One of the horses come up lame back yonder and they're sitting up there waitin' on us to ride in."

Before anyone could stop him, Lou Kennedy yelled, "Walt Webster! This is Lou Kennedy. Can you hear me, Walt?"

"I hear you, you big-mouth," Walt called. "You probably scared all the little critters within half a mile flappin' your gums. What the hell do you want?"

"You and me, Walt. How about it?"

"With that scum with you backin' you up, Lou?"

"No. Just me and you, Walt."

"Damnit, Lou!" Mack said. "Back off now, you hear?"

"No way, Mack." Lou shook off the other man's hand. "I want him. If I gun Walt Webster down, I can write my own ticket, you know that."

"Then go on!" Mack said, anger and disgust in his voice. "Walt. Walt Webster. This is Mack. You can have him, Walt. I give you my word, we won't interfere. You got my word on it."

"How about the others with you?" Walt called, hoping they'd fall for the question.

They did. "Walt, this is Leo Grant. We're out of it, Walt. Me and Nat'll stand clear. And that's as good as gold, Walt. If you drop him, you can get on back to cover."

"Four of them," Angel said. "And the light's fading, amigo."

"Let it go." He raised his voice. "Let's get this done, Lou. We walk out on a five count. You count it down, Nat. Draw whenever you feel lucky, boy."

Leo looked at Lou with disgust in his eyes. "You're a fool," he said flatly. "Did you ever stop to think that old man just might get lucky and blow a hole in you?"

"He ain't even gonna clear leather. Start countin', Nat."

On five both men stepped out of the timber. Walt stayed close to the timber, forcing Lou to come to him. "How's it feel, Lou?" Walt called.

"How's what feel, you old fart?"

"Knowin' you're about to die."

Lou cussed him as he walked up the slope. Walt

stood, a smile on his lips. Lou was a fool, playing right into Walt's plan. The slope was slippery, and by the time Lou got within shooting range, he'd be winded. Add to that he would have to shoot uphill—that is, should he be lucky enough to clear leather—and Walt didn't believe he had it in him to do that.

"Come on, you punk tinhorn," Walt called. "My coffee's gettin' cold."

Lou called him several very ugly names as he struggled to get up the slope.

"He's dead," Mack said. "Dead and he don't even know it. He'll be wore out time he gets into range. Ol' Walt planned it that way."

"Sure, he did," Leo said. "But I gave my word and I'm keepin' it."

"We all did," Nat said. "And we'll all keep it."

Lou stopped about sixty feet from Walt. The climb up the snow-slick slope had been hard and the much younger gunslick was winded. "You got any relatives you want me to notify, you old fart?"

Walt laughed. "When did you learn to write, you ignorant whelp?"

"Draw!" Lou yelled.

"After you, boy." Walt's words were calm.

"Drag iron, damn you!"

"Go ahead."

Lou hesitated. "You're yeller, Walt. You're scared of me, ain't you?"

"Not at all, you two-bit thief. Your momma shoulda dumped you in a sack when you was born and chucked you into the nearest river. Now pull iron, you cheap little son of a bitch!"

Lou's hand dropped to the butt of his .45. Walt's draw was smooth and deadly. His first slug hit Lou in the belly, the second one in the chest, right side, blowing through a lung. Lou managed to get his .45 out of leather and cock it. He fired once into the air before his legs buckled and he slumped to the ground.

Walt stepped back into the timber. "You want to come get him, boys, come on. We'll not fire on you."

" 'Ppreciate it, Walt," Nat said.

But they didn't have to climb the slope. Lou started slowly sliding down the slippery surface, losing his guns along the way. He was too weak to stop his slide. His hands did not have the strength to grasp anything. He rolled the rest of the way down. Leo reached out and pulled him into the copse of trees where they were hiding.

"Oh, Jesus," he blubbered the words, pink froth staining his lips. "I'm hard hit. Did I get him, boys?"

"Yeah," Nat lied. "Yeah, you got him, Lou."

"You boys pass the word," Lou said. "I kilt Walt Webster. You'll do that for me, won't you?"

"Yeah," Mack said, suddenly realizing that none of them were going to kill Ol' Walt. None of them were going to come out of this rich. None of them were going to come out of it with anything at all. Except dead. He looked down into the wide open and shuddered, seeing nothing but the eyes of Lou Kennedy.

# 17

Smoke raised his head and narrowed his eyes at the sound of the shots. "Close," he muttered, setting down his coffee cup. "No more than a mile. Probably less than that. Sound doesn't carry well in this kind of weather. Two shots."

"Does that mean something to you?" Gilbert asked.

"Sounded like pistol shots. Pistol's a poor choice of weapon to use in an ambush." He shook his head and stood up. "I don't know what it means." He picked up his rifle and checked it. "I'm heading over there to check it out. You people stay put and keep your heads down. Arm yourselves and be ready to use those weapons. And cut that fire back to coals to keep the smoke down." He was gone before any could say a word of protest.

Leo, Mack and Nat opened up on Walt and Angel, knowing that from their position, they weren't going to hit a thing. The body of Lou Kennedy lay on the cold ground behind them.

Smoke slipped through the timber, silently working his way toward the firing.

Walt and Angel lay on their bellies at the forest's edge, not returning the fire; from their angle they would have about as much success hitting anything as those below them.

"We have, I think," Angel said, a twinkle in his eyes, "a Norte Americano stand-off, hey, Walt?"

Walt smiled at the play-off of the expression. "You called it, partner."

Smoke slipped to within a few yards of the men. It was almost full dark now and he could not make out their features. He knelt down behind a tree and listened to them talk when the gunfire from below stopped.

"That loco German is going to kill everybody he thinks might know of his plan," Angel said. "Right, Walt?"

"That's right, partner," Walt replied. "That's the way I see it."

"But Al Hayre surely is out of the park and talking. So what is von Hausen's reasoning behind this madness?"

"He ain't reasonin', Angel. He's crazy. And so's them fools with him."

"I wonder if Jensen has put all this together?" Angel spoke softly.

"I 'magine he has. I just hope he can get clear and get any visitors out of this park. We've seen smoke from campfires from time to time. If von Hausen and that trash with him finds any campers . . ." He trailed that off.

"They will kill them."

"Yep. They shore will. Craziest mess I ever got myself mixed up in."

"Stand easy, boys," Smoke called softly. "I mean you no harm."

Walt grunted. Without turning his head, he said, "Jensen?"

"Yes."

"You're as good as the talk makes you out to be. Ain't nobody ever snuck up on me 'fore now. They's three pretty bad ol' boys down yonder . . ."

A burst of gunfire made him pause for a moment.

"Fools," Walt said when the firing had stopped. "They can't hit us from their position. Leo Grant, Mack Saxton, and Nat Reed. Lou Kennedy was with them. I dropped him. You got to get clear, Jensen. You got to warn any in this park to get the hell gone."

"I know," Smoke told him. "I've got a bunch of park-people about a half mile from here right now. Are you Walt Webster?"

"Alive and still kickin'."

"Angel Cortez," the Mexican gunfighter said.

"You're the two who wore the white handkerchiefs on your arms."

"That's us."

"Stay where you are. Don't get out of position and don't fire in the outlaws' direction. You might hit me. I'm going down there."

"Well, if anybody can Injun up on them, you're the one to do it." He twisted around. "I . . ."

But he was talking to emptiness. Smoke was already gone, moving like a deadly ghost through the timber.

Angel had also turned around. He shook his head in the cold darkness. "That is a bad man, amigo. I thank God that I had enough sense to see through von Hausen's crazy game."

"You and me both, partner."

"Walt!" Mack called from below them. "Give it up, Walt. Join us and live. Von Hausen will take you back. You and Angel think about it. If you get out and talk, you're signin' our death warrants. Come on, men, what'd you say?"

"Let's keep them talking," Angel suggested. "That'll give away their positions to Smoke."

"No deal, Mack," Walt called. "You boys surrender to us and we'll see that you get a fair trial. You have my word on it."

"Surrender? Us?" Nat yelled. "You're crazy!"

Nat had moved to his right. He was trying to work

156

his way up the other side of the slope. The timber side. Toward Smoke.

"Angel," Mack yelled. "Listen to me. You got good sense for a greaser . . ."

"What a compliment," Angel muttered.

". . . You don't wanna die no more than we do. Think about it and join us."

Nat ran into a long bladed knife that drove up to the hilt in his belly. Smoke jerked the blade upward with one hand while his other hand was covering Nat's mouth, to prevent any screaming. The blade tore into the gunslinger's heart and Nat Reed would hire out his gun no more. Smoke silently lowered the body to the cold earth, wiped his blade clean on Nat's jacket, and moved on toward the voices.

"We're just gonna outwait you, boys," Mack called. "We got food and blankets and coffee and time. You boys ain't got nothin'. You can't slip away. You got a lame horse. Think about it. Don't be fools and die for Smoke Jensen. He ain't never done a damn thing for either of you."

"What has von Hausen done for us?" Angel yelled. "What the hell have any of *you* done for us?"

"They ain't gonna give it up," Leo said. "We're gonna have to take 'em. Nat oughtta be in position about now. What'd you say, Mack?"

"He said he'd chunk a rock over this way when he got in place. I ain't heard no rocks, have you?"

"Naw."

"Will .44's do?" Smoke asked from behind the men.

They spun around, lifting their rifles. Smoke's twin .44's belched flame in the darkness. Mack was thrown backward, the slug tearing into his heart. Leo took his high in the chest, left side, and managed to lift his rifle. Smoke fired again, the slug lifting Leo off his boots and turning him around in a strange dance. He toppled over.

"That's it," Smoke called. He collected the rifles and

157

gunbelts of the men and joined Walt and Angel on the crest of the small hill.

"I'll switch saddles and ride one of their horses," Walt said. He took off his hat and ran his fingers through silver hair. "Mack had a decent streak in him at one time. I've knowed him for years. I don't know when he turned vicious."

"He can explain it to God," Smoke said.

"The ones that are left, Senor Jensen," Angel said. "They are vicious. All of them. Through and through. You heard us talking about von Hausen's plans?"

"Yes. We'll stop him. Bring the other horses along. We might need them. We're camped just over that ridge. Come on. I'll help you pack up."

When they got back to the camp Smoke checked over the short guns and the rifles taken from the outlaws. They were well supplied with ammo and Smoke divided that up and passed it around, then assigned the guns. Now everyone was armed, and well armed, for the four men who lay unburied on the cold ground a half mile away had each carried two six-guns tied down and each one had a rifle.

"What do we do now?" Carol asked, looking around her at the dark timber.

"Have something to eat and get some rest," Smoke said. "From here on in, it gets interesting."

The next day was clear and warm, the temperature climbing into the sixties before mid-morning. Roy Drum pointed to the carrion birds circling just ahead and to the west of the trail they were on. Von Hausen sent a man to check it out. He was back quickly.

"You best see this," he said, "all of you." He did not add: except for the women. The outlaw was well aware of how vicious these so-called ladies were. Especially that damned cold-actin' Marlene.

The flesh-eating birds had started their feasting and the men had to kick them away from the bodies. It was a gory sight.

"Took their guns and horses," John T. said. "I don't believe Walt and Angel done this."

"Found where a whole bunch of people camped last night," Cat Brown said, riding up. "And Smoke and Walt and Angel was among 'em.

"How many people?" Von Hausen asked.

"I'd say 'tween twelve and fifteen, countin' Smoke and Walt and Angel."

Gunter cussed and Hans looked worried. He wasn't liking any of this. It had turned too bloody, too savage. They had lost sight of the spirit of the hunt. It was out of control. It never occurred to him that it was out of control the instant they chose Smoke Jensen as the man they were to hunt.

"They're pilgrims," Cat said. "And they got some women with 'em.

"Interesting," von Hausen said.

"Frederick," Hans said. "I think . . ."

Von Hausen spat out rapid-fire German. Hans shut his mouth. Andrea came to him and took his arm. They walked away together.

"This has got to stop, Andrea," Hans said, when they were out of earshot of von Hausen. "It's gone much too far."

"It can't stop, Hans. We have no choice but to hunt those people down and be rid of them."

"My God, Andrea! Listen to you. You sound like some bloodthirsty crazed person. How many deaths do you want? How much blood on our hands?"

"Have you lost your stomach for the hunt, Hans?" Her words were cold and borderline contemptuous.

"This isn't a hunt. What this is . . . I don't know what it is. But I do know that it is out of control."

"Hans," she said, touching his arm. "Listen to me.

This is the American west. Not New York City. Despite our having diplomatic papers, do you think the western men out here—who tamed this country—would let us leave without punishment? Think about that. This is the wild west, Hans. And it's still wild. Justice comes down very hard and fast out here. We wouldn't get ten miles before some vigilante group would have us hanged. And they do hang women out here, Hans."

Hans clenched his hands into fists. He took several deep breaths. "All right, Andrea. All right. You do make a presentable case. Let's just get this over with and get out of this dreadful place."

Hans went back to his horse and rode up to the trail to be alone. The sight of those disgusting birds tearing at dead human flesh was nauseating. He lifted his hands. They were trembling.

Von Hausen came to Andrea's side.

"He'll stay," she told him. "But this better end quickly, Frederick."

"He's that close to breaking?"

"He's very close, Frederick."

"I know you two care deeply for each other, Andrea— since childhood—but I will not let one man put all of us in prison. Do you understand that?"

"Perfectly. And I feel the same way about it."

"Good. We are of like mind."

Mountains loomed in front of them, miles away through rugged terrain. Smoke halted the parade north at a spring. While the surveyors and scientists were watering their horses and taking this time to rest from the saddle, Smoke waved Walt and Angel to him.

"We're not going to make it like this, boys. These folks are just not able to push it any harder. Von Hausen's party has got to be slowed up some. Walt, you and Angel stay with these folks . . ."

Walt opened his mouth to protest and Smoke waved him silent. "If von Hausen caught up with them, they wouldn't stand a chance. None of them have ever been in a gunfight. Probably a full third of them couldn't take a human life. That's not a short-coming on their part; they just weren't raised out here and really don't understand the pickle they're in or the men they're up against. With you two along, they stand a chance."

"And you, Smoke?" Angel asked.

"I'm going to buy you people some time."

"Where?" Walt asked.

"West of here at the creek. Walt, get these people out of this country and over to the trail. It'll take you a few hours, but you'll more than make up for it once there."

The old gunfighter nodded his agreement. "Yeah, I been thinkin' on that myself."

"Rest them up and get gone. When you get to the headquarters, get with that small garrison of troops left and either make a stand or get the hell out of the park. That's up to you folks. But get word out."

The men shook hands. "Luck to you, boy," Walt told Smoke. "You damn shore got a passel of bad 'uns comin' up quick."

"Vaya con dios," Angel said, then walked to his horse.

Smoke stood as the men and women saddled up. Gilbert looked down at Smoke, standing in dirty, blood-splattered clothing, unshaven and in need of a hair cut. He was an awesome-looking figure of a man. "You are a very brave man, Smoke Jensen, and I speak for this entire group."

"Yes," Blanche said. "I know the President personally, Smoke. I shall see that you get a medal for this."

"That's good," Smoke told her. "But for now, just get any civilians out of this park. If you don't, there's going to be a blood-bath. I'm only buying you people a few hours; so don't waste any of it. Get out of here."

Charles Knudson saluted him and lifted the reins. The

others did the same. Two minutes later, Smoke was alone. That was the way he liked it. Alone with and a part of the high lonesome.

He knew he didn't stand a prayer of stopping the whole group. Close as he could figure it, there was still about twenty or so coming up hard behind him. Maybe none of those he'd sent on before him would make it. But he had to try.

"Von Hausen," he muttered to the gentle breeze blowing over the land. "I've hated mighty few things in my life. But I definitely hate you."

He looked at the sky. Clear and blue and cloudless. High above him, an eagle soared on the winds, gliding gracefully toward the north. He remembered years back, after his first wife, Nicole, and their baby son had been murdered. He'd started to Idaho, to avenge them, and he'd seen an eagle, seeming to guide him. He smiled. Eagles lived a long time; might be the same one. He liked to think so.

He gathered up his reins, then paused, wondering what month it was. Summer, for sure, and Smoke was almighty weary of this hunt. With a sigh, he swung into the saddle and made his way after those who'd gone ahead of him, mixing his tracks in with theirs. Once, resting in the saddle on the crest of a hill, he could make out mounted figures, far below and behind him. They were closing in fast.

He knew he would never make the creek. Von Hausen and group were too close. He pushed on, his eyes constantly searching for a good ambush spot. He finally said to hell with it and swung down in a copse of trees on a rise that faced a meadow. The back of the hill touched a flat that offered him an escape route. He couldn't stay here any length of time, for he couldn't watch three sides for very long. But he might be able to empty a saddle or two and buy Walt and his bunch an hour or so.

He had handed the lead rope of his pack horse to Angel, so Smoke was traveling light. He picketed his horse and patted him on the rump.

"Stand easy, old boy. Relax. I'll be back soon. Right now, I got some work to do."

He got into position and checked his rifle. Full up. He levered a round into the .44-.40 just as the point man for von Hausen's group entered the broad meadow, all bursting with new life under the warm sun.

Smoke had every intention of leaving some old life on the meadow. Forever.

The point man stopped and Smoke sighted him in through long lenses. He was still a good mile off. The scout raised his arm, and turned his head to another rider, his finger pointed toward the hill and the timber. Von Hausen rode up and joined the two outriders. He uncased his binoculars.

Smoke lowered his field glasses and hunkered down. "Come on, you crazy son of a bitch," Smoke muttered. "Be a big brave man and ride up with your scouts. If I can knock you out of the saddle, I'll have half the battle won."

When Smoke again lifted his binoculars, von Hausen's group was swinging down from their saddles to take a rest and to water their horses at the narrow little creek.

"Good enough," he said. "Take them north, Walt. Get them clear." Smoke took a sip of water from his canteen and chewed on a biscuit. He waited.

# 18

Someone among them smelled the ambush. Smoke knew it was going sour when the group split up into three's and four's and began skirting the meadow on two sides, staying well out of rifle range of the timber on the hill.

Smoke watched them for a moment, and then wormed his way back into the timber to his horse. "Not our day, fellow," he said, swinging into the saddle. "I'm not going to push you, boy. I know you're tired. So let's just lope for about a mile and see what we can come up with."

Von Hausen's group was right on his tail and the horse seemed to know it. If he was tired, he sure didn't act it when they hit the flats. That big Appaloosa stretched out and was flying like a young colt, his powerful legs eating up the distance.

Smoke grinned, even through the race was deadly. He loved to sit a saddle when the horse loved to run and was doing so. Enjoyed feeling the power of a horse that was doing what he loved to do. Smoke hung on as the 'paloosa scrambled up a ridge and leaped into the timber. Smoke cut left and weaved through the timber, smiling when he spotted the ravine that the north boundaries of the meadow ran into. Far in the distance, he could see riders entering the wide mouth of the ravine.

He heard a shout, but it was too faint for him to make out the words. If those coming up the ravine heard it, they did not seem to pay any attention to it.

Smoke grabbed his rifle and found adequate cover on the rim. He eased the hammer back and waited.

Paul Melham didn't like the looks of this ravine and told those behind him so, in blunt words. He ended with, "I'm tellin' y'all I heard a runnin' horse."

"Then how come none of the rest of us heard it, Paul?" Cat Brown challenged. "I'll tell you why: 'cause there wasn't no runnin' horse, that's why. If Jensen was in that timber back yonder, he wouldn't have come this way. That ambushin' bastard would have flanked us and picked us off. Relax, Paul. He's miles ahead of us."

"If you're so damn sure of that, then you come up here and take the point."

"Oh, hell, Paul!" Cat said. "If you're that skittish I might as well. You got fear sweat runnin' into your eyes. You wouldn't be able to see a grizzly if he reared up in front of you."

Smoke pulled the trigger and Paul was nearly knocked out of the saddle. He managed to hold on with his good right arm. His left arm dangled useless.

Smoke knew he'd shot off the mark. A fly had landed on the end of his nose just as he'd pulled the trigger. Probably shot the man-hunter in the shoulder by the way he acted.

But the ravine was void of man-hunters now, except for their horses, and Smoke wasn't about to shoot a horse. All in the group had left their saddles and found what protection they could in the rocks. Smoke smiled and started putting rounds close to the horses' hooves. That set the already panicked animals off and running. The last he saw of them they were running hot and hard out of the ravine.

Smoke ran back to his horse, swung into the saddle, and was gone.

Paul crawled back to Cat and Utah, pulling himself along with his good arm. He was cussing to beat sixty.

"Fall back!" Cat yelled. "Stay close to the sides and get back out of range. Somebody holler for von Hausen to get the medicine bag." He looked at Paul's shoulder. "You're lucky, Paul. Bullet punched right through. I don't think nothin's broken."

"When we catch up with that damn Jensen," Paul panted, his face shiny with pain. "I swear I'll skin him slow."

If any of us are left alive to catch up with him, Utah thought. That sudden thought startled him, for he'd never even considered quitting this bunch. He shook it out of his head. After killin' them soldiers, he couldn't quit. This was a race to the end—for all of them. Them who was runnin', and them who was chasin'.

"It's a painful wound, I'm sure," Gunter said, after cleaning out Paul's bullet-punctured shoulder. "But nothing appears to be broken and there is only the expected bleeding. Can you ride?"

"I can ride," Paul said grimly. "I want a shot at that damn Jensen."

No one among them, it seemed, could speak of Smoke in any other manner except 'that damn Jensen.'

"Let's find us a way around this ravine," von Hausen said. "He's probably still up there, waiting."

"He'll just move when we do," Hans pointed out. "He's got the high ground." That damn Jensen seemed to *always* have the high ground.

Von Hausen looked at Hans. The spirit seemed to have gone out of the man. He cut his eyes to Andrea. She was staring at Hans with a decidedly disgusted look in her eyes. "Round up the horses. We're riding until dusk."

Walt pushed his group as hard as he figured they could stand it. But by dusk, when he broke it off to make camp, he had a sinking sensation in the pit of his stomach that they were not going to make the park headquarters.

"They are worn out," Angel whispered to him, out of earshot of the others.

"I know. We're not going to make it, Angel."

"I could ride for the headquarters."

"And do what? Bring back six soldier boys who are engineers first and soldiers last. I ain't puttin' them down—they got a job to do like everybody else—but they ain't cavalry. We'll push on tomorrow and get as close to the park entrance as we can before we have to stand and fight."

"And then?"

"We'll just pick us the best spot we can find and show von Hausen and his boys and girls that we ain't gonna go down without one hell of a fight."

Gilbert walked up. "The ladies are exhausted, gentlemen," he said. He looked very tired. "And for that matter, so are the men in my party. The young surveyors seem to be holding up well."

"Yeah," Walt said. "We was just talkin' about that. The horses are tired, too. We'll push on at first light. When we find us a good spot to fort up—with water and graze and shelter—we'll make a stand of it."

"Might I make a suggestion?"

"Shore."

"We ride only a brief time tomorrow. There is a spot not too far from here that I know of—I've been in this park several times. It's almost a natural fort. We spend the rest of the day digging in. And I mean that literally."

Walt nodded his head. "That's fine with me, Gilbert. Angel?"

"Suits me. With us in front of them and Smoke coming up behind them, we could put them in a bad spot."

"Yes," Gilbert said, obviously pleased that the two gunfighters approved of his plan. "That was my thinking."

"Let's have some coffee and get some rest," Walt said. "We'll see what the others have to say about this."

Walt and his group were about four miles north of Smoke. Smoke was camped only about five miles ahead of von Hausen's party. Neither had any way of knowing what the other was planning.

Smoke boiled his coffee in a small and beat-up coffee pot and chewed on jerky and hardtack for his supper. He was just about out of coffee. He'd have enough for in the morning, and then that was it. And when Smoke couldn't have his coffee, he turned short-tempered.

Smoke drank his coffee and then carefully cleaned and wiped down his guns in the dying light of the small fire. He tried not to think about Walt and his group and their desperate race for the park headquarters and the tiny garrison of army engineers stationed there. He tried not to think about Sergeant Major Murphy and his patrol, lying stiffened and ravaged by animals and carrion birds in the timber by the creek, shot down in the coldest of blood by von Hausen and those who followed him.

"You're scum, von Hausen," Smoke muttered. "Nothing but scum."

"I hate that damn Jensen," von Hausen said to Marlene. "The man has ruined a perfectly good hunt."

"He's a savage," Marlene said. "No class or breeding." John T. was walking by the tent and heard that. He shook his head and walked on, wondering how in the hell he ever let himself get tied up with such a pack of fools. He walked over to the cook tent and poured a cup of coffee, carrying it over to his bedroll, close to the fire. He sat down, his back against his saddle, and looked at Montana Jess, sitting drinking coffee next to him. The man had a strange expression on his face.

"Time's runnin' out for us, John T.," Montana spoke the words softly.

"What do you mean?"

"I mean, them champagne-suckin', hoity-toity folks over yonder is takin' us to our deaths. That's what I mean. And you know it, John T."

"Spit it all out, Montana."

"We ain't got no choice left in the matter, John T. We can't come out of this unless'n we kill everybody in this park. Everybody."

"We've talked about that, Montana. What's left to talk about?"

"That ain't what I mean." He paused as others moved closer in. "We're not gonna get Jensen. You know it, I know it, and so do the rest of the boys. It's only them fools over yonder eatin' high off the hog that thinks we will. And if we do manage to kill them folks we're follow-in', and we don't kill Jensen—which we ain't gonna do—he'll spend the rest of his life trackin' us down. We'll have to change our names and get the hell gone to Ver-mont or Massesschewits or some damn other foreign place, and hope to God he don't find us."

John T. realized then that Montana, and the rest of the men, too, he supposed, were not talking about quit-ting and pulling out, but just letting off steam, with Montana being the spokesman.

That thought was dashed when Mike Hunt said, "Why don't we kill them princes and barons and what not over yonder, have some fun with them cold-actin' women,

169

take their money and jewels and just get gone from this place?"

"That thought entered my mind too," Gil Webb said. "But that'd just make it worser."

Mike looked at him. "I don't see how."

"The German government would get involved in it then, and there'd really be an investigation."

Mike nodded his head. "I hadn't thought about that. You're right."

John T. did not enter into the conversation. Only when and if he was asked. Best to let the men hash it out among themselves, he concluded.

Paul Melham moaned in pain in his sleep.

"We best stick with what we planned," Nick spoke up. "With the money bein' paid us, we can disappear for a good long time if we're careful with it. This'll blow over after awhile. It always does, don't it?"

"Not no killin' like we done and like we're plannin', it don't," Utah Red said. "But I agree with Montana that we ain't got no hell of a lot of options left us. We just got to go on and do it, that's all."

Valdes tossed another stick on the fire. "I am more fortunate than most of you. I can head back into Mexico and vanish. And that is exactly what I plan on doing. With my money, I can buy a cantina and quit this business."

"You mighty quiet, John T.," Ray Harvey said.

"Just listenin' to you boys talk, that's all."

"Ain't you got no opinion a-tall?" Tony Addison asked.

"I reckon not, Tony. I'm goin' on, so there ain't much point in talkin' about what's behind us. We just do the deed we all agreed to do."

"Oh, I'm in, John T.," Tony was quick to say. "Don't worry 'bout that."

"I was wonderin', after listenin' to all this talk," John

T. said, pulling out the makings and rolling a tight cigarette. "Just had me a little curious, that's all."

The men were all quick to speak up that John T. could count on them. Yes, sir. All the way.

"Good, boys, good." He smoked his cigarette down and tossed the butt into the fire. "I'm gonna turn in. I got a funny feelin' in my guts that tomorrow is gonna be a damn busy day."

"Why do you say that, John T.?" Valdes asked.

"Just got a hunch is all." He rolled his gunbelt and took off his boots. "I pay attention to my hunches, boys. They've saved my bacon more'n once."

"Good idea, John T.," Gil said. He got up and wandered off toward the bushes.

John T. Matthey went to sleep counting all the men they'd buried on their back trail. Thanks to that damn Jensen.


Smoke was up and drank the last of his coffee before dawn ever thought about opening its eyes. As he had done before rolling up in the blankets the night before, he climbed up on a ridge and looked to the south. Fires, and a lot of them. Von Hausen and his pack of hungry, rabid skunks were very close. He turned and looked to the north. Several small fires; that had to be Walt and his bunch.

He walked to his camp, made sure his fire was out, and then packed up, saddled up and pulled out. He had to find a place to make a stand this day. If he didn't, Walt's group wouldn't have any more days left to them.

Dawn was just breaking when Smoke rode out. He flirted with the idea of just picking a spot and make a stand to the death. But he didn't flirt with it for very long. The will to live was too strong in him. And just as strong was his will to win against seemingly insurmountable odds.

He'd have to admit he'd done a pretty fair job of doing just that so far.

No, Smoke would not make any stand-or-die move. No, what he would do is catch up with Walt and the others and then fight a rear guard action after seeing what kind of shape they were in.

They were going to win this fight, by God.

His horse sensed its rider's excitement and the big 'paloosa quickened its step. "That's right, boy," Smoke said. "You feel the same way, don't you?"

The Appaloosa snorted and swung his head. Smoke laughed.

Above him, an eagle soared.

# 19

Smoke put some distance between himself and von Hausen. Smoke's 'paloosa was a mountain horse and as sure-footed as a puma. Many times Smoke just gave him his head and let him go, so strong was the bond between horse and rider.

Smoke pulled up short when he heard voices and the sounds of an axe. "What the hell?" he muttered.

He urged his horse on, knowing that whoever was making all that noise wasn't setting up any ambush for him. When he climbed up the ridge and made the clearing, Smoke sat his saddle amazed at what he saw.

Just behind the dozen frantically working people, there was a falls, the water cascading down a sheer rock face. He could hear the sounds of running water closeby. Then he saw the stream.

"Hello, Smoke Jensen!" Robert waved and called to him. "Come on into our fort."

Smoke returned the wave and muttered, "You damn sure got that right. It's a fort."

"You can put your horse right back there," the government scientist said, pointing. "It's a tiny valley that is accessible only from the front." He smiled. "Unless you know the back way in. And even Angel and Walt couldn't find that until Gilbert pointed it out."

"But . . ."

"You look tired. There is fresh coffee in the pot. Walt made it," he added.

"But . . ."

"And there is food being prepared now."

"But . . . what about . . ."

"They might dig us outta here, Smoke," Walt said, strolling up on his bow-legs, "but they'll have one hell of a battle on their hands doin' it." He waved to Charles Knudson. "Take his horse, will you, son? Thanks."

"Damnit!" Smoke yelled. "Von Hausen couldn't be more than two or three hours behind me. What the hell are you people doing? I thought . . ."

"The hosses couldn't go no more and neither could 'bout half the people," Walt said. "Gilbert knowed of this place, so here we are. Come on. I think you'll like what you see."

He did.

Montana got his hat blowed off when he rounded the bend in the trail. He left the saddle hollering for the others to lie back and get down.

From his position in the timber, Montana stared up in amazement at the sight on the ridge. It was a fort. A gawddamned fort in the middle of the wilderness. And they had 'em a regular United States flag just a-flappin' in the breeze, all stuck up on a tall pole.

Von Hausen crept up to Montana's side and looked. And looked. Then he started cussing in several languages. He finally wound down and waved for John T. to join them.

John T. looked and shook his head and sighed mightily. "This ain't worth a damn, boss. This just ain't no good at all. I betcha there ain't but one way up there and we're lookin' at it. It'd be suicide."

"Yes," von Hausen agreed. "I'm afraid you're right.

But there is one point in our favor. They can't get out."

"True. But how long will it be 'fore the Army sends in troops lookin' for them soldier boys we killed?"

"Not long," von Hausen reluctantly said.

"Where'd you get the flag?" Smoke asked, belly down behind the ramparts on the ridge.

"We always carry a flag with us," Gilbert told him. "Anytime we're doing expeditionary work in the wilderness, whether it be in Africa or in the territories."

Smoke had agreed that the fort was solid and very nearly impregnable. While the men were busy fortifying the site, the women had busied themselves gathering up firewood, and not just for use as cooking. Both Walt and Jensen knew how to make smoke 'talk.' If they could hold out for a couple of days, the Army would, very probably, be sending patrols in to find out why the initial patrol had not returned and they would, hopefully, see the talking smoke.

Smoke had inspected the hidden opening at the rear of the falls. Nature had done her work very well. The entrance/exit had to be pointed out to him. Still, Smoke had insisted upon posting a guard near the entrance. If any of von Hausen's people found their way into the valley, those inside the natural fort would be in real trouble.

"Standoff," Smoke said to Gilbert. "At least for as long as there's light. They'll try to rush us as soon as it's dark." He thought for a moment. "Gather up any clothing you don't need and tear it into rags. We'll make torches. When they rush us, we'll light them and throw them over the side."

The stone ramparts were high and any openings between the huge rocks had been plugged with timber and dirt, gun slits added. Smoke walked the line of defenders, making certain all had plenty of ammo.

"Don't fire at shadows," he told each one. "We've

175

plenty of ammunition, but not so much that we can afford to waste it. If you're not sure of a target, don't fire. We can wait them out. Tonight is going to be our biggest test of nerve. I want every other person to nap for a couple of hours. Then stand guard and let the others rest. Do that until dark."

Smoke walked to his blankets and laid down, a saddle for a pillow. He called, "If anything important happens, wake me up."

"There does not appear to be a nerve in his body," Blanche remarked.


Smoke awakened several times during the afternoon, when one of von Hausen's men would throw a shot at the fort on the ridge, the bullet thudding into wood or dirt or howling off a boulder. He would close his eyes and go back to sleep. As the shadows began to lengthen, Smoke rolled from his blankets, put on his hat, buckled his guns around his lean hips, and walked to the fire, pouring a cup of coffee.

"It's quiet," Angel told him. "But I think when the darkness comes so will they."

Smoke sipped his coffee. Hot and black and strong. "Yes. Von Hausen is fighting out of pure desperation now. But if we can beat back the first wave—and I see no reason why that can't be done—those gunslingers down yonder will have second thoughts about doing it again. Did you get some rest?"

"I napped off and on. I feel fine. I made sure the others got some sleep."

"Good. There damn sure won't be much sleeping come the night. Was the guard changed behind us?"

"Every two hours, to relieve the boredom."

Smoke drank his coffee and ate a biscuit. He checked his .44-.40. He shoved in a couple of rounds, then checked his .44's. He walked to the stone and timber walls. "How are you doing?" he asked Gilbert.

"Fine. Wonderful, in fact. The excitement is building among us, almost to a fever pitch. All of us here have gotten over our fright, for the most part. Now a sense of deep anger and resentment toward those below us has taken its place. Our rights have been violated and we are all prepared to use force to get them returned."

Walt grinned. "In other words, y'all are ready to kick some butt."

"That sums it up rather well," Carol said.

Smoke looked at the woman anthropologist. He still wasn't all that sure what it was, exactly, that she did. And he was afraid to ask. He thought it had something to do with old bones. Carol wore a pistol in a military-style holster and held a long-barreled shotgun.

"I'm really quite good with the shotgun, Smoke Jensen," she said. "If I can hit a bird on the wing, I can certainly hit a man. And believe me when I speak for all of us here, sir: there will be no shirking among us. If those murderers down there come up that ridge, we will not hesitate to shoot."

There was a set to her chin and a determination in the woman's voice that gave Smoke no reason to doubt her. These gentle people had been pushed to their limits. Now they were going to do some pushing of their own.

Smoke smiled, patted her on the shoulder, and walked on. He stopped at Charles Knudson's position. Harold Bailey was a few yards from him, manning another post. The young surveyors smiled at him, Charles saying, "We're ready, Smoke."

"Good men," Smoke told him. He walked the interior of the fort which formed a crude half circle, stopping to talk for a moment with everybody. Paula and Thomas had left to guard the rear exit of the valley, relieving Robert at the lonely post. Two were sent so one could sleep while the other stayed awake during the long night. It might get so busy that they could not be relieved for many hours. And Walt had wanted the shift changed while there was still light to see.

He found Angel cleaning his rifle. "Senor Smoke," the Mexican gunfighter greeted him with a smile. "I think for some out there," he pointed toward the edge of the ridge, "this is going to be a good night to die."

"It might be a terrible thing to say, Angel; but I sure hope so."

"Not so terrible a thing when bad men chase good people," Angel said soberly.

"You do have a point, Angel." Smoke returned to his bedroll, slipped into a jacket, for the late afternoon was turning very cool, and filled his jacket pocket with cartridges. He poured another cup of coffee and then took the plate of food that was handed to him. He ate with a good appetite and rinsed out his plate in a pan and returned to the ramparts.

Walt had done a really bang-up job in securing the interior of the fort. The tents were set well back, too far back for anyone to throw a torch into them. A stray bullet might ricochet and scream off the rock of the sheer face behind them and hit someone, but that would be a long shot. All things considered, their position was a secure one.

"I have always heard that this was the hardest part of a battle," Gilbert said. "The waiting."

"You heard right," Smoke told him. "When the shootin' starts, a man doesn't have time to be scared. Scared-time is over. You don't have time to think about anything except staying alive."

"Would it make me sound callous if I said I believe I am actually looking forward to this fight?"

Smoke smiled. "No. It's like you said: you folks are feeling a lot of anger and resentment toward that pack

178

of hyenas down the ridge. With good reason. You want to strike back at them. That's understandable. I do too, believe that."

"Sometimes you speak like a very well-educated man, Mister Jensen."

"I married a schoolteacher," Smoke said with a smile. Gilbert chuckled as Smoke moved away, making yet another round inside the fort.


Roy Drum returned from his afternoon's circling around the mountain. He poured a cup of coffee and shook his head. "There ain't no other way in. If you want them folks, Baron, we got to go up that ridge and take 'em. And before you ask me if I'm shore about there bein' no other way in, yeah, I'm shore."

Von Hausen looked disdainfully at the man. "It isn't just a matter of *me* wanting them, Roy. It's you and all the rest of the men as well."

"Yeah," Roy said wearily. He sat down on the ground with a sigh. "I know that. But I ain't makin' no suicide charges up that ridge. And it would be suicide. I just ain't gonna do that, for nobody."

"If we done it durin' the day," John T. said," I'd agree with that. But they can't see no better at night than we can. We can look at the damn ridge and see there ain't no traps set for us. That's as plain as the nose on your ugly face."

"I'll con-cede the trap part," Roy said with a smile. "But they's some ladies who think I'm right cute."

"They must be blind," Montana Jess said.

Von Hausen stood quietly, letting the men banter back and forth. This was not something he could just flatly order them to do.

"It might work to our advantage to let them stew for one night," Gil Webb said.

John T. shook his head. "You're forgettin' about all them dead soldier boys back down the trail that probably was supposed to have reported back in a long time ago. Every hour we stall, means we're that much closer to a hangman's noose."

"I'll stick a gun in my mouth and pull the trigger 'fore I let myself be tooken in alive," Utah Red said. "I don't favor stretchin' no rope."

The men were unanimous in that.

"Well," John T. said. "Let's talk this thing out. We all know what we got to do, it's just when that's gotta be settled."

"I'll leave that up to you men," von Hausen said. He returned to his tent and closed the flap against the chill of the approaching night.

"Damn big of him," Cat Brown said.

Smoke had gone to where Angel had stacked his gear from the pack horse and dug out the sack of dynamite and caps and fuses. He prepared a dozen sticks and using thin strips of rawhide, tied them to nice-sized throwing lengths of branches he'd cut off. He gave three to Walt, three to Angel, and kept six for himself. He went to the pile of torches and passed them out.

"Put out the fire," he ordered. "That will give us better night vision."

"It'll be cold," Perry said.

"I'd rather be cold alive than cold dead," Smoke put a stopper in that kind of talk quickly.

Gilbert grinned at him in the waning light. "Very aptly put, Smoke."

Smoke watched as Carol broke open her double-barrel shotgun and checked the loads. She had a bandoleer of shotgun shells looped over one shoulder.

She was not a big woman, and had elected not to use

buckshot. She was afraid the charge might knock her down. But she was using a heavy load of birdshot that would make life miserable for anyone who caught a load of it.

Smoke smiled, thinking if she caught someone in the butt with that birdshot, they'd be damned uncomfortable sitting a saddle for some time.

He peered out through one of the gunslits. Night was gently closing in around them. Nothing moved below. That he could see. But they would come this night. He was sure of that. He'd bet on it.

They all were, with their lives.

# 20

Smoke caught a glimpse of a shadow moving near the base of the hill. He stared; there it was again. "Here they come," he whispered to Gilbert, manning a post a few yards away. "Pass the word."

The alert was quickly and quietly passed up and down the line of defenders.

"I can't see a thing," Gilbert whispered.

"They've probably blackened their faces with mud," Smoke returned the whisper. "For sure they've taken off their spurs and dressed in the darkest clothing they had with them. Those down there might be trash, but they're professionals, too."

"And desperate men," Blanche added. She was posted only a few yards to Smoke's left.

Smoke had not had to tell the women what would happen to them should the man-hunters breech the ramparts and get their hands on them. The women knew.

"I see something moving down there," Blanche whispered hoarsely.

"Let them get closer," Smoke said. "Make damn sure you've got a target. The closer they are, the better your chances of a good hit."

A figure loomed close to the ramparts. Carol's shotgun roared twice. An outlaw screamed over and over in pain. The birdshot had taken him on the shoulders, neck, and the lower part of his face. He dropped his rifle and put both hands to his birdshot-peppered cheeks and jaw. He screamed again, lost his footing on the slope, and went rolling elbows over butt down the hill.

"One down," Carol muttered, and pulled out the smoking hulls, tossing them to the ground and reloading.

Smoke's lips moved in a warrior's smile. No doubts now as to how Carol would react.

"Good," Gilbert said. "Very good shot, Carol." He lifted his rifle and fired at a shadow. The bullet howled off a rock and the outlaw dropped belly-down on the ground.

Angel found a target and drilled a man-hunter in the leg, the force of the bullet knocking the man down and sending him rolling and squalling down the hill.

"Back!" John T. called. "Back down the hill."

"Let them have it!" Smoke yelled, and the cool night air thundered with the sounds of rifle, pistol, and shotgun fire from the defenders on the hill.

Out of range, von Hausen stood tight-lipped, his face white with anger and his hands clenched into big fists, as John T. gave the orders to retreat. He watched impassively as Jerry Watkins came staggering in, the lower part of his face and his neck bleeding badly from the birdshot that had peppered him. The man was fortunate that the blast had not taken him a few inches higher and blinded him. Had that occurred, one of them would have had to shoot the man. Von Hausen was in no mood to waste any time with a blind person.

Tony Addison came hobbling in, his arm around the shoulders of Cat Brown. Tony's leg was bleeding from a .44 Winchester slug that had taken him in the thigh and his face was pale and tight against the pain.

John T. walked up. "No good, boss," he told von Hausen. "It looks like it's suicide day or night. They just flat stopped us cold. You can't get no footin' up that hill."

Frederick stared at him, then nodded his head curtly and walked away.

Utah grumbled, "Why don't he take his royal ass up that hill and try it one time?"

" 'Cause that's what he's payin' us big money to do," John T. told him. "Or have you forgotten that?"

"Don't crowd me too hard, John T.," Utah warned the man.

The two skilled gunhandlers stood in the close darkness and stared at each other for a moment. A very tense moment since feelings were running high and the surging blood of each man was hot for killing.

"You boys cool down," Montana said. "Just back off. This ain't no time for us to start squabbling amongst ourselves."

"Montana's right," Pat said. "That's what them folks up on the hill want; for us to turn on each other. Now settle down. We got wounded to look after."

Utah nodded his head. "Sorry, John T."

"It's OK, Utah," John T. replied. "We're all on a short string this evenin'. Come on. Let's see about the boys and get us some coffee."

The defenders on the hill were quietly jubilant.

"Do you think we killed anybody?" Charles asked. No one had left their post.

"I know we put some out of action," Smoke said. "How hard they're hit I don't know. Good shooting, Carol."

"Thank you. Now if you all will excuse me, I have to throw up." She beat it to the bushes behind the camp.

"Natural reaction," Smoke said, punching out empties and reloading his six-guns. "I think I did the same thing first time I killed a man, back in '65 it was. In Kansas, I believe. I was about thirteen or fourteen. Bunch of Pawnees jumped us. Me, my dad, and an old mountain man called Preacher. If I didn't upchuck, I damn sure wanted to. Nothing to be ashamed of."

"You think they'll be back this night, Smoke?" Blanche asked.

"It wouldn't surprise me."

"Let's get out of here and get out of America while we still can," Hans urged.

"Shut up, Hans," Gunter told him.

"No. No, I won't shut up," the man said. "I'll have my say and you all can be damned! We're not that far from a port in San Francisco. We can board ship and take the long way back. By that time most of the outcry will be over. What we're doing now is foolish. We won't be extradited out of Germany. So we take a few jokes at our expense; we're all grown people. We can endure that. Isn't that better than facing western justice? All I'm asking is that you give it some thought."

"What about the men?" Maria asked.

"Pay them off as agreed and let them go. They certainly aren't going to talk about this. They'd be putting a noose around their necks."

"Has the thought occurred to you, Hans," Marlene said, "that the men might not let us go?"

Hans looked startled. "What do you mean?"

"She means, Hans," von Hausen said, "that we have as much to lose as the men, and the men aren't going to just let us ride out of here and get away. If there is punishment to be had, it will be shared equally."

"The Americans have a phrase for it," Andrea said.

"It's called being between a rock and a hard place."

Gunter laughed at that.

Hans shook his head. "There has to be a way out of this for us."

Von Hausen looked hard at the man he used to call his friend. If Hans kept this up, he thought, he knew of one way out for Hans Brodermann. He met the eyes of the others and knew they felt the same about it.

"Every other person try to catch some rest for a couple of hours," Smoke passed the word up and down the line. "If you feel yourself nodding off, wake up the person next to you. We've got to stay alert." He walked back to the coals—all that was left of the fire—and poured a cup of coffee. It was still hot and tasted good.

Smoke knelt by the fading coals and drank his coffee. Those below them had to try again this night. Time was not on the side of Baron von Hausen and those with him.

The defenders had scored two hits so far. But Smoke didn't think they were killing hits. That light load Carol was using would kill, but it would have to be at fairly close range. More than likely, the man she shot was very uncomfortable, but still able to fight, unless she blinded him. In that case, Smoke felt certain von Hausen would finish him off—or one of those cold-hearted women with him.

Smoke tossed the coffee dregs to the ground, and walked back to the ramparts, rifle in hand. He stopped by Walt's position. "Anything moving down there?"

"Nothin' that I can see," the old gunslinger said. "And my eyes is about the only thing I got left that's workin' worth a damn."

"According to Angel, your gunhand still knows what to do."

"Hell, that comes natural to us, Smoke. You know that as well as me."

"I know it isn't a blessing."

"You shore got that right."

"What will they do next?" Smoke muttered. Walt didn't reply because he felt Smoke didn't expect any. "I don't think they have dynamite. Even if they did they have no way of delivering it up here. They might try to make bows and arrows and shoot fire up here. But they couldn't hit the tents using any bow that hasn't been cured out. And even if they did burn the tents, we won't be hurt."

"This was a good move on our part, I'm thinkin'," Walt said. "If we can hold out, we'll make it. Them down yonder knows they're runnin' out of time."

"And they just might get careless."

" 'Xactly."

"I got an idea," Smoke said. He explained it to Walt and to Gilbert, who had walked over.

"Let's try it," Gilbert said.

"You men down below!" Smoke shouted. "This is Smoke Jensen. Can you hear me?"

After a moment, a voice shouted, "Yeah, Jensen. We can hear you. What do you want?"

"I want you to listen to me. And when I'm finished, give some thoughts to my words. OK?"

"Let 'er bump, Jensen."

"That's John T. Matthey," Walt said.

"He's good," Smoke said. "I've heard a lot of talk about him."

"Yeah. He's good, and he's careful. Man don't get to his age without bein' careful. But they's several down there just about as good, or maybe as good as John T.

Utah Red. Montana Jess. Cat Brown. I'd have to include Gil Webb in that bunch too."

Smoke grunted. "Some rough ol' boys you just named, Walt. And fast. I've met John T. a time or two."

"So he said."

"All right, boys," Smoke shouted. "Here it is: way I got it figured, there can't be any more than fourteen or fifteen of you left . . ."

"He's close," Utah said. "They's fifteen of us still able to shoot, and three of them are wounded."

". . . Draw your money and pull out. I give you my word, and you all know that my word is my bond, I won't seek revenge. It ends right here. What the Army does is the Army's business. But I'll have no hand in it. None of the civilians up here know any of your names or faces. So they can't talk or be used as witnesses against you . . ."

"He's got a point," Tom Ritter said. "A damn good point."

"For a fact," Mike Hunt agreed.

"Damn him!" Marlene said.

"But Walt and Angel know us," Montana yelled. "What about them?"

"This here's Walt! I'm speakin' for both me and Angel. Haul your ashes outta here and we sudden got a loss of memory. And you got my word on that."

"But they're murderers!" Carol protested.

"They were murderers before this, ma'am," Walt told her. "And they'll be murderers after this. Right now, we're tryin' to save you folks' butts. Pardon my language."

"They'll meet their just end," Smoke told her. He raised his voice. "How about it, boys?"

"We'll think on it, Jensen," John T. called.

"Fine. You do that."

"Now what?" Robert asked from out of the darkness of the stone and wood enclosure.

"We wait."


"What do we do, Frederick?" Marlene asked.

"Do you have your checkbook with you?"

"Of course. One of them. It's the account we set up with Wells Fargo."

"Do you have thirty thousand dollars in that account?"

The look she gave him silently informed the baron that meager amount would be a mere drop in the bucket.

"Make it out payable to bearer, if you would, please."

When the ink had dried, von Hausen walked over to the group of gunslingers and handed John T. the check. "Let everyone see it, please, John."

John T.'s eyes bugged out. He carefully held the check up for all to see in the campfire light.

"That is, of course, in addition to the monies already paid you and is waiting for you in separate accounts back in Dodge City. And remember this, your share of that money has greatly increased over the past weeks due to the demise of several of your fellow hunters. The attorney handling that money knows to divide it equally among the survivors. Think about that. But one of my group has to give him the signal, in person, to do so." He smiled. "That was done in case any, or all of you, got it into your heads to kill us. With the addition of this thirty thousand, those of you who are left when this hunt is concluded, stand to walk away with a very large amount of money. Enough to retire on; buy a ranch or a business." He plucked the check from

John T.'s fingers. "Think about it, gentlemen. Give it careful thought." Von Hausen carefully and with a lot of dramatic gestures, folded the check and put it in his pocket. He walked back to his tent.

"Any questions, boys?" John T. said.

Cat Brown picked up his rifle and punched in a couple of rounds. "I reckon it's time for us to go back to work, boys. I always did have a hankerin' to own me a whore house."

"Sit down," John. T. told him. "I got a plan that just might work. See what you boys think about this."

"It's been more'un an hour since you made your offer," Walt said. "They must be really talkin' it over."

"Or planning to hit us again," Smoke said.

"You cowardly sons of bitches!" the shouted voice of von Hausen drifted up the hill. "You agreed to stay on until the end. You have no honor. None of you!"

A lot of cussing followed that.

"What in thunder is going on down there?" Charles asked.

"Sounds phony to me," Walt grumbled.

"Both of us," Smoke said.

"Damn you all to hell!" a strongly accented voice shouted.

More cussing.

"They're really putting on a good show, aren't they?" Smoke said with a smile.

"I thought you western men were brave?" a female voice was added. It was filled with contempt. "You're all cowards. Everyone of you."

"I think they're overdoing it a bit," Carol remarked.

More cussing.

"Smoke Jensen!" the shout cut the night.

"Right here," Smoke called.

"This is John T. We'll take your deal, Smoke. And to

show you I mean what I say, you can watch us ride out at first light. Unless you want us to pull out now."

"That's good, John T.," Smoke called. "I think you made the right choice. No point in you boys losing a good night's sleep. You can pull out in the morning."

"That's fine with us, Jensen. Good night."

"Lying scum," Smoke said.

"We're all in agreement with that," Gilbert said. "That scenario was staged if I ever heard one."

"Von Hausen!" Smoke called.

"Right here, Jensen."

"You want to settle this right now, you and me?"

"I think not, gunfighter," his voice sprang out of the darkness. "But there will be another time and place for us, be assured of that."

"I imagine so, von Hausen." Smoke turned to his group. "This ought to be good." He raised his voice. "And your plans come the morning?"

"We'll be striking camp and pulling out, Jensen. I no longer have any appetite for the hunt."

"He's lyin', an' John T. is lyin'," Walt said. "So what the hell are they up to?"

"No good, and that's for sure," Charles Knudson said. "Now I'm getting worried."

"No need for that," Smoke told him. "I think we'll just let them outsmart themselves."

"What do you mean by that?" Carol asked.

But Smoke would only smile.

"Do you agree the hunt was a good one, Jensen?" von Hausen yelled.

"It was interesting, von Hausen," Smoke called.

"Oh, quite!" the man shouted. "Good night, Jensen. We'll all wave auf Wiedersehen in the morning."

"Yeah, you do that," Smoke muttered.

"Could it be they are actually leaving?" Perry asked.

191

"Oh, they'll pull out," Smoke said, "and set us up for an ambush."

"And you have a plan to counter that?" Blanche asked.

"Oh, yes, ma'am," Smoke said. "I sure do."

# 21

"Oughta shoot 'em dead if they show themselves," Walt said. "And to hell with all their lies."

Silver was streaking the eastern sky. Those inside the fort stood by the ramparts, drinking coffee and waiting to see if von Hausen's party were really going to pull out.

"I know we should," Smoke agreed with him. "But there is that one chance in a million they're really going to leave."

"Of course, you don't believe that?" Gilbert asked.

"No. I sure don't."

"Yo, the fort!" came the shout.

"We're still right here," Smoke called.

"For reasons of security, none of us will step out into the open," von Hausen called. "You understand, of course?"

"Sure, von Hausen. I understand."

"You really have nothing to fear; any of you. After we've pulled out, and since you have the high ground you'll be able to see us cross the meadow to the south, and you will, of course, inspect the remnants of our camp. You will see that we are keeping our word. We'll have our coffee, and then we shall be gone. Goodbye, all."

"And good riddance," Walt muttered. "Even if you are lyin' through your teeth."

"They won't be going much further than those ridges past the meadow," Smoke said. "Just as soon as they enter the meadow, I'm gone out the back way, on foot. I'll carry some supplies with me in a pack. I'll stick to the timber on the ridges and make a half circle. You'll be able to hear the battle."

"You want some company?" Angel asked.

Smoke shook his head. "No. They started this. I'll finish it."

Smoke went to his supplies and packed a few items in a rucksack while breakfast was being cooked. He did not even look up when Robert called, "There they go."

Smoke checked his high-top moccasins. The soles were getting thin, but they'd hold out for this run. He tucked his jeans inside the leggins and wound the raw-hide tight around his ankles and calves. Then he went over and had breakfast.

"Now listen to me, people," Smoke said, squatting down by the fire and fixing a biscuit and bacon sandwich. "You stay on the alert. Head's up at all times. Just as soon as von Hausen makes the timber on those ridges, he's going to send people back here, on foot, swinging wide through the timber to avoid being seen. They'll be getting into position and they'll have supplies to last a day or so, to wait you out. Stay behind these walls and don't expose your-selves. Just as soon as those he sends back here hear the shooting, they'll know it's gone sour for them. I don't know what they'll do. But I'll bet that von Hausen offered them big money to reject our proposal and to stick it out. Don't leave this fort after the shoot-ing stops. For any reason. Don't leave the protection of these walls."

Smoke walked to the ramparts and looked down at the seemingly deserted timber.

"They're entering the meadow," Gilbert said, holding binoculars to his eyes.

"Count them."

"I count twenty-two."

"That's the whole bunch of them, then. OK, Gilbert. Keep the people behind these walls. I'm gone."

"You be careful out there, boy," Walt said.

"I'll do that. Take care of them in here."

"We'll do that," Angel said. "Vaya con dios, Smoke."

Smoke slipped into his pack, picked up his rifle, and left the fort, jogging across the tiny meadow and coming up to where Thomas and Paula were standing guard. Charles Knudson had visited them before dawn, telling them what was planned, so they were expecting Smoke.

They greeted him, wished him luck and God speed, and Smoke slipped through, being careful not to disturb the natural look of the exit.

He set out on a distance-eating lope, staying in the timber whenever possible, keeping low and moving swiftly when he had to cross short expanses of open terrain, using every bush and shrub for cover.

He had steeled his mind for this mission. He had offered them all safe passage last evening. If they were planning an ambush—and he had no doubts in his mind about that—there would be no mercy shown them. None. For any of them. Including the women if they turned hostile, and he was sure they would do just that. This was the most savage, cold-blooded, ruthless bunch of people he had ever encountered. He did not pretend to comprehend what went on in their demented minds.

As he neared the far ridges, Smoke slowed his approach. He slipped from tree to tree, his carefully-placed feet making no noise when they touched the earth.

He stopped, still as a sturdy tree when he heard the first whisper of voices filtering through the lushness of untouched forest. He worked his way closer, moving only when someone was speaking. Von Hausen and party had stopped in a small clearing, well hidden from the eyes of those back at the fort.

Smoke counted those in the clearing. Six were missing. And he'd bet those six were the top guns in the bunch. So be it. He would deal with them later.

"How long you reckon it'll take the boys to get into position back yonder?" The question, or at least a part of it, reached Smoke.

He worked a few yards closer.

"Give 'em a good two hours," his question was answered.

"I don't 'spect Jensen and them will stick their noses out of the fort for several hours," another said. "Maybe longer than that."

"This is wrong!" a very accented voice reached Smoke. The words were almost a shout. "The man gave his word and we gave ours. What we are doing now is despicable!"

"Oh, stop your whining, Hans," a woman said. "I'm sick of it. We all are."

"This is a good plan," a man said. The words were just audible to Smoke.

So von Hausen and his immediate party were some distance away from the hired help. Figures, Smoke thought. Heaven forbid they should have to associate with the lower classes.

Smoke moved closer. He was very near the edge of the clearing now. He thumb-nailed a match into flames.

"Shut your goddamn mouth, Hans!" von Hausen said. "We're all tired of your silly whimpering. Now sit down over there and be quiet. Give us all a break. Those people back at that fort have to die. All of them. That's final, and it's settled."

Smoke stepped to the edge of the clearing, lit the fuse on a charge of dynamite and tossed it into the center of the men, sitting and squatting in a circle.

"Jesus H. Christ!" one bellowed.

"Run!" another squalled, and took off like his long handles was on fire and he was in them.

Smoke laughed, threw back his head, and howled like a great gray timber wolf.

"What in the hell is that?" Marlene screamed.

Three sticks of dynamite blew. One man had been nodding off and was slow to move. The blast and concussion lifted him off the ground and moved him about thirty feet, one of his legs bent in an impossible angle.

Smoke started shooting, working the lever on his .44 carbine as fast as he could. Nick took a round in the belly that doubled him over. He fell to the shattered ground, screaming as the pain rode him down like a surging tidal wave.

Tom Ritter reached his frightened and rearing horse, got into the saddle, and Smoke put a slug in his shoulder as he was galloping off. He jerked in the saddle but stayed on.

Mike Hunt got to his boots, both hands filled with six-guns. Smoke shot him in the center of the chest just as Pat Gilman started throwing lead in Smoke's direction. Smoke dropped to his knees at the edge of the clearing and pulled the trigger. The slug was low and caught Pat in the hipbone, knocking him down. Pat hollered and began crawling for a horse, any horse.

Smoke dropped his carbine and jerked his six-guns.

197

Tony Addison screamed obscenities at him and leveled his guns. Smoke sent him to hell carrying two .44 slugs, one in his belly, the other one in his chest.

Smoke stepped back into the brush and squatted down. He could hear hard-running horses, the sounds of their hooves rapidly fading away. The little meadow was filled with flowers and gunsmoke and blood and death.

Smoke waited for several minutes, waiting for the dust to settle. He could see one man moving. He took that time to reload his carbine. He stood up, still in the timber and brush at meadow's edge, and surveyed the scene. He was startled to see the wounded man was dressed like he was on an African safari. His stupid looking hat—what were they called, yeah, pith helmets—lay off to one side.

Smoke checked the dead. Two of them. Even the one who appeared to have a broken leg got away. But Smoke knew he'd put several out of action.

He walked over to the wounded man. The blood was dark as it oozed from his wound. Probably shot in the gizzard.

"I didn't shoot you," Smoke said. "A .44 round would have made a bigger hole than that."

"My . . . wife shot me. Andrea Brodermann."

"Your *wife* shot you?" Smoke knelt down beside the man.

"Yes. I'm . . . going to die, aren't I?"

"Probably. Looks like she drilled you through the liver. Small caliber pistol. Those small slugs tend to wander around in a person's innards; do all sorts of damage."

"You're Smoke Jensen?"

"That I am."

"Please accept my . . . apologies for this . . . insan-

198

ity. Long days back I . . . tried to stop this. They would . . . have none of it." He closed his eyes and gritted his teeth against the pain. He sighed and said, "She shot me . . . just as the dynamite blew. I should have been . . . more careful."

Smoke started to tell him that when you run with hyenas, you shouldn't expect to get the best cuts of meat, but he decided against that. Man had enough troubles right now.

"I am a Prince," Hans said.

"Do tell?"

"Yes. The men left . . . alive. They will not give up, sir. They . . . have money deposited for them . . . and they will hunt you . . . down."

"Well, I shortened the odds some this day." Hans' face was deadly white. Smoke figured the man didn't have much longer. "You got family you want me to write, Prince?" He did not slur the title.

"In my wallet. My jacket . . . pocket. Inside. If you would be . . . so kind as to write my parents."

"Sure. I'll do it. You have my word."

Hans tried a smile. "With that tremendous dynamite . . . charge, you shouldn't have much of a . . . hole to dig."

Smoke returned the smile and wiped the sweat from the man's brow with a bandana. "I'll bury you better than that, partner. That's a promise."

"Be careful of the . . . women in our," he grimaced, "*that* group. They are vicious, sir. I think we have married too closely . . . over the years. It's beginning to . . . show."

Smoke said nothing. The man's time was running out. Let him talk until he shook hands with the devil.

"I have a considerable sum of greenbacks in . . . my wallet and . . . several small sacks of . . . gold coin in

199

my saddlebags. That's my horse . . . over there. The . . . there is no word for it in my language." He cut his eyes. The horse was grazing not far away.

"Roan," Smoke said.

"Yes. That is it. I want to compensate you for all the misery we have caused you . . ."

"There is no need for that."

"I want to."

"All right."

"Take it . . . now. Let me see you do it. Please. A final request."

Smoke walked to the horse, spoke to it, and opened the saddlebags, all the time keeping an eye on Hans. He took out three small but heavy leather sacks of gold coin. When he returned to Hans, the man was holding out a wallet.

"It will not make up for what . . . we have done to you and the others. But it is a step. I did not fire upon the soldiers."

Smoke believed him. He took the wallet.

"I told . . . Frederick last night it was a stupid plan. That you would . . . not fall for it. He slapped me. My wife . . . laughed. They are perverted people. Twisted. I . . ."

Prince Hans Brodermann died surrounded by the magnificence of Yellowstone. Smoke reached out and closed his eyes. He found a shovel on one of the pack horses that had wandered back into camp and dug a deep hole. The earth claimed Prince Brodermann just as it eventually claims all, making no distinction of class.

Smoke piled rocks on the grave, picked up his rifle and gathered up a saddled horse and the two remaining pack horses. He rode slowly back to the rear entrance of the fort.

He told what happened while the others were going through the supplies.

"My God!" Blanche said. "Champagne and caviar."

"I'd let it settle down some before I popped that cork," Gilbert said. "The bouncing it's taken, that stuff would go off like a shot."

"What did you do with the other dead?" Thomas asked.

"Left them for the varmints," Smoke said shortly. "Any activity out front after the fireworks started?"

"Yep," Walt said. "They was men out there just like you suspected. But I don't think they ever got in place. They pulled out. Angel climbed up yonder," he pointed to a ledge off a-ways from the falls, "where the rocks wasn't so wet he couldn't get a hand-hold, and seen 'em leave. Then we used field glasses and seen 'em way over yonder ridin' hard." He pointed. "They musta picketed their horses and walked in the last mile or so."

"Pack it up," Smoke said. "Now. And do it fast. We're pulling out of here."

"But . . ." Carol said.

"No buts, lady. We're moving. Now."

"Yes," Gilbert said. "I see the logic in that. Our horses are well-rested. We have regained our spirits and strength. So while the opposition is running chaotically, in total disarray, we make our final dash to freedom."

Smoke smiled. "Took the words right out of my mouth, Gilbert."

# 22

The final ride to park headquarters was uneventful. The acting park superintendent had already sent a messenger to the Army, advising them of the missing patrol, and a full mounted platoon was only a day away and riding hard.

The ladies immediately went off for a hot bath and a change of clothing. The small garrison of Army Engineers went on full alert. All six of them.

"They won't come here," Smoke calmed the acting superintendent down. "Once they see we made it, they'd be riding into a death trap, knowing we got word out. But let the Army stay on alert. It'll be good for them."

"Well, the law will now take care of this von Hausen and those hooligans with him."

"No, sir, they won't."

"I beg your pardon, Mister Jensen?"

"I will," Smoke said flatly.

The man took one look into Smoke's hard eyes and backed up a step. "Yes, sir. I do believe you will."

Smoke had told no one about Hans Brodermann's money. That evening, after supper, he took Angel and Walt aside and told them. He gave them the money.

"My God, Smoke," Walt said, after looking into the sacks and the wallet and finding his voice. "There must be four or five thousand dollars in here."

"Probably more than that," Smoke said. "There's two thousand dollars in greenbacks and several thousand more in signed checks on Wells Fargo. That's not counting the gold. Why don't you two buy you a little spread somewhere and settle down?"

"That's a good idea," Angel said, looking at Walt. "How about it . . . partner?"

The three men shook hands.

"Keep in touch," Smoke told them. "I'll be pulling out at first light."

"You want some company?" Walt asked.

"No. This is something I have to do myself. You both understand that."

They did.

When the others awakened the next morning, Smoke had already left. When questioned, not even the Army guard on the last duty watch had heard him leave.

"He's going to track them all down, isn't he?" Gilbert asked.

"Yep," Walt said. "To the last person. They could have pulled out. Smoke gave them that option. But they turned their backs to it. And they messed up real bad when they done it. They made Smoke mad."

"That is quite a man," Carol said.

Walt glanced at her. "All man, lady. Some say he's the last mountain man."

"The lard's done hit the hot skillet now," Montana said, lingering over the last of the morning coffee. "And she's a-bubblin' and a-spittin'."

"He is just one man," Valdes said.

"I used to think you had good sense," Montana replied. "Now I'm beginnin' to think you fell off your hoss and landed on your head one too many times. He's acomin' after us, Valdes. And he's mad clear through.

203

And when he's mad, and knows he's in the right, Smoke Jensen don't give a damn about the law. They's been a dozen times over the years when more men than us tried to stop him. When the gunsmoke cleared, Jensen was still standin'."

"I think I am in the company of old women," Valdes said scornfully.

John T. Matthey smoothed out the saddle blanket, slung his saddle on and cinched it up. He said nothing. But he felt that Valdes' pride was setting the Mexican gunfighter up for a killing. His own.

It had been four days since the fight at the fort on the ridge, and the men had swung wide and then cut east. Dodge City, Kansas, where their money was being held, was a long way off. And those of them with any sense knew that Smoke Jensen was coming hard after them.

"Where are we?" von Hausen asked, walking up to the men.

"Wyoming," Roy Drum told him. "Just a few miles south of the Montana line. 'Bout twenty miles south of us, on the Shoshone River, they's a little settlement. It ain't got a name. 'Least it didn't have last time I was through there."

"Is there a railroad there?" Gunter asked. "We have to get east as quickly as possible."

"Don't know. But I'd fight shy of railroads, was I you," Roy told him. "I got me a good strong hunch that the word's done gone out on us. The law'll be lookin' hard at folks buyin' train tickets."

"That doesn't leave us many options, then, does it?" von Hausen asked.

"We done run out of options," Gil Webb said. "Slap dab out of them. All but one."

"And that one is? . . ." Andrea asked, a haughty note in her voice.

"We run, lady," John T. said. He was tying his bedroll

in place behind his saddle. "We ride hard for Dodge, you folks pay us off, and then we all scatter like leaves in the wind. Jensen's comin', lady. Comin' hard. And he's mad. Killin' mad. He's snarlin' like a big lobo wolf, sniffin' the ground and stayin' on our scent. We run."

"You ever seen a buffalo wolf, lady?" Roy Drum asked. "No. 'Course you hadn't. They 'bout all gone now. Folks killed them out. Big one would weigh a hundred an' fifty to hundred an' seventy five pounds. One— just *one*—could bring down a buffler. Jump on its back and kill it. That's what Smoke Jensen is, lady. Are we afraid of him? No. But only a fool don't respect him. Now if you folks don't mind, get them hosses of yourn saddled and let's go. Like right now!"

"We have to have supplies," von Hausen said. "We'll travel to that settlement you talked about."

Roy opened his mouth to argue. John T. cut him off. "We're out of coffee, Roy. We lost several pack horses back yonder in that meadow. We ain't got no bacon, no flour, no beans. We'll head for the settlement."

"All right!" Drum said savagely. "Then damnit, let's ride."

They managed to get Ray Harvey on his horse. His broken leg was swollen badly and it was all he could do to keep from screaming out in pain.

"We got to leave you when we get to the settlement, Ray," John T. said. "You got to get some doctorin' on that leg 'fore gangrene sets in and you die. We'll make sure you get your money. And that's a promise."

That was a lie and both men knew it. Ray's leg was stinking from infection. Gangrene had already set in and his blood was poisoned by it.

The party provisioned at the trading post and pulled out that same day, leaving Ray Harvey in the barn on some hay. Jerry Watkins took all the man's money. So much for honor among thieves. The settlement had no doctor. Smoke rode in the next day, early, and found Harvey nearly gone.

"Shoot me, Jensen!" the hired gun begged. "Put me out of my misery. I can't stand the pain no more."

Smoke shook his head. "I won't do that, but I will buy you a case of whiskey. You can die drunk if you like."

"I'd appreciate it. That'll help a lot. They've gone for Dodge, Jensen. You ain't but about a day behind them. They stole my money and left me here to die. I don't figure I owe none of them a damn thing."

Smoke bought a case of whiskey and arranged with the livery owner to let Harvey stay there until he died. Which was not going to be long. His leg had turned black and vivid streaks of infection were shooting out from the poisoned leg.

Smoke rested his horses, feeding them all the grain they wanted. He had a bath and a haircut and a shave and had his clothing washed and ironed. He left his packhorse, taking only a few things he could carry in his saddlebags and rolled up behind his saddle.

At dawn, he swung up into the saddle. "Let's go, boy," he told his big Appaloosa. The horse stepped out eagerly, knowing the hunt was on.

The livery owner watched Smoke ride out in the darkness. He told a buddy, "I'd not want that man after me. They'll be hell to pay when he catches up with them folks that wronged him."

"I hope he gut-shoots Watkins," Harvey said, his words slurry from the whiskey.

Roy Drum had cut south from the small settlement, and Smoke knew then the route he was taking. They would angle southeast and cross the North Platte at that little town just east of Emigrant Gap. From there, they would touch the corner of Colorado then turn due south toward Dodge.

"Looks like I don't buy any bulls this summer," Smoke told his horse.

Once von Hausen and party crossed the Greybull, they had about fifty or sixty miles of nothing until they hit the north/south stagecoach road. Smoke remembered a trading post—that by now might be a settlement of sorts—on the old Bridger Trail, at the confluence of Fifteen Mile Creek and the Big Horn River. They would have to stop there—the ladies would want that—and resupply. Sixteen or seventeen people went through a lot of groceries on the trail. Then too, there was another point to consider: from the trading post to the next settlement, that being on the North Platte, there was about a hundred miles of nothing.

Smoke frowned as he rode. If they stayed on the route that he, himself would take, it would put John T. Matthey about twenty miles south of the Hole-In-The-Wall. John T. just might know some pretty salty ol' boys who would like to pick up a few bucks—namely by killing one Smoke Jensen.

It was something to keep in his mind.

Von Hausen and party, with Roy Drum at the point, crossed the Greybull and pressed on. Some of the swelling in Jerry Watkins' face had gone down, but he still looked like someone had taken an icepick to his face. Many of the birdshot had been picked out; the rest he would carry for the rest of his life. Which, with Smoke Jensen hard on them, might turn out to be very short.

Tom Ritter's left arm had to be carried in a sling, due to a .44 slug that had passed right through his shoulder. Pat Gilman had been wounded in the hip. He could ride, but his face was pale and his lips were tight against the pain. Paul Melham's left arm was out of commission; like Tom, he toted that arm in a sling.

It was a sad-looking bunch that rode toward the Big Horn.

"You know any boys at the Hole, John T.?" Pat asked, riding alongside the man. They were walking their horses to save them.

"Could be. I been thinkin' on it. That's a good hundred miles down the trail. But I don't know how many of them would want to tangle with Smoke Jensen."

"If we could just slow him up some . . ."

"Yeah. I know. Jensen gave us more breaks during this . . . craziness than I figured he would. That's over now. He sees us, anywhere, anytime, he's probably gonna drag iron. For a fact, he ain't gonna give us no more breaks."

"I give up on tryin' to ambush that feller. Seems like he can smell a set-up."

"He was raised up by mountain men. Preacher, in particular. He ain't got no better honker on him than we do; but he senses danger. Preacher schooled him good."

"We're just gonna have to make up our minds to stand and face him, John T."

"I been thinkin' on that, too."

"And? . . ."

"You best keep in mind that if we do that, we're gonna take some lead. Jensen ain't gonna just step out in the street and face fifteen of us. He's the farthest thing from a fool. He faced them old boys at that silver camp—eighteen or so of them—and he rode off after the dust settled. And he wasn't nothin' but a kid hisself. He's a ring-tailed-tooter, Pat."

"Sounds like you sort of like the man, John T."

"Oh, I do, in a way. I ain't really got nothin' agin him. I'm just gonna kill him, that's all. How's your hip?"

"Hurts bad. I'm gonna pull out at the settlement on the river. Maybe I'll get lucky with Jensen."

A couple of days later, when they swung down from the dusty saddles at the settlement on the Big Horn, Valdes pulled his rifle from the boot and said, "No more of this for me. I am staying here and settling this affair once and for all. I am weary of running like a frightened child."

"Count me in on that, too," Jerry Watkins mumbled through still-swollen lips. "I got a real personal score to settle with him."

"I can't ride no more," Gilman said. "I was plannin' on pullin' the pin here anyways."

The others just looked at the men and shook their heads. John T. said, "I wish you boys would think on that some. I'm goin' to head for the Hole later on and round up some more boys."

Valdes shook his head. "No. This is as far as I run." He handed von Hausen a slip of paper. "That is my mother's name and address in Mexico. You will see that she gets my share of the money, por favor?"

Von Hausen nodded his head. "Yes, I will, Valdes. I give you my word on that."

"This is adios, then." He solemnly shook hands with everybody and led his horse to the stable.

"See you, boys," Pat said, meeting the eyes of the men and the women. The women seemed indifferent about the whole matter. Then limped off, following the Mexican gunslick.

"I reckon that about sums it up," Jerry mumbled, and followed Pat and Valdes.

"We'll resupply and immediately move on," von Hausen said. "We can't afford the luxury of bathing and grooming. Let's buy what we need and get out!"

Valdes, Jerry, and Pat watched the party ride out of town from a table by the window in a saloon. Pat had not sought the advice of the local doctor about the festering wound in his hip, because he didn't figure he had much longer to live anyway.

He took out a pen and started laboriously printing on a piece of paper he bummed from the bartender, who was nervous about the men being in his place of business. He had heard about von Hausen—news traveled swiftly in the west—and wanted no part of Smoke Jensen.

"What are you doin'?" Jerry asked.

"Makin' out my last will and testament," the gun-for-hire said. "Then I'm gonna give it to that lawyer acrost the street."

"I didn't know you had anybody to leave nothin' to."

"I don't. I'm leavin' it to my horse."

"Your *horse?*"

"Yep. He's a good'un. I ain't worth a damn; but that shouldn't be no reflection on my horse. I'm gonna see to it that he lives out the rest of his days eatin' and gettin' fat and bein' lazy."

"That ain't a bad idea," Jerry said. "Do it for my hoss, too. How about you, Valdes?"

"I don't give a damn what happens to my horse," he said sullenly. "And how do you know we're not gonna ride out of this dismal place?"

" 'Cause the telegraph down the road says Smoke Jensen is about a half a day behind you boys," a rancher spoke from a couple of tables over. "That's why. I'll see to it that you boys' horses are put out to pasture and live a good life, if you want me to. I admire a man who takes care of his horse."

"Thanks," Pat said.

The rancher looked at Valdes. "You can go to hell."

Valdes started to get up from the table. He stopped halfway out at the sound of several hammers being eared back. Four of the rancher's hands stood at the bar, six-guns in their hands.

"Sit down," one told him. "Way I figure it, you got maybe six or eight hours to live—at the most. You might as well enjoy that time. 'Sides, I don't want to miss this fight."

Valdes sat, being very careful to keep both his hands on the table.

"I'll take care of your horse, too, Mex," the rancher told him. " 'Cause I like horses."

"You serve up food in this place?" Jerry said.

"Got a stew that's good," the barkeep told him.

"That'll suit me just fine," Pat said. "Then I'm gonna take me a snooze under that tree yonder." He pointed. "I reckon I'd better get in the habit of bein' stretched out," he added drily.

# 23

The day wore on with its usual never-deviating pace. But to the three hired guns in the saloon, time seemed to drag. The saloon filled as word spread around the area. Buckboards and wagons rattled into town, carrying entire families; many had packed box suppers. This was the biggest thing to happen in the community since the outhouse behind the church collapsed and dumped the minister into the pit. Took twelve men half the day to haul him out. Folks never dreamed that a man of the cloth would know all those bad words.

A cowboy galloped into town and jumped from the saddle in front of the saloon. He slapped the dust from him and ran inside. "Rider comin'! Big man on a big Appaloosa."

"That's Jensen," Jerry Watkins said.

Valdes stood up and slipped the thongs from the hammers of his guns. Jerry rose and slipped his guns in and out of leather a couple of times. Pat Gilman shifted his chair around. His hip was hurting him so bad he was afraid if he stood up, he'd fall down.

Smoke rode slowly up the short street. Jerry started to pull iron and shoot him through the window. He froze as the rancher who had stayed at the table through the long afternoon eared back the hammer on his Colt.

"I'll shoot you myself, boy," he said. "Lord God, you

got him three to one as it is. What kind of lowdown snakes are you people?" He shifted his gaze to Gilman. "Git up and take it like a man."

Pat got to his boots and stood with an effort. "I'm surrenderin'," he said. "I want a trial."

"We ain't got no badge-toter here," a cowboy said. "Law's a hundred miles away, near 'bouts. 'Sides, we heard all about you boys ambushin' that Army patrol and tryin' to murder them women in the park. You're gonna get a trial, all right. And the judge is comin' through the door right about now."

Spurs jingled on the rough boardwalk and the batwings were slowly pushed open. Smoke stepped inside, and there was no doubt in anyone's mind that this was Smoke Jensen. He seemed to fill the whole doorway and his cold eyes put a sudden chill in the room. Smoke sized up the situation and deliberately turned his back to the hired guns, walking to the bar.

"Beer," he told the nervous barkeep.

Every inch of space along the front of the saloon was filled with people. The minister who had first-hand knowledge of excrement and knew it when he saw it, began praying for the lost souls of the hired guns.

Smoke drank his mug of beer, wiped his mouth with the back of his hand, and turned to face the trio. "Mighty good beer. Tasted good."

"I'll buy you another," the rancher said.

"I'll take you up on that in just a few minutes," Smoke said. He stared at Valdes. "Valdes," he said softly. "The backshooter. Angel told me about you."

Valdes spat on the floor and cussed his former friend until he was near breathless.

"Pat Gilman," Smoke shifted his gaze. "Raped and then killed your stepsister. Broke jail and killed a deputy in the process."

"You writin' a book, Jensen?" Gilman asked. His face was shiny with pain and fear.

Smoke smiled and looked at Jerry, with his birdshot-peppered face. "One of the women you big brave boys were trying to kill did that to you. I don't know your name."

"Watkins. Jerry Watkins. If I'd a got my hands on that woman, she'da been fun for a couple of days."

"Yeah," Smoke spoke softly. "That's just about what I figured. Scum, all of you."

"I don't take that kind of talk from any man," Valdes said. His voice was high-pitched, and he was sweating. He was in a half crouch, tensed, his hands over his guns.

"Then I guess it's time, Valdes," Smoke uttered the quiet, deadly words. That was his only warning that their time was up. He drew his right hand .44 and let it bang.

The reports of the .44 were enormous in the room. Smoke fired six times, the shots seeming to be as one long, thundering roar. Valdes took two slugs in his chest and fell back against a wall, his hands empty. Smoke's draw had been so swift that the Mexican gunfighter had not even seen the initial move.

Pat Gilman took a round in his chest and another slug in the hollow of his throat as he was stumbling backward. He went crashing through the window to fall on the feet of those gathered on the boardwalk.

Jerry Watkins did not have to worry about his birdshot-peppered face any longer. He had a bigger hole right in the center of his forehead and another hole in his cheek.

The barroom was very quiet after the thunder of the deadly gunfight. Smoke ejected the empties and they fell tinkling to the floor. He reloaded calmly. No one spoke. No one even moved. Outside, the minister was shouting to the heavens.

"Sweet Jesus," a cowboy breathed. "I never even seen his pull."

The rancher, western born and western reared, shook his head in disbelief. Up to this point, he thought he'd seen it all.

The barkeep stood rooted to the floor, his mouth hanging open, his hands on the bar.

Smoke holstered his .44. "They have plenty of money on them," he said to no one in particular. "Von Hausen was paying them well to kill me. You can either give them a fancy funeral, or roll them up in a blanket and dump them into a hole. I don't give a damn." He looked at the rancher. "I'll take my horse over to the stable and see to his needs. Then I'll be back for that beer."

The rancher nodded his head. "My pleasure. Jim, take his horse and see to it, will you?"

"Right now, boss," a cowboy said, and stepped gingerly around Smoke.

"Grain, hay, and have him rubbed down good."

"Yes, sir, Mister Jensen," the cowboy said. "I'll see to it personal."

"Get that crap outta my saloon!" the barkeep finally found his voice. It was high and shrill with excitement. "Drag 'em over behind the barber shop."

Some of the good ladies of the town started singing church songs, still standing on the bloody boardwalk.

"When we heard about this von Hosensnoot feller," the rancher said, "I sent a hand down to the nearest wire office and telegraphed the sheriff's office. Told him I'd be glad to round up some boys and tend to this matter personal. He wired back and told me that couldn't nobody arrest this feller. Is that right?"

"I'm afraid so," Smoke said, sitting down just as the bodies of Valdes and Watkins were being dragged past his table. "I don't really understand it all. Something about being immune from prosecution."

"Well, that don't make a damn bit of sense to me!"

"It doesn't me either. But I guess it's the law." The barkeep sat his mug of beer down on the table, gave Smoke a nod, and quickly backed off.

The church ladies were singing the Lord's praises loudly, as they all trooped across the street, following the men dragging the bodies. The minister, when he'd heard Smoke telling about the dead outlaws having lots of money, was really pouring on the shouting and preaching and planning an elaborate funeral. He followed the singing ladies. A giggling gaggle of young boys and girls followed the minister. A pack of the town's dogs followed the kids, barking and playing and rolling in the dirt. All in all it was quite a parade.

"The sheriff said that you'd probably be in trouble if you killed this von Hossenhoof," the rancher said.

"Well, I'll just have to get in trouble then. 'Cause I'm damn sure going to kill him."

"What about them women?"

Smoke shook his head. "I don't know. I'd sure hate to hurt a woman. If I can help it, I won't." Then he told the rancher about Andrea killing her husband, and how she shot him and left him to die.

"You don't mean it!"

"Sure do. I talked with the fellow for a few minutes before he died. He was a real prince."

"I seen 'em when they come in this mornin'. Them was some hard ol' boys ridin' with the no-bility. I recognized John T. and Cat Brown. Funny thing, Smoke, that von Hossenheifer and them folks with him all dressed up like nothin' I ever seen . . . they didn't none of them look crazy." He thought about that; took off his hat and scratched his head. "Well, them hats looked sort of stupid."

"Pith."

"Oh. Sure." He pointed. "It's out back."

"No," Smoke said. "That's what they call those hats."

"You got to be jokin'!"

"No. Pith helmets. P-I-T-H. I think that's the way it's spelled."

"Well, that makes it some better," the rancher said.

"I've got to rest my horse," Smoke said, after draining his mug. "Then get something to eat and rest."

"They may try to recruit more men at the Hole."

"Yeah. They probably will. These people seem to have money to burn. I'll just have to deal with that problem—if it arises—when I come to it." He pushed back his chair and stood up.

The rancher sized him up. 'Bout six, three, and probably two hundred and twenty or thirty pounds. One hell of a big fellow.

Smoke smiled at the man. "Thanks for the beer."

"Luck to you, Smoke."

"What exactly is the Hole?" Gunter asked.

They had camped for the night, eaten supper, and were drinking coffee before turning in.

John T. said, "It's about fifty miles south of a brand new town called Buffalo, and due east of the Powder River. Used to be run by a man called Poker-Face Carey. I don't know whether he's still there or not. It's a shanty town of shacks and a couple of saloons. I'll angle over that way in a couple of days and see if anyone's interested in hookin' up with us."

"How many days to Dodge City?" Marlene asked.

"Long-hard ride, missy," Utah Red said. "I'd hate to even guess. We're days away from Dodge."

"Get ten men," she told John T. "Ten good men who are fast with a gun and who aren't afraid of Smoke Jensen. We'll pay each one a hundred dollars a day and a thousand dollar bonus apiece if they'll get us to Dodge City."

John T. smiled. "I don't except I'll have much trouble gettin' ten pretty good ol' boys."

"One-Eye's there," Gil Webb said. "I know him. And I'm pretty sure Dick Dorman's still there."

"You know Dick?"

"Sure."

"Soon as we hit the Bighorn's, you angle off and beat it for the Hole. We'll meet up on the south fork of the Powder. You know the crossin'?"

Gil nodded.

"I had me a partner once. Name of Slick-Finger Bob. He'll do to ride the river with. He was usin' the Hole 'fore it became so known. Get him if he's there."

"See if an ol' boy named of Barton is there," Paul Melham said. "Henry Barton's his name. Tell him to come on; mention my name."

"Ask around for Sandy Beecher," Utah Red said. "He's a good one, too."

Later, Marlene lay beside von Hausen. They talked in whispers. "Getting to Dodge City is only part of the trip, *mein liebling*," she said. "What happens to us after the men are paid off and gone?"

"Gunter will go in alone. You've noticed the beard he's growing? He'll be dressed like a cowhand. He'll contact that attorney and get the money. We'll pay the men off and one by one go in and catch the train. Jensen will be looking for us east. We won't go east. We'll head back west, to San Francisco, and take the long way home. By the time we get back, all this will have been forgotten."

"I wish we did not have to go to Dodge City. We are placing ourselves in a great deal of danger by doing so."

"So do I. But we couldn't risk taking that much money with us. These desperadoes would have killed us the first night on the trail. I had to set it up this way for our safety. I think with the men from this Hole place, we'll make it. If nothing else they'll buy us some time."

"Do you suppose Valdes and the others might have killed Jensen?"

"I doubt it. But it's a nice thought to go to sleep on, isn't it?"

She laughed. But it was an ugly laugh.

When Smoke crossed the Bighorn River he cut slightly south, skirting the Bighorn Mountains and angling down to catch the stagecoach road that led to the settlement slowly being build around Fort Caspar on the North Platte.

He had a plan, and he thought it would work. Alone, with the big strong Appaloosa under him, he was making about ten miles a day more than those in the large von Hausen party. He'd get to Fort Caspar at least two days ahead of their planned arrival. At Fort Caspar, he would resupply and then head back west and see what damage he could do, plus he wanted to turn the party more north.

Von Hausen would not dare show his face at the Fort, so the only flaw in Smoke's plan was if the party decided to change directions on him. But he didn't think they do that. They had to have supplies. Von Hausen and party would camp well away from the fort and send some of their hired guns in for supplies.


Fort Caspar was named for Lt. Caspar Collins, who was killed by Indians while trying to rescue a wagon train. Casper came about due to the misspelling of the railroad clerk who filed the plat for the town.


Gil Webb rode to the Hole and came away with ten salty ol' boys who thought they could handle Smoke Jensen. What they were were thugs and petty thieves and riff-raff and horse-stealing bums. They were good with a gun, give the devil his due, and any of them would kill for the pennies off a dead man's eyes.

Smoke had found a tinker on the stagecoach road who was more than willing to sell him coffee and bacon and flour for inflated prices. Since he did not have to go to Fort Caspar, he headed straight north about the time Gil was leaving the Hole with his band of thugs.

The rendezvous on the Powder was going to be very interesting. And quite lively.

# 24

"This here's One Eye Slim," John T. introduced the man to von Hausen.

Von Hausen looked at the man. Both his eyes seemed fine.

"He likes to gouge out the eye of anyone he fights," John T. explained.

"It's my trademark," One Eye said proudly.

"Wonderful," von Hausen replied. "We all have our little quirks."

He was introduced to Dick Dorman. "He can do a border roll faster than you can blink," John T. said.

Von Hausen and company did not have the foggiest idea what a border roll was and none of them were particularly interested in finding out.

"Slick-Finger Bob," John T. pointed to another man.

Von Hausen waited for some explanation for the nickname.

John T. shrugged his shoulders. "I don't know why they call him that."

Von Hausen sighed.

He was introduced to Henry Barton, Sandy Beecher, Frank Clover, John Flagg, Joe Elliot, Terry Smith, and Ed Clay.

They were the most disreputable-looking human beings Von Hausen had ever seen in all his life. He was loathe to turn his back on them. "We pull out in the morning," he said.


Smoke stopped to chat with a drifting cowboy on the trail.

"They's some bad ol' boys camped up yonder by the crossin'," the cowboy said. "That many bad ones all in a bunch spells trouble for somebody."

"How far ahead?"

"No more'un five miles. You'll see their smoke. Altogether there must be twenty or twenty-five of them. I got the hell outta there."

Smoke thanked him and rode on. When he spotted the smoke from their campfires, he found a good place to picket his horse. Smoke took off his boots and slipped into his worn moccasins. He took the .44-.40 from the second saddle boot and moved out while he still had about an hour of light. He stopped about five hundred yards from the big camp and looked it over.

Then he threw back his head and howled like a great gray timber wolf.

"What the hell!" John Flagg said, as the wild howling came again.

"That ain't no wolf," Utah Red said. "It's real close to it, but not quite."

"Jensen," John T. said. "He's found us."

The howling stopped for a few minutes. Everyone in the camp had armed themselves and taken cover where they could find it.

The howling came again. This time it was coming from a different direction. The men and women in the camp looked at each other nervously.

"He's playin' games," Cat Brown said. "The dirty son is playin' games with us."

"Then he's a damn fool," Dick Dorman said. "One man

against all of us. Who the hell does he think he is?"

A .44-.40 slug from Smoke's rifle screamed off a rock about two inches from Dick's head. Rock fragments bloodied Dick's face and sent the outlaw hugging the ground. A second slug tore into his exposed boot and shattered his ankle. Dick screamed in pain and doubled up, both hands to his bullet-broken ankle.

Another slug punched a hole in the coffee pot and coffee spewed out into the fire. Another round from the .44-.40 whined wickedly off the big cook pot and started it rocking.

Paul Melham jumped up and jerked his rifle to his shoulder. That move got him a slug right between the eyes that blew out the back of his head. He fell backward without a sound.

"Damnit!" von Hausen yelled from his position behind a tree. "Rush him. Drive him back. If you don't he'll pick us off one at a time. It's our only chance. Come on, let's go!" von Hausen leaped from his position and zig-zagged a few yards forward.

The hired guns could not hang back while the man who was paying them risked his life. They charged, running and ducking and twisting.

Smoke faded back and slipped away into the waning light of early evening.

Roy Drum found his tracks. Cautiously, the men followed the tracker. "He's runnin' hard," Drum pointed out. "See how his moccasins is diggin' in? He's way ahead of us."

The men pressed on, cautious, but eager for the kill.

Smoke jumped into the saddle and headed straight back for the camp while the main body of men were a good three quarters of a mile away and getting further. Smoke hit the camp screaming like a wild man.

Marlene shrieked and grabbed for a rifle just as the shoulder of Smoke's horse hit her and knocked her sprawling. She fell hard to the ground, knocking the wind from her.

Smoke rode right over a big tent, the Appaloosa's hooves shredding the canvas and destroying equipment.

Andrea ran screaming from the onslaught. Smoke leaned over in the saddle, grabbed her by the belt and lifted her off the ground. She was wailing in fright. He dumped her unceremoniously on her butt into the river and left her splashing and sputtering and screaming. He turned and headed back for the camp. Maria was lifting a rifle to her shoulder when Smoke started putting rounds from his six-gun into the ground around her feet. She shrieked and made a run for it. She didn't get far.

With the reins in his teeth, Smoke grabbed her by the seat of her pants and turned her flipping and rolling, her aristocratic posterior catching up with her boots. She landed on her belly and went sliding in the dirt.

He stampeded the horses, sending them racing in all directions, then made a final pass through the camp, tearing down the second big tent and dragging it into the fire. The barons and princes and princesses would have to sleep under the stars from now on.

Marlene was just getting to her feet, screaming her rage and calling Smoke some really terrible names, when Smoke turned and raced toward her. She reversed herself and took off. He grabbed her by the shirt collar and dragged her toward the river just as Andrea was reaching shore. He tossed Marlene into Andrea and the two women got dunked.

Smoke headed out, driving the frightened horses ahead of him and screaming like a Comanche.

When the men got back into camp—or what was left of it—they were out of breath from running. Von Hausen jerked his pith helmet off his head and threw it on the ground. "He's taken the women!" he shouted.

"He's damn welcome to 'em," John T. muttered.

223

"There's two of 'em," Utah Red yelled, pointing to the river.

Marlene and Andrea were climbing out of the river, slopping and sloshing to the bank.

"I'll kill him slow!" Marlene screamed. "I swear it'll take him days to die."

Maria groaned and got to her feet. Her face was skinned from her abrupt hard slide on the ground. Gunter ran to her side. She shoved him aside and screamed, "He put his goddamned hands on me!" she squalled. "Treated me like dirt! *Me!*" She whirled at the men. "Five thousand dollars for the man who kills Smoke Jensen."

"I'll add five thousand more!" screamed Marlene.

"And I'll add five thousand to that!" shrieked Andrea.

"I'd fight a grizzly bear and make love to an Eskimo woman for that," Slick Finger Bob said. "Or vicey-versey," he added.

"Now, ladies," von Hausen tried to calm them. "Our mission is to get to Dodge City. We simply can't . . ."

"You go right straight to *hell!*" Marlene screamed. "I want Smoke Jensen's . . ."

She named a couple of things she wanted cut from Smoke.

"Whoa!" Montana Jess whispered. "That there's a real mad woman."

Smoke rounded up as many horses as he could and cut the cinch straps off the saddles. Then he slapped them on the rump and sent them running off, free and happy. He emptied out the men's saddlebags and took what food they had and threw the rest of the contents in the river. Then he swung back into the saddle, recrossed the Powder and found him a good campsite, high up on a mesa and tucked behind some huge boulders.

His supper that night was sandwiches of biscuits and

salt meat he'd taken from someone's saddlebags. He went to sleep smiling at how furious he'd made those fancy women.


There was no placating the women, so von Hausen soon gave up trying. They had been manhandled and humiliated by Jensen, and none of them were forgiving creatures. But, von Hausen thought, sitting and drinking coffee that night, perhaps they were right. The women maintained that they would never reach Dodge City; that Smoke Jensen would track them down and kill them all. That it was just a matter of time.

John Flagg recollected that Smoke had traveled clear across country to New Hampshire one time to settle a score, so why not just deal with him now?

Von Hausen had started to argue that surely Jensen would not come to Europe to settle a score. But he'd shut his mouth before the words could form. Jensen probably would do that.

And von Hausen was going to do something else. He'd set up a code word with the lawyer in Dodge City; a code word that would release the money to the men. A little item he had kept from everyone. As soon as they got to a town with a telegraph office, he'd free up the money and take his party into Canada. They would travel east and sail out of a port there . . . even though he would have to be friendly with those damnable French for a time. He felt better now that that was settled in his mind.

Now all they had to deal with was Smoke Jensen, von Hausen thought ruefully. And for the first time on this long hunt, he admitted—to himself—that he had made a mistake in chasing Smoke Jensen.


Frank Clover felt his guts churn and sweat pop out on

his face when the cold voice spoke from behind him.

"Get off your damn horse."

Frank froze in the saddle. He didn't want it in the back. He'd shot men in the back, but he didn't want to go out that way. "I'm gettin' off. Jensen?"

"Yeah. Turn your horse so I can see your moves."

"Whatever you say, Jensen. Slow and easy. You gonna give me a chance?"

"Oh, yeah."

Frank dismounted and turned to face Jensen. Lord, lord, but the man was dangerous looking.

"Slap your horse on the rump," Smoke told him. "Get him out of the way."

Frank slapped his horse and the animal moved off a few yards. He grinned at Smoke. "I don't want to hit him too hard. I'm gonna need him to ride out of here."

"You're not riding anywhere, hombre. This is your last day to do anything. You should have stayed at the Hole."

Frank looked puzzled. How in the hell had Jensen known about that?

"My name's Frank Clover."

"Heard of you. Two-bit thief and back-shooter. Like to slap women around. You're a real brave boy. Drag iron, punk."

Frank tried. He got as far as closing his fingers around the butt of his .45. Two shots rang out, twin lightning and thunder bolts that slammed into his chest and knocked him down. The last thing Frank Clover remembered was that the sky was so blue. So blue . . .

Smoke unsaddled the horse and turned him loose. He left Frank Clover stretched out on the trail. Both his guns were still in leather. He should have listened to his mother and stayed on the farm in Minnesota.

John Flagg found the body and looked nervously around him. He was growing increasingly nervous until

Joe Elliot and Terry Smith rode up. That made him feel better.

The howling of a wolf sent chills scampering up and down their spines. The wolf howl came again, and their horses got jittery at the sound.

A rock about the size of a grapefruit came hurling down from a mesa and slammed into Joe Elliot's shoulder, knocking the man to the ground.

"Jesus Christ!" he bellered. "My shoulder's broke. Oh, damn, it hurts."

Another rock about the size of a big fist came flying down and hit Terry Smith in the head, knocking him flat on the ground and unconscious.

John Flagg hit the saddle and got the hell gone from that crazy place.

Joe Elliot looked up and saw Smoke Jensen standing in the rock above him.

"Strip," Smoke told him. "Right down to the skin. Then get your canteen and pour some water on your buddy on the ground."

Elliot peeled down to the pale buff. He was in very bad need of a bath. Terry could not talk due to his badly swollen and very busted jaw. But he could strip down and did. He was even nastier than Elliot.

"Throw your guns in the bushes," Smoke told them. "Then start hiking."

"This ain't decent!" Elliot hollered.

Smoke jacked back the hammer on his .44. The naked pair started hiking back to camp.

"And take a damn bath when you get to the river," Smoke shouted at them. "You stink!"

Dick Dorman saw them coming. His wound had been cleaned out and his ankle set and he was in camp with the women. "You ladies best turn your heads," he called. "We got some company comin' and they're nekkid as a new born."

"Tell them to take a bath in the river before they come in," Andrea said. She picked up a bar of soap and hurled it at the limping men. "Bathe, goddamnit!" she yelled at them.

Dorman, using a sturdy branch for a crutch, hobbled over to the men's bedrolls and found clothing for them.

"And tell them not to put on those stinking pile of rags until they wash them, too," Andrea screamed.

"Yes'um," Dorman said.

"And it wouldn't hurt you to take a bath, either," Marlene squalled at him.

"Yes'um," Dorman said, thinking for the umpteenth time that day that if he could find his horse he'd leave this crazy bunch 'fore Jensen kilt them all. Never again would he be so stupid as to tie up with anybody who wanted to hunt down Smoke Jensen.

Von Hausen and Gunter rode in and looked at the men, bathing in the river.

"Jensen kilt Frank Clover and took our clothes," Elliot said. "We had to walk back."

Von Hausen had a dozen questions to ask about that. But he only shook his head and walked his weary horse over to the picket line. Marlene met him.

"Any luck?" she asked.

"We couldn't even find his trail," von Hausen admitted. "The man's hid his horse somewhere and is on foot. And he's not leaving any tracks."

All the women were bruised and somewhat the worse for wear after their brief encounter with Smoke, and they were in no mood for excuses.

Marlene said, "We have hunted man-killers all over the world. We have always been successful. Tomorrow, *we*," she waved at Andrea and Maria, "shall take to the field and show you big, brave men how to hunt."

"Marlene," von Hausen said, his temper barely under

control, "as of this moment, I do not give a damn what you ladies do."

Marlene tossed her head and stalked off, Maria and Andrea with her.

Von Hausen had to clench his fists in order not to give the backs of the ladies a very vulgar gesture.

# 25

Smoke shook his head when he spotted the women the next morning. They were riding without men. Smoke concluded they were either the dumbest females he had ever run into, or just so arrogant they did not realize the danger they were in. He decided on the latter. He flattened out and let them come on. His clothing blended with the earth and Smoke had the patience of an Apache. Ol' Preacher had drilled into his head that many times movement gives away position more than noise.

Smoke did not want to hurt the women. A dunk in the river and a good shaking up was about the limit he was prepared to go with them, even though they were as vicious as any man he had ever encountered. What would he do if they started shooting at him? He didn't know.

As they drew closer, Smoke thought again that this was not his favorite terrain for fighting. He liked the high mountains and deep timber. Where he was now was rocky and sparse. There were peaks here: Roughlock Peak was to his north, Deadman Butte lay to the west, but nothing to compare to the High Lonesome.

Andrea made up his mind.

The women reined up about ten feet from him and Andrea said, "This is a good spot. I'll stay here. Marlene, you ride on about two hundred and fifty yards. Maria, you ride on an equal distance past Marlene.

We've got rocks behind us and a good field of view in front of us. As long as we stay within shouting distance of each other, we'll be fine."

Maria and Marlene rode on. Andrea dismounted. The last thing she would remember for about an hour was something crashing into her jaw and the ground coming up to meet her.


"What the hell do you mean, she's gone?" von Hausen roared.

"I mean she's vanished," Marlene screamed at him. "One minute she was there, the next minute she was gone. The tracks lead straight north."

"Break camp," von Hausen ordered. "Jensen's got her."

The men had found most of their horses and repaired the cinch straps. They quickly saddled up and broke camp. Dick Dorman could sit a saddle. But he had to have help dismounting. He gritted his teeth against the pain and rode. Joe Elliot's left arm was in a sling, and he was hurting something awful, but he followed along, riding Frank's horse. Searchers had found Terry's horse and brought it to him.

Henry Barton was riding a pack horse that had the worst gait of any animal he had ever tried to ride. Sandy Beecher rode a mule that tried to bite him every time he mounted and tried to kick him every time he dismounted.


"You are the most despicable man I have ever met in all my life," Andrea told Smoke. "This is outrageous. I have never been treated like this in my life. This is kidnapping. I will have you arrested."

"Shut up," Smoke told her.

He had tied her hands to the saddlehorn and was seriously considering wrapping a sack around her mouth.

"I suppose you intend to violate me," Andrea said.

Smoke looked back at her. "You have to be kidding! I'd sooner bed down with a skunk."

She spat at him. She wasn't a very good spitter. With spit on her chin, she said, "You are certainly no gentleman. You are a brute and a boorish oaf."

"Lady, shut up."

She screamed so loud it hurt Smoke's ears.

"Go right ahead and squall, lady. No one's going to hear you. In case you're interested in geography, that's Roughlock Hill right over there."

"I hate you, I despise you, I loathe you!"

"This is really going to be a fun trip. I can sense that right off."

"Where are you taking me, you pig?"

"To the mountains, lady. I'm glad you had sense enough to bring a coat with you. You're going to need it."

"Why did you kidnap me?"

"So the others will follow."

"I shall have you whipped to death, you barbarian."

"Right, lady."

"If you attempt to violate me I shall give you no satisfaction."

"You're as safe with me as you would be in a nunnery."

"Don't you find me beautiful?"

"In the same way a rattlesnake is pretty."

"These bonds are too tight. My hands hurt."

"My ears hurt."

She cussed him.

"You have a very dirty mouth, lady."

"I'm hungry."

"We'll eat this evening."

"I have to go to the bathroom."

"Later."

She cussed him.

"I'm not so sure this was such a good idea," Smoke muttered.


On the third night out, Andrea finally got it through her head that Smoke was not going to violate her precious wonderful flawless perfect body. And that made her madder than the kidnapping.

The man was infuriating. He seemed to sleep with one eye open. She could not escape because Smoke tied a rope around her waist and the other end to his arm before they went to bed. Three times she'd tried to slip away. Three times Smoke had jerked her back to the ground so hard her eyes crossed, her teeth rattled, and her butt hurt from the impact.

While the fire burned down to coals, Andrea asked, "Why don't you sleep with me tonight?"

"I'm married, lady."

"She isn't here."

"Yes, she is. In my mind."

"Is she beautiful?"

"Yes."

"She probably weighs three hundred pounds and has a head like a hog."

Smoke laughed at her.

"You find me amusing?" she flared at him.

"I find you dangerous, Andrea. Vicious and unfeeling and very dangerous."

"It was only a game, Mister Jensen," she said softly.

"Lady, you people were going to *kill* me."

"When this started, we thought of it as the ultimate

233

hunt. You are depicted as a notorious gunfighter. A killer. We assumed there would be arrest warrants on you. That no one would care if you got killed. We . . ."

"Stop it, Andrea. You're lying. Stop lying. You found out about me before the hunt started. You could have stopped it before you left Dodge. And you killed that Army patrol. A cold-blooded ambush. So stop lying and making excuses for yourself and your lousy damn friends. And Andrea, I buried your husband. We talked at length before he died. You shot him with that little hide-out gun I took from you. And he didn't die easy."

She refused to meet his eyes. "If you turn me over to the police, I won't be prosecuted."

"I know that. I don't know what I'm going to do with you. But believe this, Andrea, if you believe nothing else: if you try to kill me, I'll hurt you."

"Big brave man, aren't you?" she sneered the words at him.

"No. Just a man who is trying to survive. Now shut your mouth and go to sleep."

"And if I don't?"

"I'll stuff a gag in your big mouth."

She lay down and closed her eyes.


"He's leadin' us back into the mountains," Roy Drum said. "Just as sure as hell that's what he's doin'."

"And then? . . ." Gunter asked wearily.

"He'll start killin' us," John T. said, his voice flat. "That's why he grabbed Andrea. So's we'd follow him."

"Heading back to the mountains," von Hausen said, scratching his unshaven chin. "And he'll make his final stand there, won't he?"

"You better believe it," Utah said. "Howlin' and snarlin' and spittin' and scratchin' and shootin'." He looked back at the group. "If any of you boys feel you're comin' down with a case of the yeller belly, git gone now. 'Cause once we git up in the high lonesome, there ain't gonna be no runnin'."

No one left. They sat their saddles and stared at the man, defiance in their eyes.

"Don't say you wasn't warned," John T. told them. "Let's ride."

Smoke rode through Powder River Pass and took a deep breath of the cool clear air. He smiled, smelling the fragrance of the high country; he was home. Halfway between there and Cloud Peak, he set up his first ambush point, after securing Andrea's mouth so she could not scream and warn her blood-thirsty friends.

She tried to bite him and kick him, but he was expecting that and got her secured with only a small bruise on his shin.

"Now you be a sweet girl now," he told her, after stepping out of kicking range.

She bugged her eyes and fought her bonds and tried to kick him again.

"Relax, Andrea. You're making your bonds tighter."

She soon realized he was right and ceased her frantic struggling. She fell back on the ground and glared hate at him.

"Hans was probably glad to die after being married to you," Smoke muttered. He picked up his rifle and moved to a spot several miles away.

Smoke watched the long, single-file column come up the old trail, Roy Drum watching the ground, tracking Smoke like the expert he was. Roy passed within ten feet of Smoke.

Ed Clay was the last man in the column. When the

rider in front of him had rounded the sharp bend in the trail—a place Smoke had deliberately chosen—Smoke leaped from the ledge and knocked Ed out of the saddle, clubbing him with a big fist on the way to the ground. He threw Ed across his shoulder, grabbed his rope from his saddlehorn, and slapped the horse on the rump, sending it back down the trail. Smoke slipped into the brush and climbed back up to the ledge.

There, he hog-tied Ed and gagged him with the hired gun's own filthy bandana and picked up his rifle, slipping back into the brush, paralleling the trail.

"I sure will be glad to get shut of this damn mule, Ed," Sandy said. "You wouldn't like to trade off for a spell, would you?"

He got no reply as they rode further into the dimness of thick timber and brush.

"Did you hear me, Ed?" Sandy asked, twisting in the saddle.

Ed wasn't there.

"We got trouble!" Sandy called. He looked up in time to see a stick of dynamite come sputtering out of the ridge above him. "Oh, hell!" he yelled.

The charge blew, the mule walled its eyes and bowed up, and Sandy's butt left the saddle and he went flying through the air. He landed on the west side of the trail and went rolling down the slope, hollering and cussing all the way down. He landed in a creek and banged his head on a rock, knocking him silly.

Marlene's horse reared up at the huge explosion and threw her off. She landed hard and immediately started bellering.

One Eye's horse fell against the slope and Smoke took aim and conked One Eye on the noggin with a fist-sized rock. One Eye slid off the saddle, out cold.

Smoke added more confusion to the riders on the narrow trail by jerking out his left-hand six gun and empty-ing it in the air. Then he threw back his head and howled like a wolf and screamed like a panther. The horses went crazy.

Smoke found some good-sized throwing rocks and started pelting those below him. One cracked von Hausen's pith helmet and knocked the Baron slap out of the saddle. He landed belly-down on the edge of the trail and about fifteen seconds later, he joined Sandy in the creek, sitting in the cold water, addled goofy by the blow to his head.

Smoke had had his fun, but he wasn't going to play games with skilled gunhandlers like John T. and those of the original bunch. He pulled his rifle to his shoulder and blew Tom Ritter out of the saddle. The outlaw was cooling meat when he hit the ground and went slowly tumbling down the slope to the creek.

"Damn you, Jensen!" John Flagg screamed, struggled to get his horse under control and finally managing to jerk his .45 out of leather.

Smoke shot him between the eyes.

John Flagg's horse bolted and ran right over Maria, knocking the woman over the side of the slope. She rolled and tumbled down the bank and hit the creek just as von Hausen was getting to his feet. She hit him squarely across the knees and both of them went under, flailing and waving their arms and slipping and sliding on the slick rocks in the creek.

Smoke lit another stick of dynamite and dropped it to the trail below him. Then he cut out at a fast run through the timber.

The charge blew and knocked Utah Red off his horse. The hired gun went rolling down the slope and slammed into von Hausen and Maria just as they were crawling out of the creek. They returned to the creek.

Slick Finger Bob was tossed out of the saddle and landed on his belly on the trail. He had just enough wind left in him to roll frantically off the trail to avoid having his head smashed by the hooves of the panicked horses. He felt himself going over the edge and grabbed at an ankle. Marlene's ankle. The two of them went over the side of the steep embankment and began the fast tumble down.

Von Hausen had just enough wind left him to crawl up the bank of the creek. He almost made it. Slick Finger Bob and Marlene banged into him and knocked him clear to the other side of the fast-rushing mountain stream. Von Hausen's head hit a rock and he was out.

The mountain trail grew quiet. John T. peeped around a tree trunk and took in the sight before him. Two men were down and dead as a hammer. Tom Ritter lay on his belly and John Flagg was on his back, a hole right between his eyes. One Eye looked dead; then John T. saw his fingers began to twitch. A whole bunch of people appeared to be in the crick below, squallin' and bellerin' and cussin' and hollerin' for help. John T. couldn't see Ed Clay nowheres. Dick Dorman had been tossed from his horse and landed on his bad ankle. He had passed out from the pain.

John T. motioned toward Cat Brown to take the south end of the trail while he climbed the bank on the north end. It only took a couple of minutes for them to see that Jensen was gone.

Marlene was crawled up the slope, her eyes wild with hate and fury, her mouth working overtime, spewing out every cuss word she knew in several languages. She was mud from head to boots.

John T. looked around and finally found his horse and tied a rope to the saddlehorn, dangling the other end down to the creek. "Tie it around his majesty's shoulders," John T. called. "We'll pull him up."

"What about me!" Maria shrieked.

"Drag your own ass up here," John T. muttered, "We'll git to you," he hollered. "Just take it easy."

Von Hausen was hauled up the slope. He lost his boots and his pants during the salvage effort.

Slick Finger Bob was crawling up the slope, pushing Maria ahead of him.

"Get your hands off my backside!" she screamed at him.

"Well, goddamnit, lady, what else am I gonna push against?"

"Don't touch me!"

"All right," Slick Finger said, and removed his hands and got out of the way.

Maria hollered all the way back down.

# 26

Smoke put the muzzle of a .44 against Ed Clay's head. "I'll give you a choice, partner," Smoke told him. "Leave or die. What's it going to be?"

"You give me a chance, Mister Jensen, and I'm gone. I won't join up with the others. You don't have to give me a horse, a gun, or nothin'. Just let me leave and you'll never see me again."

"Head straight east," Smoke told him. "There's a settlement on the Clear. If I see you in these mountains, I'll kill you."

"The only people that's gonna see me from now on is my momma and daddy, back in Nebraska."

"Get gone."

Ed Clay got gone. Smoke doubted he'd return to Nebraska, but he also felt he'd never see the man again.

Smoke tossed Andrea into the saddle, tied her hands, and swung aboard his Appaloosa. He headed north, deeper into the Bighorns.

"Found Ed's horse," Henry Barton said. "But there ain't a sign of Ed."

The camp looked like a field hospital. Dick Dorman and von Hausen were stretched out side by side. Maria was off to one side, badly shaken and bruised up from

240

her trips to the creek. Utah Red had hurt his leg on the way down the slope and was bitching and moaning. Slick Finger Bob had a cut on his face and a knot on one knee. Sandy was still addled and acting goofy from his head impacting against a rock. One Eye had a egg-sized lump on his noggin from Smoke's thrown rock.

Marlene finally got von Hausen awake and was pouring hot soup down his throat. Roy Drum had retrieved von Hausen's boots and pants, falling into the creek himself. The pith helmet was ruined, cracked wide open.

Gunter knelt down beside von Hausen. "Two dead," he told him. "Ed Clay's missing. Several of the men are injured, but not seriously."

Von Hausen coughed up creek water. "The spirit of the men?" he questioned.

"As long as we keep paying them, they'll continue."

"We'll continue," von Hausen said. "As long as he has Andrea, we really have no choice, now, do we?"

Cat Brown rode back in and swung down. "I found Jensen's tracks. He's headin' straight north. The woman's still with him."

"And leaving tracks a fool could follow," von Hausen said, not putting it as a question.

"That's right, boss."

"We'll rest here and push on at first light."

Marlene glanced at him. There was a grimness in his voice that she had never heard before. She wondered what it meant.


"When are you going to turn me loose?" Andrea asked.

Supper was over, she had the rope around her waist, the knots so tight she had broken off her nails trying to loosen them—to no avail.

"When the hunt is over," Smoke told her.

"You mean, after you've killed them all."

"I didn't kill that fellow this morning, now, did I?"

"I could talk to Frederick. I'm sure he would cease immediately once he sees I am safe and unhurt."

"Frederick is mine," Smoke told her. "I'm going to kick his face in."

"You!" she said mockingly. "Frederick will destroy you. He is a skilled pugilist."

"We'll see."

"I've seen him fight two men at once and whip them both."

"Good for him. In a ring?"

"Certainly. One of Frederick's opponents would tire and the other would come in."

"Rules to it, hey?"

"But of course."

"I'll have to say a little prayer before bed tonight that when we do lock horns, Frederick doesn't beat me up too bad."

"Now you're being sarcastic."

"Go to sleep, your ladyship. Tomorrow is going to be very exciting."

Sandy Beecher heard a rustling behind him. He left the saddle and stared hard at the thick brush. The midmorning was cloudy and cool, with the skies looking like rain. The bushes did not move again.

For the first time he noticed the thin vine that stretched across the trail. From ground level, he could see that it was attached to the bush that had moved. Sandy got to thinking on that. Now if the vine was attached to the bush, that meant that whoever jerked on it was . . .

"Oh, hell," he muttered. "Behind me."

"That's right," Smoke whispered. "You're a mighty young man to die."

"Do I have a choice?"

"You might. That's up to you."

"The others are fanned out all over this mountain, lookin' for you. You let me get back on my horse, and I'm gone. That's a promise."

"Why should I believe you?"

" 'Cause I'm tellin' you the truth. Where's Ed Clay?"

"If he's not dead on the trail, he told me he was heading back to Nebraska."

"That's him. Me and him was pards. You let me go and you'll never see me no more, Mister Jensen. Never."

"Tell me about the others."

"They're bad ones. They got big money in their eyes. I got me a couple hundred dollars from that Baron or whatever he is, and that's enough to get me back to Missouri."

"That your home state?"

"Sure is! About thirty miles east of Springfield."

"I was born not far from there."

"You don't say? You know the Blanchard's?"

"Doc Blanchard tended to my ma when she was sick."

"Well, I'll just be damned. He's my momma's brother."

"He still alive?"

"Was when I left, about five year ago."

"Tell him Emmett Jensen's youngest boy said howdy."

"I'll sure do it. Smoke?"

"Yes. Them others'll kill you if you get careless. I've stole from time to time, but I ain't never killed nobody."

"I hope you never do. Take off."

"You want my guns?"

"No."

Smoke watched him leave, and true to his word, Sandy headed south without so much as looking back.

Smoke stood up and began stalking those who hunted him. Henry Barton sat his gray and studied the stillness of the timber. He wished Jensen would step out and challenge him. He'd like to be the man who killed Smoke

Jensen. He could write his own ticket after he done that.

"Looking for me," the voice came from off to his left.

Henry knew he'd been suckered. He was right-handed, and Smoke had studied him, waiting for just the right moment. If he drew now, he'd be shooting across his body. "Jensen?"

"That's me."

"Do I get to turn my horse?"

Smoke chuckled. "Why sure you do."

Henry said to hell with it and jerked iron. Smoke's .44-40 roared and Henry was knocked from the saddle, the slug taking him just under his rib cage and blowing out the other side.

Terry Smith came galloping up the mountains trail, hollering for his buddy. He reined up when he saw the gray, standing riderless in the timber.

"Here I am," Smoke called.

Terry cussed, wheeled his horse and lifted his six-shooter. Smoke blasted him out of the saddle, the big slug taking him in the center of his chest.

Smoke faded back into the brush on the mountain and jogged to a small knoll set in the middle of the timber. He punched two more rounds into his rifle and eared the hammer back, waiting.

A yell came to him, faint but understandable. "This here's Dick Dorman, Jensen. Joe Elliot's with me. We're gone. You hear me, Jensen. I got a broke ankle and Joe's shoulder is busted and swole up. We're out of it and gone."

"This ain't no trick, Jensen," Joe hollered. "We're headin' back to the Hole. Just let us pass and you won't hear no more from us."

Two rifles crashed. Smoke heard the sounds of bodies falling to the earth.

"Good shooting, darling," von Hausen said.

"And the same to you, sweet," Marlene said.

Smoke shook his head. Fine people to work for, he thought. Very caring about the hired help.

Montana Jess, Gil Webb, John T., Cat Brown, and Utah Red and Roy Drum were by now old hands at chasing Smoke. None of them were about to expose themselves and enter those dark woods. But the two left of the men from the Hole just weren't that smart. Slick Finger Bob thought he was slicker than he was. He slipped into the timber unseen, so he thought. It was his last thought.

Smoke drilled him at two hundred yards, the slug punching right through Slick Finger Bob's head.

"I'm a-gonna tear both your eyes out, Jensen!" One Eye called. "Then I'm gonna let you stagger around blind a couple hours 'fore I shoot you."

What a nice fellow, Smoke thought. I wonder what he does for an encore?

"Jensen!" he hollered. "You're surrounded. You can't get away. Step on out here and fight me."

Smoke picked up a rock and tossed it to his right. It thudded to the ground and One Eye fired. Smoke put three fast rounds in the area of the gunsmoke. One Eye staggered out, both hands holding his belly. He grunted in pain and slumped to the earth. He was still on his knees when Smoke backed out and disappeared into the lushness of the timber.

John T. sighed. "Anybody seen Sandy?"

"Not since breakfast," Montana told him.

"Well, that means he's either dead or pulled out."

"Do we go in there after him?" Utah asked.

"Not me," John T. said. He slipped back and into the timber on the other side of the game trail Smoke had been using. One by one, the others joined him.

They grouped together, very conscious of the bodies of Dorman and Elliot, lying not thirty feet away, back-shot by their employers.

"Comes a time, boys, when a man's got to use some common sense," John T. said. "Personal, I think we should have used it about a month ago."

"What are you sayin', John?" Gil asked.

"That it's time for us to go. We got some money out of this. More'un we'd have made in five years ordinarily. Boys, we've left bodies all over the place durin' this so-called hunt. It's time to pull out."

"That's what Dorman and Elliot tried to do," Cat pointed out.

"That ain't gonna happen to us, now that we know what to expect."

"How about our money down in Dodge?" Gil asked.

"Hell with it. We can take that check that Miss Hoity-Toity wrote us back yonder in the park. How about it?"

"You boys go on," Roy Drum said. "I want Jensen and the real big money."

"It ain't worth dyin' for, Roy."

"I'm with Roy," Cat Brown said. "But we'll see to it that you don't get back-shot."

"I'm stayin'," Utah Red said.

"I'm goin'," Montana Jess said.

"I'm with Montana and John T.," Gil Webb said.

The six men walked over to von Hausen. "I'll take that big money check you offered back in the park," John T. said. "We're pullin' out."

"Who is 'we'?" Gunter asked.

"Me, Montana, and Gil. Hand over the check."

Von Hausen noticed that the gunfighter's hand was close to the butt of his six-gun. He reached into his jacket and took out a waterproof pouch and opened it. He handed John T. the check.

John T. looked at it, then folded it and put it in his pocket. "Thank you kindly, von Hausen. Roy and Utah and Cat will see to it that you good folks don't back-shoot us on the way out. Adios, ladies and gents."

Several long moments ticked by before anyone spoke. The sounds of the hired-guns' horses faded into silence as the men left on the trail south. Finally, Gunter said, "Does anybody have a plan?"

"Hire more men?" Marlene asked.

"Forget it," Utah told her. "No time for that."

"I think I'll make a pot of coffee and fry up some bacon," Roy Drum said. "What about them bodies?"

"Push 'em over the side of that ravine yonder," Cat said. "I don't feel like diggin' no damn holes."

"We don't have a shovel anyways," Utah pointed out. "It got lost yesterday when Jensen ambushed us."

Roy built a fire while Utah and Cat hauled the bodies away and shoved them over the side, into the ravine. Roy had the bacon frying when the men returned.

"It might work," von Hausen said, looking at the trio of gunslicks. "Those are the hardest of the hardcases. We're a very small force now, and we'll be able to move faster and much more quietly."

He looked up, then stood up. He thought he'd heard a very faint yell.

"What's the matter?" Maria asked.

"I thought I heard something. A yell. Yes. I'm sure I did."

The faint yelling reached them all.

"That's Andrea," Gunter said. "She escaped!"

"I doubt it," Utah said, not getting up from his position by the fire. "Jensen probably got tired of listenin' to her complain and cut her loose."

"You men go get her," von Hausen ordered.

"You hired us to kill Jensen," Roy said. "Not find lost females. Just give a shout or two. She'll wander over here."

"Heartless brutes," Marlene said.

"Right, lady," Utah replied.

Von Hausen and party began shouting and waving

their arms and jumping up and down. After a few minutes, Andrea staggered in, collapsing by the fire, telling all sorts of wild stories about being beaten and raped by Smoke Jensen.

"You're a goddamn liar," Roy Drum said flatly. "He wouldn't touch the likes of you with a coup stick. I hate Smoke Jensen, but he never raped no woman in his life. I'd be willin' to bet everything I own he ain't never even been unfaithful to his wife. So why don't you just shut your lyin' damn mouth."

Andrea glared hate at the man, but she said no more about being assaulted. She slurped at a cup of coffee and said, "He said he was going to whip you in a fight, Frederick. Said he was going to kick your face in."

"Nonsense!" von Hausen said. "The man has better sense than to think he could best me in a ring. I've fought the best of fighters and never lost. He was just blowing off steam, that's all."

"Don't tangle with Jensen in a fist-fight," Utah said. " 'Cause you'll lose."

"Ridiculous!" von Hausen snorted.

Utah shrugged his shoulders. "Don't say you wasn't warned."

"What else did he say, Andrea?" Gunter asked, getting a blanket and draping it around her shoulders. The day was growing increasingly cool and damp.

"That tomorrow you all die."

# 27

It was a sensation, an emotion, that all skilled gunhandlers experience at one time or the other; that feeling of knowing that today is the day.

Utah and Cat and Roy knew it. They did not speak of it, but each knew the other was sharing the emotion.

Cat almost dropped his coffee cup when the wild howling of a wolf cut the early morning air. It was from the throat of someone very close to the camp.

"Let's do it!" Roy Drum said. "Let's by God get this over with once and for all."

He picked up his rifle and walked to the edge of the timber that surrounded the camp. A single shot rang out. Roy slumped to his knees and leaned up against a tree. His rifle fell from his lifeless fingers.

Cat looked at Utah. Both men shook their heads. They rose as one and saddled their horses.

"What are you men doing?" Marlene screamed at them.

"Pullin' out, lady," Utah told her.

"What about your money?" von Hausen asked. There was a tremor in his voice that no one among them had ever heard before.

"I 'spect that John T. knows a way to shake it out of that Dodge City lawyer feller. If he don't, I do," Cat said. He rolled his blankets and groundsheet and tied it back of his saddle.

"Smoke!" Utah called. "Me and Cat are the only ones left. We're pullin' out. I'd be obliged if you'd keep these foreigners from back-shootin' us."

"I'll do that," the call came from the damp woods. "I let a couple of others go. I'll do the same for you boys."

" 'Ppreciate it. See you around, Smoke."

"I hope not," Smoke called. " 'Cause when you do, you better drag iron."

"It was just a job of work," Utah called.

"Get out of here before I change my mind," Smoke called.

They got.

"Either strap on guns or toss them all in a pile," Smoke called.

"Kill him, Gunter!" Maria yelled, grabbing at his arm. "Kill the arrogant bastard."

But Gunter had lost the taste for the hunt. He unbuckled his belt and let his sidearm fall to the ground.

"You coward!" Maria screamed at him. She jerked up a pistol and emptied it into the dark timber.

"You missed, lady," Smoke told her, his voice coming from behind her.

Marlene grabbed up a rifle and fired at his voice, working the lever until the weapon was empty.

"Over here," Smoke called, from a new location.

Andrea put her face into her hands and began sobbing.

Marlene threw the rifle to the ground and stood trembling with rage.

"The Army's coming," Smoke called. "I saw the patrol about an hour ago from a ridge. They had some rough country to get through, so I figure they'll be here in about an hour or so. Then I'll do what somebody should have done a long time ago."

"And what is that?" von Hausen called.

"Stomp your damned guts out."

Von Hausen laughed at him. "I accept your challenge, gunfighter. But why wait until the Army gets here? I don't understand that."

"Because I don't trust any of you back-shooting bastards and bitches."

Von Hausen removed his gunbelt and tossed it to one side. "All of you, put your weapons in a pile. Every weapon. All the military can do is escort us to the ship. We might as well have some fun waiting for them to get here."

Every weapon, including hunting knives was piled onto a blanket. Von Hausen pointed to a long flat rock about three feet high. "All of you sit over there," he told his friends. "And do not, under any circumstances, try to assist me in any way during this brief boxing match." He raised his voice. "Is that satisfactory, Mister Jensen?"

"Suits me," the voice came from behind von Hausen and it startled him. Smoke hung his gunbelt on a limb and pulled on a pair of leather work gloves.

"We'll now set the rules," von Hausen said.

"No guns or knives," Smoke said. "Those are the rules. No time limit, no neutral corner, no knock-down rules. So anytime you're ready, you pompous, over-bearing, arrogant jackass, come on and fight."

Von Hausen assumed the boxer's stance: his left fist held out from his body, elbow bent, his right fist up, protecting his jaw. "You may approach and make the initial move, Jensen."

"OK," Smoke said, then jumped at the man and hit him in the face with both fists.

Von Hausen backed up, not really hurt, just startled at such a move. He flicked an exploring punch at Smoke. Smoke ducked it and busted von Hausen in the belly. That got Smoke a hard fist to the side of his head. Smoke spun around and kicked von Hausen on the knee.

The German yelped and backed up.

"Oh, foul, foul!" Gunter yelled.

Smoke ignored them and pressed von Hausen, hitting him with a combination that bloodied the man's mouth. Smoke followed that with a hard left to the man's belly. The German tried to clench. Smoke threw him down to the dirt and backed up.

Von Hausen jumped to his boots and charged Smoke. Smoke tripped him and clubbed the man's neck on his way down. The German got up, spitting dirt. Now he was mad, which is exactly what Smoke wanted.

"You peasant!" von Hausen hissed at him.

Smoke put one of his peasant's fists through the nobleman's guard and busted von Hausen's regal nose, sending blood flying. Smoke ducked a punch and waded in, smashing both fists against the man's belly and landing a vicious uppercut that snapped von Hausen's teeth together. The German was having to breathe through his mouth; his honker was busted.

Smoke caught a fist to the side of his head, another got through: a glancing blow on his jaw. Smoke back-heeled von Hausen and sent the man crashing to the rocky ground. Von Hausen came up snorting and bellowing. He came at Smoke, both big fists flailing the air. Smoke caught von Hausen's forearm, turned slightly, and flipped the heavier man, sending him hard to the ground.

With a roar, von Hausen was up and trying to get set. Smoke never let him. Smoke stepped in and smashed the man's face with hard left's and right's. The blows staggered von Hausen and tore his face. Smoke timed one perfectly and sent von Hausen to the ground, on his hands and knees.

"Time, time!" Gunter yelled.

"Shut your damned mouth," Smoke told him.

Gunter shut up.

"Get up, Baron," Smoke said. Then all the rage he had kept under control for weeks boiled to the surface. He cussed the man, calling him every filthy name he could think of. And being raised among mountain men, he knew more than the average fellow.

The Baron was a little slow getting up. Smoke kicked him in the belly, the blow lifting the man off his hands and knees about six inches. Von Hausen rolled and slowly got to his feet. He raised his hands and Smoke started a punch about a foot behind his shoulder and gave it to von Hausen. The German's teeth flew from his mouth under the right fist and Smoke tore one ear off with a thundering left that whistled through the air. It sounded like a pistol shot when it landed.

When the man was sinking down to his knees, Smoke came under his jaw with an uppercut. All present could hear the jaw pop when Smoke hit him. Frederick von Hausen hit the cool damp earth and did not move. Marlene screamed and ran to his side.

Smoke walked over to Gunter and before the startled man could move, Smoke knocked him slap off the rock. Gunter tumbled over the flat rock and lay unconscious on the ground.

Smoke pointed a finger at Maria and Andrea. "If you two even so much as twitch, I'll shoot you." He walked over to von Hausen, jerked off the man's wide leather belt and grabbed Marlene by her long blonde hair. He dragged her over to the rock, sat down with her across his knees, and proceeded to give her fanny a long overdue beating with the belt.

When Smoke finally released the woman, her screaming had been reduced to low whimpering moans of pain. He knew he had blistered her butt; he also knew it would be a long, painful ride for Miss Marlene, sitting a saddle out of the mountains.

"You brute!" Maria hissed at him.

Smoke smiled and jerked her across his knee. He gave her fanny the same workout he had given Marlene's derriere, reducing the woman's squallings to tiny whimperings for mercy. When he finished, he dumped her on the ground and dangled the belt for Andrea to see.

"You have anything to say to me?"

She shook her head and kept her mouth shut.

Gunter was moaning and crawled around on his hands and knees, his mouth a bloody mess. He got to his feet, leaning against the rock for support. He didn't need it.

"Oh, no," Gunter said as Smoke approached him.

"Oh, yeah," Smoke said, and popped him again. Gunter kissed the ground.

The Army patrol, which had arrived at the scene just seconds after Smoke and Frederick squared off, and whose members had thoroughly enjoyed every moment of the thrashing and spankings, rode into the clearing.

"Captain Williams, sir," the officer said, saluting Smoke. "We've come to escort these people to the nearest train depot and to see that they leave this country."

"You can sure have them," Smoke said. "No way they can be held accountable?"

"I don't think so, Mister Jensen. Their families have a lot of political influence in this country. Statesmen and diplomats and that sort of thing."

Smoke told the Captain about Hans and where he was buried. "I'll write Prince Hans Brodermann's parents personally. He really wasn't a bad sort of fellow."

"Why did he get mixed up with this bunch?"

Smoke looked over at the now not quite so haughty Marlene. "Well, I reckon, Captain, that the man had a good eye for horses and mighty poor judgement when it came to picking friends."

# Epilogue

Smoke rode into Sheridan and sent a wire to Sally, assuring her that he was all right. He told her he was going to ride back to the Sugarloaf, sit on their front porch, play with his dogs, and wait for her to join him. He closed with: I'll stay here in town and wait for your reply.

The next morning, over breakfast, a boy brought him the reply from Sally. It read: Taking next train. Will be there long before you. I'll play with the dogs. You can play with me. Love Sally.

# William W. Johnstone
## The *Mountain Man* Series